Michelle Aung Thin was born in Rangoon and brought up in Canada; she now lives in Melbourne. *The Monsoon Bride*, her first novel, was shortlisted for the Unpublished Manuscript Fellowship of the Victorian Premier's Literary Awards 2010.

The Monsoon Bride

Michelle Aung Thin

TEXT PUBLISHING MELBOURNE AUSTRALIA

The Text Publishing Company
Swann House
22 William Street
Melbourne Victoria 3000
Australia
textpublishing.com.au

First published by The Text Publishing Company 2011

Cover by W. H. Chong
Page design by Susan Miller
Typeset in Adobe Caslon 11.5/17pt by J&M Typesetters
Printed in Australia by Griffin Press, an Accredited ISO AS/NZS 14001:2004 Environmental Management System printer

National Library of Australia
Cataloguing-in-Publication entry:

Author: Aung Thin, Michelle

Title: The monsoon bride / Michelle Aung Thin.

Edition: 1st ed.

ISBN: 9781921758638 (pbk.)

Dewey Number: A823.4

To Peter, Pam-Anne, George and Julian

Heat

Rangoon, 1930

Of course Winsome could not sleep. She marvelled that anyone else in the compartment could. She had been woken from a fitful doze hours ago when the train jolted over the points somewhere past Toungoo. She had felt a violent lurch to the left and when she looked out the window into the dark night, there was the gleam of a new track running alongside them.

That glimmer was a sign the city was close and indeed she could feel this imminence in the train's momentum. 'Soon, soon, Rangoon, Rangoon,' and she glanced about the carriage to see who else shared her excitement in the nearness of the city, in the miracle of speed that was both polished and perilous, in the sense that something was gathering beneath them, washing them all forward.

One or two of the other passengers had blinked briefly against the sulphur-yellow emergency light. But once the train righted itself, they slept on. She alone sat with her hands cupped against the glass, tracing the dim outline of the second track in the night.

It was not only the city's proximity that kept her awake but also the pleasure of solitude; since the second track appeared and the train swung violently across the points, she had been turning her thoughts like planets in a soft sky. At their final marriage lesson, when the priest talked on and on, Desmond bent his head to hers and whispered, 'Our world is newer, faster and better—you will see.' She took his hand in hers then, and squeezed it.

His skin had a peppery, meaty sweetness, a smell that seemed to stick to her dress, her hair and skin. She named it 'the scent of men'. Now he snored gently beside her, his face no more than an outline rising and falling in the dim light. A man snoring—she decided that she liked the sound.

Desmond stirred and his knees spilled apart, coming to rest too warm against her side, pushing her into the wall of the train. He was a big man, tall—taller than the priest, taller than the men she had seen on the train, taller than the other young men standing shyly outside the convent, those sons of white fathers come looking for brides, their hands and faces brown or yellow against their good linen shirts. In his wedding suit Desmond had seemed substantial, a man meant to be, and when they boarded the train together he moved with such sureness she thought that he must have walked along this carriage many times before. She felt herself very small then, not a wife but a girl, with little behind her except stale convent air. Winsome McLintock that was. Winsome, the name her father had given her, his only gift.

But now, as Desmond slept, those long legs and arms were too solid for this cramped space. Flattened against the darkened window, she caught her own reflection—her wide mouth, her mother's flat nose and dark skin—while his bulk loomed behind her. She pushed her knees back against his—and none too gently either. He shifted once more, tossing his head as if he might wake. His arm brushed against her breasts and she found herself holding her breath; what if he did wake, what if he demanded his rights here on the train, amid the rhythmic sighing of sleepers? He might slide

4

his hand beneath her dress, he might draw his fingers along her thighs, he might cup her face to his, his touch unbearable, liquid.

The air in the carriage was sour with the breath of strangers, their sweat and their half-eaten meals. Winsome pulled away from the heat of Desmond's body. She stood up and rested her face against the smooth glass. Beyond the train, the night was moonless and without colour.

She had been warned by the experienced travellers against opening the windows, but the longing for a breeze overrode their advice. The teak frames were stiff in their tracks and so heavy it took all her strength to move them, but it was worth the effort; she was immediately rewarded by a rush of air across her skin. Gazing blindly into the night, it seemed minutes before she was able to make out the varying densities in the dark; there were feathery moving shapes that must be trees, an occasional shimmer that could only be water, perhaps a field under paddy. She imagined villages, women and men sleeping, dreaming too. Further still, there would be a solid, opaque blackness that was the rise of the Pegu Yoma marking the edge of the delta and the beginning of the city.

High up on those hills was the ridge where the Shwe Dagon Pagoda sat. She had heard that the golden dome received the very first light over Rangoon, and shone with a coral gleam, visible above the hills, as true as any star. Leaning out over the edge of the window, she felt the air flow faster across her arms, the delicious coolness raising the hairs on her skin. There! She saw it. A tiny orange sliver. But then there was another and another, as embers, still glowing, streamed from the engine to sting her arms and face. She screwed up her eyes against them, but it was no use—she had to draw back into the stuffy carriage and close the window. Resting her face against the glass once more, she murmured, 'Rangoon, Rangoon, soon, soon.'

5

Those were the same words she had repeated to herself as she walked along the nave of the convent chapel—was it only that morning, or a whole day ago?—and as she moved, she understood why they veiled your face; it was for fear of what might be seen there, what you might show them. That veil, a scrap of patched lace, felt rough against the fingers, and when it swirled around her head it reminded her of ice on the wash basins in winter, of the miraculous snow that had fallen around the convent once when she was very small. A rare, joyous thing.

Assumpta, the sewing mistress, had pinned the veil to her scalp with clumsy fingers. It hurt.

When it was done and the veil was wanted for Maisie Maung, the next bride (her mother a Shan village girl, her father long returned to the Lincolnshire fens), Winsome pushed Assumpta's hands away and unpinned the lace for herself, feeling gingerly through her hair, trying not to ruin the upswept style that Maisie had told her looked so elegant.

'My darling girl.' Assumpta's voice was sad and sentimental as she put out her hand for the veil. The same fingers had gripped her shoulder long ago, when they took her to the man they said was her uncle. Small and brown, silent because he did not speak their English. Go with him, Assumpta said. Your mother is dead. But all along, those fingers holding her flesh so that she knew what was expected and, with her own voice, refused.

As Winsome returned the veil, Assumpta bowed her head in an awkward and formal gesture that seemed to acknowledge the past, Winsome's departure; the way things changed, would always change. Handing it back Winsome felt she was taking another kind of vow and wondered if she ought to say something. Before she could speak Assumpta, wearing a sly and knowing grin, giggled. 'You are an old married woman now,' she said, 'you'll have breasts like a cow.' Then she turned away, ready to pin the mended bit of lace onto Maisie's head, Maisie who was already waiting in the little anteroom. Winsome felt her cheeks burn.

'Silly old fool.' The vehemence in Desmond's voice took her by surprise. He took up her hand, and she felt his fingers on her own, a heavy pressure as he led her into the hall of the chapel to take their place among the other newlyweds, waiting to eat their wedding breakfast.

There was a loud crack. The train swerved briefly to one side, throwing Winsome off balance again. A new set of tracks ran alongside them. Then another appeared, and another, until she could no longer keep count. Grey light seeped across the sky and a coral gleam showed above the dirty dark green of the Pegu Yoma.

'Soon.' Her body was as warm as that coral flame. She wanted to share their arrival in the city, this brief dawn. But no one was awake. She looked to Desmond and caught her breath.

A shaft of pink light fell across his face and he was beautiful. It was not the evenness of his features or the European roundness of his eyes that made him so, but rather the delicacy of the brows, the triangular nostrils, the high, scalloped cheekbones in the peach-brown of his skin.

She sat down beside him and placed her hand flat against his warm flank. She leaned in a little closer to him, felt the morning light across her own cheek now. 'Rangoon,' she whispered in his ear, 'we are in Rangoon.'

Desmond's eyelids convulsed mechanically and he recoiled, his fists flying up in front of his face. She gave a little involuntary cry and it seemed to rouse him. He blinked and then looked at her, rubbing his eyes. He gave her a half-smile and murmured, 'Good morning, funny thing.' His voice was warm and fond as he stretched his arms up to the roof. 'Are we in Rangoon yet?'

On the eve of his wedding Desmond Goode paused for a moment at the verandah of the Civil Administration building to take in the view across town. In his hands he held the thick buff envelope containing his letter of appointment to the Indian Medical Service (Coroner's Assistant, Rangoon General Hospital) and two train tickets (Third Class, No Berth)—one for him, one for his bride. She would be waiting for him at the convent school's chapel in the morning. Not the prettiest, but certainly the best academic results of her year. A good, biddable convent girl. Eager to please every time he'd met her. He tapped the envelope against the heel of his hand and permitted himself a moment of self-congratulation in this shady, auspicious place.

Someone—an Englishman, he supposed—had planted a climbing rose in the red soil at the steps and the plant had colonised the wooden rail with its glossy leaves and white blooms, each of which gave a clean, sweet scent that filled the warm air, attracting bees in numbers. Beyond the neat circular driveway the hill station unfolded, a tidy, whitewashed little town strung along a broad declivity. All around, the Shan Hills were the same purple as smoke.

Desmond tore a small, half-blown bud from the plant and threaded the stalk into the buttonhole of his jacket. He was not entirely surprised to find himself standing here in this position—a future before him, possibilities, perhaps even a certain prestige. In life, one made one's chances; his personal experience was certainly evidence of this. After all, had he not risen far above the rest of the recruits in his intake to the Indian Imperial Police? Who else among them had made such a success of things? Who else could? No one. Except perhaps for Sawyer.

Sawyer had cut a dash in his police uniform. Although he was locally born, and therefore a déclassé white despite his pure

English blood, he was still invited to play tennis at the club when they were down in numbers, or when a tournament was got up. He never gave up on a point and was quick at the net. 'I have good hands,' he explained, 'that's what we say in tennis.' Desmond remembered those hands; they were smooth and long fingered, like a woman's. His own hands were big and brown, strong too. A boxer's hands, made for dealing out the law.

A bee landed at the edge of his envelope and curled its abdomen against the creamy vellum. Gingerly Desmond shook it away, worried it might mark the paper. It flew off towards the railing where he could see many more bees crusting around the pale flowers. The air was full of their persistent hum.

On his way home from the police training yard, Desmond used to pass the chummery where Sawyer boarded. There was a neem tree at the gate and occasionally he stopped to rest in its shade. One evening, as the cicadas throbbed in the dusty summer air, Sawyer appeared, his white tennis sweater and flannels glowing in the last rays of the sun.

'Constable Goode,' his voice was flat and without expression, as if he'd expected to see Desmond at his gate, as if it had been prearranged. He stopped, his feet square in the dust of the road, twirling his racquet in his hands.

'Sawyer,' he replied. Sawyer was close enough for Desmond to smell the salty tang of his sweat, feel the coolness radiating from his skin. A film of red clay clung to his cheeks and forehead, to the fair hairs of his eyebrows, and Desmond's fingers itched to brush the particles away. He had to shift his gaze, to focus on the racquet instead. He watched the strings blur as Sawyer spun it clockwise then stopped, spun it anti-clockwise, then stopped again. The cicadas pulsed around them. 'Been playing tennis?' he asked and felt a fool as Sawyer smirked. That was the thing about Sawyer;

he was fluent in the lexicon of silences and gestures that separated all white men from the rest, from Desmond's own kind, no matter what their rank. He was something.

'Yes,' he said; and then, 'I've enjoyed our little talk, Desmond,' before he turned and disappeared up the path.

Desmond's ears still pulsed at the memory. He touched a hand to the rough teak rail. The roses were now covered in an untidy mass of bees, dry little bodies colliding against one another, directionless, drunk with perfume. One or two droned around his buttonhole and he sprang back; pulled at the rose, dropping it on the wooden floor where the same bees crawled between the pale petals. He stamped down on them hard and took the steps at a run, waving the envelope around his head. It was only when he was standing on the gravel drive, the stones sharp beneath his feet, that he felt he was truly clear of the swarm.

He smoothed his hair with his hand. He shouldn't be standing here idle, there were things to be seen to. His wedding suit, for example, and his packing.

It was a few months after their encounter outside the chummery that Desmond heard the news about Constable Sawyer. 'Dysentery,' someone said, shaking their head. 'Nasty.' Later on that same day, Desmond was sent home with a suspected bout of fever; he'd begun to shake uncontrollably, a sure sign that something malign had taken hold of him.

'A damnable waste.' He said it out loud now as he pocketed the envelope. Then he turned to walk along the driveway towards the road and his digs.

The European Refreshment Room was near the up-country platform at the far end of Phayre Street Station. Its entrance was a green panelled door with a brass handle, shaded by a zinc roof. Here

Desmond stopped, straightened his tie and turned to Winsome, his eyes bright. 'I thought we might stop for tea, just the two of us. Our own little celebration.' Then he opened the door and, with a wave of his hand, invited her to walk through.

Inside, it took a moment for Winsome's eyes to adjust to the dimness of the room, which was vast and cool. She had never been anywhere like this before. Ceiling fans rotated of their own accord. Barefoot bearers lined the walls, their faces and feet the colour of teak. Rangoon's early morning light, already brassy, flared off the silver cutlery. And the faces—a handsome Indian in a plum-coloured sash stood behind a high bench and sent the bearers gliding between the tables with a gesture of his hand; pink-cheeked travellers bent over their china cups, eyes sliding towards the silhouettes of coolies at the windows, waiting with the bags.

Winsome could smell beeswax polish and sunlight on wood, the sourness of butter, dirty feet, unwashed flesh. But it was the noise of the room that most struck her; the clatter of crockery was indistinguishable from the murmuring voices, the impatient scrape of chairs, the hissing boilers heating water for tea, all of it reverberating from the ceiling and walls, converging and diverging until the din seemed to well up from inside her, to saturate her skin like the Rangoon heat.

'Look at this place,' Desmond whispered as they sat down, his head turning this way and that, 'so modern, so *tasteful*.' He sat back in his chair, ran a palm over the tablecloth. 'We will come here once a month. After mass.'

Winsome nodded stiffly, the days and weeks and months spinning before her, the blazing sun crossing the sky.

'Sir. Madam. Tea?' It was the Indian from the door, face as glossy as his silk sash, and Winsome thought of the man on the train, his skin the colour of sugar syrup.

When they had got off the carriage that morning she nearly fell down the steps, hurrying to keep up with Desmond. A fellow passenger caught her hand and saved her. Beneath the brim of his hat his eyes were dark blue in golden skin. He smelled of English tobacco and that same pepperiness she had noticed on Desmond's skin—the scent of men. When his hand grasped hers, she felt her blood rise.

'Tea.' Desmond dismissed the Indian simply by looking away but she watched as the man signalled, saw a bearer leap from the wall. Beneath the table, her ankle brushed against Desmond's and his touch rippled out across her skin. Everything between them was still to come. She blushed as he pulled his leg away.

The tea arrived in a bone china pot. The cups were stamped with the Burma Rail insignia, the B and R entwined in silver; it was a detail she would have delighted in sharing with Maisie Maung or one of the other girls back at the convent. When she took a sip, the liquid scalded her tongue and the sweetness set her teeth on edge.

Above her the fans circled, the breeze like a breath on her hair. She tried to picture ordinary things. Folding rags, sewing a button, washing the floor, but it was no good. The hem of this tablecloth, the letters on this cup, only these were real.

Desmond cleared his throat. 'Winsome,' he began. His voice rose with importance (yet she had to squeeze her eyes to hear him). 'Perhaps you are wondering what we will be for one another.' He smiled. 'You see I know only too well what you are feeling.' As he spoke, he waved his hands and knocked the spoon from the sugar bowl. White granules littered the cloth. Flies would come. She looked away.

Over Desmond's shoulder the doors to the European Refreshment Room swung open and white light flooded across the floor. A woman stood in the brightness, dust motes swirling about the shoulders of her tweed travelling suit. She had a proud face; a superior expression framed by grey hair. Winsome recognised her as the sort who gave out the school prizes once a year, an English grande dame accustomed to obedience. As she peeled off her gloves, the Indian with the plum sash hurried to her side.

'I will of course have certain expectations of you, just as you will of me…respect, a sense of your duty, a certain modesty and delicacy of manner…'

The grande dame was speaking briefly to the Indian without looking at him and he bowed with elaborate courtesy, then made a show of scanning the room. She must be looking for a table, but Winsome could see they were all taken. The Indian held up his hands in apology.

'…in turn you can rely on me for guidance in all matters. My role as a husband is to instruct you, to train you, to lead you.'

The grand lady compressed her lips and with an irritable shrug raised her face to search the room herself. Her grey eyes met Winsome's only briefly. Then, with the Indian in her wake, she began to move purposefully between the tables.

'I am a man of experience and you will find that I do not cower before life's blows. I have courage enough for both of us. Let me be your guide; take me as your model.'

She stopped a little distance away, the superior lady, and although she did not speak in a loud voice, Winsome could hear her instructions to the Indian quite clearly. 'Move the chi chis. My train is at twenty past.' She turned her back to let him do his work.

'…if you do, then you will see that there is so much before us, so much will be possible…'

'Thakin…' The Indian bowed smoothly at Desmond's elbow, startling him.

'*Sir,*' Desmond corrected, scowling. 'Can't you see we are drinking our tea? That we are having a conversation?'

The Indian shook his head from side to side and smiled. 'Of course, sir. Beg pardon, sir. But the memsahib. Sir.' He gestured towards the grand lady, who kept her eyes on the wall, then raised his hand. A bearer with a metal tray jumped from the wall and hurried to the table.

Winsome watched as Desmond looked from the lady in tweed to the Indian, then around the room. His movements were stiff, uncertain, and his eyes seemed to bulge. Like her, he must feel this sucking stillness, the cold prickling of the scalp, the eyes of others. Like her, he would feel this rising anger, this wonder and fear.

Desmond rose decisively to his feet.

On the previous morning he had stood close beside her to pronounce his vows; his profile smooth as a river stone, his words low but clear as the convent bell. Now his voice was theatrically loud and his face flushed, his complexion becoming darker, browner. 'Madam,' he said, 'please, take our table, we are quite finished.' He gave a little bow and pulled out his own chair for her, but the superior woman did not make the slightest sign she had heard him. The bearer, his head bent over the table, smirked as he brushed up the stray grains of sugar. Teapot, milk jug, saucers rang against his metal tray. He turned to Winsome and held out his hand for her cup.

Winsome looked down into her tea. Around the room, white men and women in expensive travelling clothes watched from over their own cups while along the walls, behind the boilers, black eyes stared out of impassive brown faces. The bearer waited. Desmond stood stiffly, his arms at his sides.

'But I haven't finished.'

Nobody moved. Nobody spoke. The grand lady's eyelids did

not even flicker as she studied that wall, standing tall and straight; such impeccable posture.

Desmond's smile tightened. 'Come, Winsome.'

She looked into his dark eyes. This was how he would look when he was very, very old.

'Winsome.'

Did she want to see him crushed?

He moved around the table and put a hand to her shoulder. 'Come, funny thing.' His voice was gentle, but his touch was firm. 'You must be tired after our journey.'

She saw herself—an obstinate girl with a flat nose in a shabby homemade dress. She surrendered her cup to the bearer; bent to collect her carpetbag (so light). The bearer swept the rest of their tea things from the table as the venerable lady waited for all evidence of their presence to be removed. She sat down only after the Indian had wiped the seat with a cloth.

'Ridiculous little cranny,' she remarked loudly, leaning back against her chair.

As they threaded their way back through the tables, Winsome kept her face low. There was no need because now no eyes met hers, yet she knew they were watched. She knew there would be knowing little smiles, little shakes of the head. When Desmond tried to take her elbow she swung her arm away and quickened her pace, refusing to stand in the way that women stand with men. So what if he looked a fool?

Desmond caught her as they neared the door, his fingers digging into the soft part of her upper arm, his voice just audible in her ear. 'Do not cause a scene.' His tone made her catch her breath.

Arm in arm they walked through the swinging doors of the European Refreshment Room and back onto the platform, past the coolies and bags, past the cheap tea-carts, the waiting passengers and over the wooden bridge. Quickly they moved through the concourse and out of Phayre Street Station. At every step she wanted to give herself over to the salty, scalding comfort of tears. She wanted to die. She loathed the clip of their shoes on the wooden floor, the fluidity of her body as she moved forward until they were through the station's big double doors.

Outside, a clock struck the hour and the light was sharp as a blade. They both blinked, momentarily blinded. Beyond them, Rangoon traffic was already at full throttle. There were cars and trucks, trams and bullock carts; further still the metallic gleam of the river where the ocean-going liners moored and, over it all, a cloud of dust, a swirling, golden haze, each particle made dazzling by the sun.

Desmond dropped her elbow and instead took her hand. She could feel him beside her, found herself caught once again between wonder and fear. 'Cleave to one another,' the priest at the convent had said.

Cleave. To bind together. To split apart. They were still hand in hand as they walked out into the heat.

As Jonathan Grace stepped outside into the grey air, the reek of burning oil catching in his throat, he was briefly disoriented and fancied himself lost in a London fog. But this air was blood-warm and as he moved along the cinder path, the shape of a Burman squatting over a glowing brazier loomed out of the haze and the vile stink of his meal, chilli and garlic and fermented fish, was sharp in the air. Further along, a stringy line of Indians trudged from the steamer that had just pulled into the dock below and beyond them churned one of the great brown rivers of Asia. Guy's Hospital and the pinching damp of London were behind him. This was Rangoon. He was in Rangoon.

Jonathan pulled the handkerchief from his pocket and held it over his mouth against the foetid air. The cloth was already soggy, rank with his own perspiration, and he felt his belly lurch. He had not stopped for tiffin, had instead come out here, crossing the Rangoon River at Ronnie's behest, Ronnie who had been on the boat from Portsmouth (friend? No, acquaintance).

'Delicate matter,' Ronnie had said, 'company doctor not quite the thing. Thought of you.'

Jonathan risked a cautious breath, then folded the handkerchief and loped along the cinder path that led down to the water. There would be a breeze on the river.

But at the water's edge the air was worse, fouled by engine oil and diesel; the paddleboat's mechanisms, open to the air, belched out stinking clouds of greasy smoke. Dark bodies (Burmans, Indians, Chinamen), hot and fragrant, pressed around him. It was little better on the topmost deck where the Europeans travelled, and he felt himself again only when the paddles started to turn, raising a cooling spray of river water. Standing at the railing, his palms resting against the worn teak, he roused himself with an effort from this waking dream of heat and brown faces.

Ronnie's friend had a house in the Burmah Oil compound, on the opposite shore from Rangoon proper. A liveried butler had answered the door and in the sitting room another servant was waiting with ice, glasses and decanter.

'Drink?' Ronnie's friend offered as Jonathan opened his bag to remove the swab, the glass plate, the little vial of distilled water. He declined politely and the man smirked. 'New to Rangoon, are you?'

In the room there was the scent of some woman's perfume. 'Boredom and loneliness,' the friend said, 'the scourge of this town, worse than the pox, really.' Jonathan didn't reply. The man's face fell when Jonathan told him he would have to come into the hospital after all. A different servant showed him out.

As a Senior House Officer Jonathan was entitled to digs, his own manservant and an Indian woman who would come in from time to time to help with the cleaning and cooking. Jonathan had never employed anyone whose sole purpose was to serve him; he had grown up in a household where it was natural to make economies. He and his mother had made do with a char and not much more and he could not imagine what he would require of a servant. He had thought to save the money and fend for himself, but in the end had done as the other single men did.

Jonathan leaned over the railing of the boat and looked down into the foaming waves. He inhaled the brackish air. With his eye he measured the angle that the draught ate into the copper-coloured water. This river was deep and in parts treacherous; the bottom would be shifting constantly, sediment collecting in drifts; its currents and tides might drag you in unexpected directions. But it was always good to be on a river, any river. He had spent his boyhood messing about on the Ouse and later rowed in the college fours and with the hospital club. These perverse and swirling Asian rivers were nothing like the waters he had known, and yet he felt he knew them; or at least, he *could* know them. He had tried to explain this—the knowing of rivers—to some of the others on the ship, but it had been impossible to find the right words.

Boredom and loneliness. He turned the words over in his mind—they were already a too-familiar refrain. Surely boredom was the province of a certain class? He would be busy, he had nothing to fear. And there was the question of his extracurricular work, for Jonathan was ambitious—he had plans of his own, a study, some sort of research that would make the most of working in a tropical hospital. All he needed—all any man in this position needed—was a comfortable bed, a quiet place to work, a reliable clerk (he would find one) and the occasional cooked meal. Everything else he could do without.

That was not all. The atmosphere of Rangoon itself both compelled and disturbed him, making it a fitting environment for intellectual effort; a new place, a strange place like this might well encourage expansive thinking. He believed the very circumstances he found around him: poverty, disease, the squalid living conditions of the Asiatics—all of this would spur him on. He had heard of this happening, of quite ordinary men stumbling upon extraordinary things. His plans, his intellectual curiosity, these would keep him busy. No, he would not be bored. And loneliness? Well. One might be lonely anywhere.

Before he'd left England, some fellow rower (Hastings? Batby?) told him, 'Flying fish, Grace, they have fish that fly...and their women...' Then Batby or Hastings had raised his eyes and whistled in mock rapture. Well, he had been here nearly a month and had travelled on or near this river almost daily, yet he had not seen a single flying fish. As for the Burmese women, he found them charmless with their narrow obsidian eyes. They seemed to be constantly assessing him, watching and judging him by some standard he did not know or understand. The mere sight of them, triangular heads above snaking hips, left him numb and astonished by his lack of desire. No cure for loneliness there. 'It's the heat,' he told himself. Yet it was not what he had expected.

The steamer nosed into the centre of the river, passing small Burmese sloops, each curved like a Turkish slipper; a motor launch; long boats crammed with sailors, those Indian sailors who called themselves lascars—he had seen men just like these in every port between Portsmouth and Rangoon, most of them famously from Chittagong across the Bay of Bengal. They were walnut brown, these men, their puny limbs wiry and incredibly tough and strong. No doubt these ones were coming ashore from one of the big liners moored further downstream in the deep central channel of the river. Like him, they were far from home and headed for the city; bound, he imagined, for pleasure. In each long boat a Burman, balanced at the stern, stretched forward to stroke the water with long-handled oars, the movement bird-like, painfully balletic; there were no flying fish—but there was this.

Jonathan turned his attention to the bank opposite. Bund,

they called it locally, a Hindi word; although he had been told it was mostly Coringhee-speaking coolies who worked the docks. (Rangoon was a city more Indian than anything else and he wondered if they minded, those remote-eyed Burmans.)

He could see them, black-backed coolies in white dhotis clustered on the shore. Two or three creeping out along the steel arm of a monstrous crane that hung over the river and glinted white in the bronze light. They ventured so far along that arm, he would not have been surprised if one of them fell, could almost see the tiny body wheeling, limbs flailing as it tumbled towards the water.

Although he was still too far away to hear the noise of the docks, he knew it would be all clamour, pounding and shouting, metal howling against metal, the kind of din that made it easy to lose your concentration and slacken your grip: such were the risks working men took, forever at the edge of scarcity.

Even when the noise of machinery stopped—if it ever did stop—there would still be the racket of people living wedged between buildings, beneath trees, beside drains; hawking a yellow bolus of tuberculoid slime to aim at your ankles. Rangoon's streets were home to that class of Asiatic who lived all of his life in public, cooking, shitting, getting drunk, copulating too no doubt, although Jonathan rarely saw their women.

Curiously, the only sound that did drift across the water was a recording of a popular song. It came from a bioscope-wallah— Jonathan could picture him too, pedalling his bicycle along the shore, the phonograph in the basket hung across the handlebars, a placard perched above, advertising a moving picture. He would be chanting (*bioscope aggh, very good bioscope today shown at very convenient times*) but what Jonathan heard was not his sonorous call, rather it was the crackling voice of the phonograph, the needle jumping so that the words were repeated over and over, bending back upon themselves, truncating the lyric. He still recognised the tune—it was one the ship's band had played so often on his way out here that he had started to dream about tiptoeing through tulips. With the chug of the motors beneath him, he was reminded of another dock, another hot and alien port, where he had leaned across the railing of a ship and looked out at the men working there.

Apart from one inexplicable lumbering mound of rock, Djibouti was flat and featureless so that, from the height of the ship's deck, Jonathan had a far-ranging view. Beneath the dark-blue sky Sufi workers stalked the docks, moving gracefully beneath their flowing robes, fuzzy hair piled high and tied in huge bundles above their heads. Past the coaling station were clusters of shabby buildings that made up the town and in the centre of these, a white square split the horizon, like a sail on land.

'That's the outdoor cinema.' It was a woman who spoke, young, English, yellow hair tousled by the wind, her gaze following his own. He recognised her as one of a group he had often seen around the games-room bar. 'Funny place for a picture show, wouldn't you say?' Then she turned to grin at Jonathan and held out her hand. 'Lesley Chapman.'

'Dr Grace.' Her lacquered nails trailed along his palm as she pulled her hand from his. 'Jonathan, actually.'

She looked into his face, her eyes screwed against the sun. She was not a first-rate sort of girl, perhaps not even second rate, but her voice had a pleasing catch to it that made the roughness of her accent charming. 'So, do you fancy the pictures, Dr Grace? We're docked here overnight just for the privilege.'

'Why not?' he replied. She grinned again, showing her teeth.

Later, as they made their way through the busy souk, Lesley took his elbow and propelled him expertly through the crowd, past the phalanx of waiting natives in their long white robes towards a small knot of Europeans queuing directly in front of the cinema's ticket office, a little tented cubicle perched in front of a tall grey wall.

'The wall's so the locals don't try to cadge a show,' Lesley told him. 'Still, it doesn't stop them.' She rocked on her heels as she held onto his elbow. The sky was still bright, but men from the cinema were already lighting torches that flared a violent orange and sent up dirty brown smoke.

When the ticket office finally opened, the crowd surged forward and they lost their place to a chattering, well-dressed Anglo-Indian family. 'Typical bloody crannies,' Lesley remarked under her breath and at the little stab of distaste Jonathan turned his head, pretending not to have heard her. They had to wait a good ten minutes before they got to the front of the queue. Jonathan paid and turned to Lesley, who led him into the cinema.

It was nothing more than a large enclosure, open to the night air, with a dirt floor packed hard through use. Deckchairs were set up in haphazard lines and people from the town and passengers from the European ships were rapidly filling these seats. All about him he could hear languid conversations about seasickness and good stopping points, punctuated by the voices of sellers with wooden trays of nuts and fried beans wrapped in paper cones. As the sky darkened, the torches glowed a more vivid orange.

Lesley directed him to a raised platform with deckchairs, towards the rear of the courtyard. 'That's for the Bibby Line passengers,' she told him. When he asked her if she'd like some refreshment, she shook her head and produced a slim metal flask, which she handed to him. 'They prefer you don't drink in front of the locals, so keep it to yourself.' She laughed in her scratchy voice before taking the flask back. 'Your health.'

The little platform was filled with Europeans as well as English; an assortment of Dutch and French, Germans and Swiss, some chatting comfortably, others anxiously watching the blank screen. The sky was now completely dark and he saw that the same men who had lit the torches were walking along the perimeter of the wall. Ushers, perhaps? The crowd, good natured, excited, shifted in their seats. A kind of singsong went up in a language he did not know, but he could imagine the meaning of the words. Start the show, start the show.

As if on a signal, the cinema screen began to shudder with light. Beside the screen an Arab in a jacket and tie put the needle to a gramophone and a thread of orchestral music rose up and echoed into the night. The crowd settled in around Jonathan, but he was distracted, his eyes continually drawn back to the wall, for in the chiaroscuro of torchlight, white-clad bodies were rolling over the top of the wall and dropping silently onto the cinema's dirt floor.

He found himself listening for the thud of landing, bracing himself as each interloper appeared. But all he could hear was the music from the film as the ushers prowled, up and down along the wall, scanning for these men in their white robes, rushing to the spot when such a man was briefly visible. Always arriving too late, for the transgressors were easily absorbed into the too-dark night, quickly lost among the crush of chairs, the faces staring at the screen.

'I suppose they cannot police the whole expanse, so it's worth a chance to jump in like that,' he whispered to Lesley, but she pushed her hand at him and shushed him, never once shifting her gaze from the screen ahead. Her eyes were opened wide, her lips slightly parted; her whole body was straining forward.

Later, in the moonlight of his cabin, her nipples looked grey against the bluish skin of her small breasts, her eyes narrow and her forehead furrowed. With her body, she measured him, gauged him, until at the crucial moment she raised herself onto her knees and cried, 'Now, pull out now.' And he obeyed, sliding his slick penis free of her, rubbing himself against her belly until his shuddering climax, leaving only a tiny sticky stain on her skin that she wiped away with his handkerchief. In the morning he found it folded on his cabin table, his ejaculate a stiffened patch in one corner.

The main feature was a comedy. Lesley laughed and laughed, but he found it tedious, his own gaze drawn away from the grey-and-white images back to the walls. He kept watch for the men but no more came. Instead he found himself looking out across the expanse of stars, moved by the strangeness of them against the edge of the screen, so much brighter than the flat night. He gazed until he was dizzy with looking, until he was taken by an old and childish dread.

He didn't see Lesley again, not even at Calcutta where they docked and he had a few days ashore. He had been slightly ashamed at his relief.

The thrum of the steamer paddles changed tone, the stroke was slower and the engine throatier as the boat neared the docks, and now the noise of landing drowned out all other sound. The steamer lurched forward then back, left and right again as the captain manoeuvred alongside. Smoke churned in the air and a galley dropped from the ship to the walkway. As he crossed, Jonathan could hear the water slapping against the wheelhouses. Those Chittagonian sailors would still be far behind.

Jonathan stepped off the walkway and onto the streets of Rangoon. There was no smell of burning oil here, no grey, acrid air. He walked up towards the centre of the city, taking his time. As he did he experienced that instability, the mal d'embarquement that always comes after leaving a moving boat, no matter how short the trip. Beneath him, the ground seemed to pitch and wheel, but it didn't stop him. He didn't even break stride, knowing that it would only be a matter of time before he felt solid again.

Scott Market was teeming with people that morning and Winsome, her basket under her arm, had to stop for a moment to get her bearings. Wherever she turned, she heard a babble of languages: Burmese and Urdu, Shan and English, the occasional burst of German. There was the squeal of handcarts and the roar of a sugarcane juicer, the sizzling of hot oil in massive black dekshis. She could smell fermented fish and the turpentine of early mangoes. Jostling, pushing, lost in the crush, she was as bold as any explorer, brave as any martyr and because of this she felt a shiver of near-perfect, private joy. She bargained with a farmer's wife for a tola of lady's finger bananas and smiled at her newfound competence while in a far corner, a Chinaman in a too-big English suit sobbed, the flesh of some pink fruit smashed across his bare brown feet.

Most mornings, it was not joy that she felt. She woke abruptly from disgraceful dreams, her thighs still sticky with an ebbing private pleasure, while Desmond snored beside her. The stripes of beige light across the crumpled sheets, the sight of his slippers neatly arranged on the floor, these made her sad beyond bearing.

Her dreams still drifting through her, she rose from their bed and into the long, flat hours ahead.

These were heaty days, when something in the thick air loosened her joints and razed her judgment so that she looked when she should have turned away, stared when she should have cast her eyes down. It was on a heaty day that she first realised Rangoon was a city of men; men pulled rickshaws, drove buses, important men in light-coloured suits rushed along Phayre Street, holding their noses against the smell of drains. White men, brown men, black and yellow men, bunched like so much ripening fruit. She imagined them falling, warm from the branch, onto the flat of her hand. But that was not all; when the yellow-haired clerk at Barnet's smirked at her, she itched to smash something stinking into his pink face. She was transfixed by a monk's bronze skin, let her fingers graze those of a black coolie as she passed him in the street. These impulses both shamed and exhilarated her; she was incapable of repressing them.

The sky was already turquoise and the air glassy when she left Scott Market. She turned towards the river, walking aimlessly, stopping only when she found herself in China Street.

China Street was one of the places the young half-caste wives of St John's would not go. Dirt gathered there; those clever Chinese merchants might cheat you; an impertinent Burman might look at you in that way. Worse iniquities were possible—whores, abortionists. One had to be careful, one had to keep one's distance. In the very air the potential for corruption was as palpable as the spice of foreign food and you held tighter to your bags, you kept your eyes on the ground, for who knew what you might tread in?

Rangoon hygienic and unhygienic, that was what those young married Catholic women discussed over tea and white baps at Continental Cakes, their noses heavily powdered so that they would not brown in the sun.

But as she walked along the dry earth, Winsome found China Street a disappointment; it was airy and open, the shuttered shop-houses too linear and sturdily built. If there was corruption, then it was obscured by bland china shops and round-bellied merchants. She stopped beside a noodle stall. Above her hung an old red lantern faded to the colour of tea. She stared up into its limp tassels.

'Move it, lady!'

Winsome felt a heavy thud as the handcart clipped her calves and threw her forward. She cried out in pain, then angrily turned and shouted, 'Idiot, come back here,' but the idiot, some clumsy, rushing coolie, was gone. She bent to rub the back of her legs.

In the air there was a new sound. Voices, fractured and discordant; and then around the corner of Dalhousie Street came a sudden surge of people. Indians mostly, of the higher castes. They moved it seemed with one purpose. A chorus, their single voice controlled by a young Burmese woman, delicately pretty, marching at the front, a tall bespectacled Indian beside her. Winsome watched as the woman, a megaphone raised to her lips, bound the crowd together with words alone.

Here then was shame of a completely different sort, shouting aloud in the street, making a public display of oneself. Yet this girl did not look like a rough sort, even though she was dressed in the plain homespun that the poorest rice farmers wore. 'Sen Gupta!' she called.

'Yes,' the crowd seemed to reply, 'he shall be free!'

Because Desmond insisted she read the English newspapers every day, Winsome knew that Sen Gupta was the Mayor of Calcutta, brought to Rangoon to face charges of sedition. She knew he was a supporter of Gandhi and those Indian nationalists who refused to buy the prints and calicos made in Manchester, choosing instead the local cloth, plain and grey. 'They wear shabby clothes,' Desmond jeered, 'and think they can govern themselves.'

But she saw nothing shabby about the young woman with the megaphone or the other young people around her, similarly dressed. Their skin was too sleek, their expressions too satisfied, and their clothes were spotlessly clean. When they called out, answering the girl, it was in English and Hindi but not Burmese; when they punched the air with their fists, it was with the expectation of the crowd's approval, even admiration.

These, then, must be the students and lawyers, the political troublemakers she had read about. The girl lifted the megaphone once more and called to them. The crowd's response was like a wind along the street.

Near Winsome a Burmese noodle-seller emptied his full pot onto the ground and ran. Up and down the street, the Chinese merchants hurriedly closed their doors. Soon the crowd would be upon her and escape would be impossible. She picked up her basket of bananas, yet she did not move—she was mesmerised by the faces and gestures, the spectacle of the crowd, wondering how it must feel to be one among so many.

And in that brief moment of hesitation she lost her chance. They were upon her, the delicate young woman near enough for Winsome to count the pins holding her dark twist of hair. She shouted through the megaphone once more and this time, when the crowd's cry resounded, Winsome felt her ribs vibrate, as if she had raised her own voice, euphoric and fearless. If she felt herself carried along by the rhythm of this mass of feet, this push of bodies, she allowed it.

Around her the marchers laughed, they joked and chanted and sang. A dark man with brilliantined hair offered her a little yellow flower, tucking it behind her ear. From within the crowd, she found that she could no longer hear the girl's words as distinctly as she had before, but that it didn't matter. She felt the sun on her face and a forward impetus that made every movement effortless. If there was one meaning she could decipher it was 'we' (or maybe 'us') and this we/us was repeated again and again. She wondered what we/us might mean—we the crowd, united by the action of marching? We who march?

But now China Street narrowed and the protesters crushed in tightly around her, a poorer sort of man at her shoulders—for they were all men, hard-eyed with thin, pinched faces. What had felt like effortless movement became forced, a relentless forward pressure. She scrambled to keep pace, hampered by their bodies, barely able to feel her own arms or legs or feet, concentrating only on remaining upright, while around her head the words we/us, we/us echoed. We/us that so easily might mean not-you.

She was being pressed up hard against some brittle emotion, it made her gasp, it grated along her skin, a high-pitched sensation that made everything strange. Something shattered, she could taste it. Glass? Someone shook a fist above his head; another banged his bamboo stave against the ground; others took up this thump, thump, thump; the chant of we/us/not-you now a threat. She thought of the noodle-seller abandoning his pot and pushed, so that she too might escape, but the crowd held her. Beneath her feet the ground was slippery.

She lost a shoe, sucked right off her foot, and she was forced to limp, her rough basket of bananas held tight against her chest. The shop signs of China Street were her new horizon—*pots, pans, kitchen implements*. Black men, brown men, yellow men rolled around and over her, engulfing her in breath and skin and hair and heat and although the crush of them was repulsive to her, she was also reliant upon it; she would fall without these men and women who were also her tormentors, she would be lost beneath them. We/us was gluey air and sweaty bodies, an animal panic, a suffocating chaos. She kicked out viciously at the give of flesh next to her, saw it was the man with the brilliantined hair.

And then they stopped and she was able to take a free breath. But the respite was brief and again the crowd surged, this time back upon itself so that she was once more enfolded in a human fabric, only pressed more tightly and from all directions. Until she was lifted from her feet. Until she could not tell where her body ended and others began. Formless and limbless, suffocating, the air about her going bright and then black, like the weave of a dream. All of them one seething skin, born from that one voice, we/us. Touch was molten, numbing, animal, urgent, insane. Yet in this madness, she was entirely alone.

Without warning the crowd eased and fell apart.

The open air like a cool breeze. The firmness of the road beneath her feet. She could barely take these things in. The buildings were dazzling, the distant sounds of traffic, musical. She still held her basket in her arms.

She took a few steps to the kerb and sat down on her own, at a little distance from the crowd. The sole of her left foot was badly cut, it felt hot and she winced when she probed the place. She calculated the steps to the bus stop, further to the tram, there was the ride home, another quarter of a mile's walk at the other end. Could she manage it? She felt for her purse. There was only enough money for the bus fare. She would have to travel with one shoe.

In her misshapen basket, the bananas she'd bargained for so skilfully were ruined; she sighed at the waste and drew a hand through her hair. Behind her ear she found the yellow flower. She threw it onto the road.

At the far end of China Street, where it met the Strand and the docks, the tall Indian blew a conch shell and the sound, loud and belligerent, hurt her ears. She heard the voice of the young woman once more. This was no longer call and response but something else, something calculated to raise the blood. Already, ranks of dark-bodied labourers had gathered along the dockyard fences to listen, Telugu labourers eager for the slightest distraction.

'My friends,' came the girl's voice through the megaphone, a little reedy for being further away, 'my comrades, we share a cause.' There were jeers from the labourers—comrades, they would be laughing at the very idea—but of course this did not deter that steely young woman, who merely adjusted the angle of her attack. 'Wealth,' she cried, 'is the foundation of all power. And we shall be poor no longer.'

Now there was an eruption of voices from the crowd, a roar of such force she barely heard the whistle blasts. Three shrill notes.

Winsome didn't see how the trouble started. Later, all she remembered was a brief, flat silence and then the sudden onrush of air as people began to run. She would have run herself, but where? To what? All about her were shouts, the thud of feet, the smell of sweat and anger, as people swarmed like insects with no centre and no direction. Those with purpose swung sticks or threw stones. She jumped to her feet.

She found herself face to face with a labourer, no older than fifteen, his black face pitted with acne like little white stars. 'Miss, miss,' he croaked, clutching at the air, turning to her as if he might hold onto her, as if she might keep him still, his terrified eyes rolling in a manner that was oddly comical.

Or at least she remembered thinking this as she saw a running man pause, his longyi awry as he raised a bamboo stave above his head and swung it against the boy's right temple. The force of the blow sprayed moisture from the boy's face onto hers and she felt the crunch of his bone, caught his look of surprise. Then he fell, legs and arms twitching. The man ran off as she dragged the boy to one side, cradling his head in her lap.

When the next police whistle sounded, the mob once again seemed to pause. At the final whistle, all who were able turned and ran while along the street came a line of police—sunburnt Britons, Anglos, Indians and Burmans, burly in their blue uniforms. With linked arms, they pushed through everything in their path, sweeping up those who were left, making no distinction between marchers and onlookers, black or brown, Indian or Burman, men or women, labourers or men of substance; anyone could be caught up and kicked down. In two charges the street was clear.

A red-faced policeman, stinking from his exertions, bent over her. 'Got an injured half a loaf,' he called out, then: 'You all right, miss?'

'Yes,' she replied, 'but this man is hurt.'

He looked down at the boy. 'He's a bit worse than hurt, love.' Colour was seeping from the boy's face and he was slack in her arms.

'Is he dead?'

The policeman shrugged.

'Will someone take care of him?'

He held out his hand to her. 'Time to get on home now, miss.' Gently she rolled the boy's head from her lap and put her hand into the policeman's. He pulled her to her feet.

But when she tried to take a step, her knees buckled. She was missing her purse, had lost her bus fare. Her other shoe was gone. Slowly, painfully she combed the street for her things.

She found an abandoned shoe on the opposite side of the road, the sole badly split, it was difficult to slip the strap over her heel. She found a slipper in a gutter and thus mismatched she struggled along. The policeman took her arm. 'Enough to get you home with, miss.' (Miss miss.) 'I'll take you to the bus stop.'

Together they walked towards the bus station, he cupping her elbow where the ground was rough. As she walked, Winsome saw over and over again the thin face of the boy, his hand clutching at the air as he fell.

'What will happen to him? Will somebody attend to him?' she asked the policeman. 'Are you certain he was dead?'

When they reached Campbell Street the policeman stopped and gestured to the depot on the other side. She turned to thank him, but before she could speak, he had caught the hem of her skirt with the tip of his truncheon. Delicately, playfully, he raised the fabric above her knees until she could feel the stick cold against her leg.

She staggered backwards, away from him, but he grabbed her by the wrist. He leaned in, his face close to hers. 'Best be careful where you walk in future, miss.' Then he flicked her skirt so that it jumped a little higher, exposing the tops of her thighs, before dropping back down to her knees. 'Rangoon isn't safe for girls like you.' He turned and left her to walk the rest of the way alone.

At the depot the other passengers stared and she realised her clothes were stained with the boy's blood. On the bus, news of the disturbance travelled up and down the rows of seats. She could hear the passengers speaking of it.

'I heard that a woman was attacked.'

'They say it was a criminal gang and the police were waiting for them.'

'Sen Gupta was there.'

'It was Indians, immigrants—it always is.'

'A lazy people.'

'Gandhi himself sent spies.'

'Three men were killed.'

'No one was hurt.'

'Dirty kalaas.'

'Fucking natives.'

On it went, as absurd as the running, sprawling bodies, the angry faces, eyes big, mouths gaping.

By the time the bus pulled into Kemmendine Station her body had stiffened and she stood up from her seat with difficulty. On the walk home, the sole of her ruined shoe flapped against the laterite road.

'A riot! How on earth did you manage it?' Desmond cried. 'What were you doing there, in that part of town?'

Wearing clean clothes, her body scrubbed, her skin rubbed with balm, she had no words to answer him. China Street was unhygienic.

The girl, Than Thint, had helped her when she got home; she had warmed the water, taken away her soiled clothes, rubbed her bruises. Winsome told her about the boy and she gasped and then whispered, 'What was it like, to see a man die?' In her soft brown eyes there was a yellow gleam.

'Someone was killed,' Than Thint said to Desmond.

He gave the girl a sharp look before turning back to Winsome. 'No one was killed,' he contradicted her, 'that's official.' But his face was guarded and Winsome felt a little throb of fear and anger. 'I saw it happen,' she said, her voice low. 'He was a boy, no more than fifteen.'

Desmond looked from Winsome to the girl and back again. He sighed. 'You are mistaken.' His tone was still firm, but soothing too. He took a step towards her and then, folding her in his long

35

arms, rested his chin on the top of her head. His body felt unyielding, his will a drag on her flesh. 'It is easy to make a such a mistake. It's the shock of things. That is all. Besides,' he added, and she could hear the sneer in his voice, the small triumph, 'if anybody should know, wouldn't it be me?'

She pushed herself away from him. 'I know what I saw.' The heat of her words made him set his face and turn away, his arms swinging roughly. She thought of the policeman's warning and flinched.

Near the door, the girl hovered. 'Put her to bed,' Desmond spat as he left the room.

All of that night she dreamed of the dead boy. In the morning, her body ached and she found she had come up in bruises, her trunk, her sides, the outside of her hips, along the back of her legs, even the small of her back was marked. At times her head throbbed with the smack of bamboo against human flesh.

When the newspapers came she scoured them for a report of the riot and the death. All she found was a brief mention of a student demonstration in between stories of Sen Gupta's trial, higher rice prices and a new building planned for the Pegu Social Club. The half-dozen lines of the report ended with 'police were called' and that was all. She sent the girl out to check the other English papers, as well as the Burmese and Indian ones. No deaths were mentioned. She reminded herself of Desmond's instructions (do not think of it, stay home, rest). 'Perhaps he did not die,' she said aloud.

She knew that was wrong because in the morning, the boy came back to her; from the corner of her eye she caught a glimpse of his slackened jaw, of his comically rolling eyes. Filling a glass with water, she was startled by the sudden flail of his hand. If she stood up too quickly from her chair, she heard his lisping voice. Always, he was there. By the afternoon she could not stand it any longer;

she snatched up her good straw hat and limped slowly to the tram stop for town.

As the tram passed the important buildings on Commissioners Road, she sensed him, loping alongside the tram's open window. She closed her eyes against him and saw instead liverish-red walls, shadows playing from electric lights swinging on long cords, Desmond standing over a sheeted body. *Miss miss, don't mind me, miss.*

She went first to the police station but they sent her to the Rangoon General Hospital. It was where Desmond worked, but she steeled herself and made her enquiry anyway, giving only the details of the boy and not her own name.

'He was young,' she told the clerk, 'about fifteen, he was a Coringhee, I think, working on the docks. He was hit on the head yesterday. He was hit here,' and she showed him with her hands. While the man consulted the records, she waited silently to one side.

'Excuse me,' the clerk called her. 'There is someone. It may be him.'

The mortuary was set apart from the hospital in a corner of the grounds studded by shade trees and palms. As she walked beside the clerk along the cinder path, her head hummed and something white fluttered at the edge of her vision. The ache in her body was worse now, and the heat felt like defeat. Desmond would be there. Of course he would.

'This way, miss.' The clerk held the door open for her and she walked into a hall. There was an annexe with an office—she recognised the jacket hanging on the rack. The clerk led her into an open room. A tall man stood with other men over the body of a child. The tall man looked up.

'Winsome?'

Desmond excused himself and walked across the room towards her. His eyebrows were furled with surprise and displeasure.

37

Beside her, she could feel the clerk's hesitation. Her face was numb.

'I came about the boy who died.' How calm her voice sounded, how serene.

'You were supposed to stay home and rest.'

'But he's here, Desmond.'

Desmond thanked the clerk, who still stood there. 'Which one?' he asked.

'Twelve.'

Desmond nodded. 'I will take her.'

The clerk turned to go.

Desmond faced her. 'Do you insist?'

She could no longer read his expression, her own face felt swollen, her eyelids too heavy. 'Yes, I insist.'

He nodded curtly. 'Then follow me.' He walked through the room and past the annexe, out of the door and along the edge of the building. He moved fast and she had to run to keep up, her breath coming in little gasps.

He turned down a cinder path; he didn't slow his pace or speak to her. She wondered where they were going, because already they had left the main buildings behind, but she felt the boy beside her and knew they must be getting close. Like her, he was forced to quicken his pace to keep up with Desmond. She could hear him wheeze, it must have been all that dust at the docks.

They reached a wide road, Canal Street, and she was forced to rest for a moment to catch her breath. She leaned against the trunk of a palm, panting, her body sagging beneath its own weight. The boy stopped beside her, hands on his knees, bent forward from the waist. Desmond stepped out onto the kerb and raised his arm. He hailed a trishaw. She turned to the boy, she wanted to tell him she was sorry, but he had already gone.

'You are unwell,' Desmond said, but he did not take his

eyes from the road as he spoke. 'Otherwise you would not go traipsing after a dead coolie. The police probably chucked his body into the river, that's the truth of it. You are to go home now and sleep it off.'

For the next few days, she did as she was told. She suspected that the girl, Than Thint, had been instructed to watch her: she brought Winsome consommé soup, the *Rangoon Times*, the Burmese newspapers, dry toast, slices of melon. But the smell of food made her gag, she had no appetite, couldn't even stomach a cup of clear tea. She picked up the newspapers and each time put them down again, unable to decipher the printed words. Every movement dragged at her body and, although the weather was hot, she felt chilled and nauseated. It pained her to pass water. When she did, her urine was dark and cloudy and it stank, as though she harboured something foul deep inside her. Sleep was equally impossible, fitful at best. Whenever she closed her eyes she felt herself closed in by bodies once more, trapped and unable to move.

The boy came back on the second night. She dreamed of him, he was tugging at her arm, trying to lead her somewhere; she shouted that she would not go, and was shaken awake by the chattering of her own teeth. Her ribs shuddered and her legs bent in on themselves, independently of her will, jerking so violently she was frightened that her bones would snap. Tremor after tremor tore through her until she had to fight to draw breath.

When the shaking stopped, she fell into a half-sleep and in her dreams began to sob. She dreamed that it was the boy's weeping she heard, but woke to find her own face wet. She had to push her nose and mouth into the pillow to stop the crying. Through it all, Desmond slept and she didn't dare rouse him. She was too frightened at what her body had become.

By Sunday morning she felt better, and even took a little tea and fruit at breakfast. Desmond was pleased. 'I think you're well enough to go to church,' he said and ordered a rickshaw, despite the expense.

As they rode, he told her he was proud that she had snapped out of it. 'None of us is able to deal easily with shocking things,' he said, 'but deal with them we must.'

St John's was warm and smelled of old wood and candles. The church's beams and joists creaked and groaned with the rising heat while all around the congregation fluttered sandalwood fans. At the end of their row a man snored softly with his head tilted back, his mouth slack and wide.

At the intercessions she began to weep and could not stop. She covered her face with her hands, trying to stifle the deep sobs that broke from her throat. But it did no good. Still they erupted from deep within her—comical sorrow, theatrical, sounding like mocking laughter. Nearby a small boy giggled.

'You have nothing whatever to cry about,' Desmond hissed fiercely. 'Stop. It. Now.'

But she could not stop. She could barely breathe. The white fluttering returned and she felt herself sinking, a waxy, flickering thing into the wooden pew. She wept. The priest droned over her, but no one was listening to him any longer. Row by row the fanning, the rustling of hymnals, ceased. Even the snoring man fell quiet. There was only a muscular, listening silence, the priest's voice, her wheezing.

Mrs De Brito stood up in the front pew. She turned into the aisle, her heels rapping against the teak floor, and stopped only when she came to Desmond and Winsome's bench. 'My dear,' she said, pointing her fan at Winsome, 'I think you'd better come with me.'

They each took a shoulder, Desmond and Mrs De Brito, and supporting her between them, took her to the small vestry just inside the porch and sat her on a bench there. She was choking now, gasping for breath yet still she could not stop, her sorrow going on without her. Desmond's face was pale and his eyes black. He bent low over her and gripped her shoulders hard.

'Funny thing,' he said, his voice almost tender. Then he shook and shook and shook her until the air was full of small bright lights.

'Mr Goode! Stop it.' Mrs De Brito pulled at his arms until Desmond, his own breath ragged, finally loosened his grip, reeling backwards. Mrs De Brito inserted her body between them. 'Can you not see that your wife is ill?' she demanded, her face shiny and pink.

'Ill?' repeated Desmond, his voice faraway, a dreamer disturbed.

Ill? thought Winsome. *Ill*, and she wanted to laugh except she hadn't the breath. *I thought I was mad.* It was the last thing she remembered before she lost consciousness.

Desmond took long, quick steps across the lawn of the mortuary compound then stopped and scraped his left foot against the grass once more.

This time the lazy little derwan, the Indian nightwatchman, had gone too far. Desmond had explained time and again that the pariah dogs must be kept out, that if they were not chased away, they would mark the mortuary as their territory. And how would it look to have mangy, hungry dogs hanging around a mortuary? The bereaved would wonder what the dogs had been eating. What would the District Inspector think? After each interview, the nightwatchman had waggled his head, plucked pathetically at Desmond's sleeve and promised to do better. 'But he has been laughing up his sleeve,' Desmond shouted out loud. Because this morning, at the building's very entrance, Desmond had found evidence that the pariah dogs were still very much at home in the grounds: he had stepped in a soft pile of shit.

The smell was the first thing he noticed. Pungent and gamey, stinking of stolen food gobbled down quickly. As he strode to the nightwatchman's hut at the edge of the compound, he could still smell it, despite the repeated rubbing of his shoe against the grass. It was an odour that clung and was offensive to a man accustomed to the vilest of odours.

As he walked, he imagined the face of the watchman shaken from his sleep. The man's yellow eyes would dart this way and that as his body twisted with remorse, his hut would be squalid and dirty. Well, Desmond would be sure that this time he learned his lesson. He would make that lesson sting.

Already he had noticed that here in Rangoon, the big city, there was an attitude about that whole class—cooks, houseboys, waiters. He saw it even in the clerks and assistants in the hospital. Some of the porters—Bengalis, Burmans—had dared to tell him that the pariah dogs were not responsible for the dung, that the derwan himself had placed it there as a charm to ward off evil spirits gathering around the dead, it was part of his job. Perhaps they took him for an up-country bumpkin; perhaps they had failed to mark his white blood, his family name—one of the old Anglo-Indian families.

No matter. He could see this was a case of shirking. That was the thing; certain natives were not always prepared to do things properly. They did not accept that there was a price for a meal, for a roof. Position, no matter how humble; prestige—these things cost.

Desmond stopped for a moment and checked his shoe again. The smear was now nothing more than a faint impression of moisture, but the leather sole would never be truly clean. 'Ruined,' he snarled and his fingers itched for the nightwatchman's neck, to squeeze him like they used to do with the dacoits, the robbers and miscreants, up country when he was still on the police. There, the law was writ on flesh. He had done the writing at the behest of his superiors. Give him another, give it to him Goode, stout fellow.

Without warning the ferrous scent of blood flooded through

him and with it, the sensation of flesh landing upon flesh, how a body gave against your fist, the watery sound of it, always accommodating, making way.

He lurched towards a spreading tree, ducking into its shade. He took out his handkerchief and dried his forehead. Across the brown lawn he could see the low mortuary building, the little window of his office. That was the thing, to look, to take a step back and look carefully. That way you could think. He pictured his desk. He pictured a neat stack of new files, tied with departmental ribbon.

When he was a child his mother had found work as a nursemaid at various well-to-do households around the district. She was always tired in her brief hours off, but he found ways to please her. He collected wild golden raspberries for her, or sweet limes. Sometimes he'd dig for water potatoes and wrap them in a leaf so they'd stay cool and keep that refreshing wetness in the mouth. He would be waiting for her at home, standing to present his gifts, wanting only for her to take him into her long, thin arms, her son, her only child.

Once he brought her a bunch of wild flowers, as he'd seen her 'other' children do, her rosy-cheeked, white charges. Irma's laugh was sour as she'd set the bunch of weeds aside. It was the same in the police; the white officers had relied on him to use his fists, but his obedience, his talent as an enforcer of punishments, had not helped him to progress any faster.

Always, during the beatings, he heard their laughter in the background and afterwards none of those white officers could meet his eye. If they did he saw mistrust, and fear. Quid pro quo. You had to understand what was *really* wanted, you had to see it, beyond your loathing, beyond your disgust. The price had to be right.

It was soon afterwards that he began helping the police surgeon with the bodies. And now here he was, in Rangoon.

Desmond pulled at his jacket lapels, shook them straight before leaving the shade. He draped his handkerchief over his head to protect himself from the sun, and continued on to the nightwatchman's hut. He knew the price that he would extract today; call it reparations. First the watchman would clean up the mess that the dogs had left—Desmond would inspect his work— then he would have to set traps for the dogs. Lethal traps. The dogs would have to be killed, and if the taking of those lives went against his God's will then so be it; a punishment should fit the crime.

But when he arrived at the far edge of the compound, the watchman's little hut was silent. Inside, he found only a folded cloth on the string bed, a stove made from an old coffee tin filled with a meagre mound of charcoal, a dented cooking pot and half a gourd of rice. There was no dirt, no squalor. With a sweep of his foot, Desmond sent the rice and charcoal spilling across the floor. He wiped his feet on the way out.

As he walked back across the lawns, he noted that the morning already had the kind of Rangoon brassiness that signalled the hottest of days. At home, his wife would be lying on the day-bed, her eyes still opaque although he knew she had recovered from her fever. Did one ever fully recover? He touched his fingertips to his palm. The gardener would have to clean up the dog mess instead, and set the traps for the dogs. The watchman would have to be let go, he would see to that.

Errors such as this did not inevitably mean failure. If he had made a few miscalculations, if some things were outside his experience, then he would see them right. He would do what needed to be done, as Irma had done (and if it pained you to do your duty, then more fool you for allowing it to hurt). He would take a view of what should be given and what expected in return. He would see to things. He continued across the lawns to his office.

On the wooden board, Winsome cut the lemon in half with the heavy cleaver. Juice leaked onto the wood. Outside, the green pigeons were whistling and calling between the branches of the mango trees. It would be dark in minutes, but it would be another hour before the heat subsided and the air cooled.

Her belly was heavy and her breasts were sore, swollen against the fabric of her dress. She was late, and now something inside her was quickening, reaching into the night and thirsting for cool air. For more than a week her body had been cutting itself from its moorings, turning away. Slipping into the centre of a river, where the current flowed fastest and the danger of drowning was acute.

Was it only a fortnight since she'd stopped to watch the ocean-going liners picking their way along the Rangoon River as it rose with the incoming tide?

She took another lemon from the bowl, the yellow skin vibrating against the greying light as she sliced into its flesh. The blade skated across the tough peel and into the pad of her finger; she gave a little cry of shock as the acid bit and her blood welled. She sucked at the cut. It tasted salty and sour.

Back in Kalaw, not lemons but limes were cut for drinks. Large, heavy, sweet limes. You found them growing wild in small clusters throughout the grey-green jungle. Saya Teresa, the women's doctor, planted some in the little garden surrounding her orange-brick house not far from the convent school.

'So she's growing wild limes, is she?' Assumpta had snorted her scorn. The small trees, bent and twisted with puny trunks, did look faintly ridiculous, splayed and staked against the wall. Not like the hydrangeas, the beds of roses, the cultivated hedges of other gardens. Even the Burmese laughed to see these tough little local trees cultivated in a European way.

But the wild sweet limes loved Teresa's garden. They produced gluts of fruit from among thick growths of glossy leaves. On the days Winsome was sent to help at the surgery, she would often find Teresa in her lime grove. She could still picture her tending those trees; gently bending a leaf to one side, checking for marks of disease, taking off the spectacles that usually sat crooked on her nose, screwing up her eyes and pushing her face close.

As soon as Winsome took her finger from her mouth, more blood leaked from the lips of the wound. It was almost black in this half-light. She was not surprised. What would be the colour of a quickening woman? Of a changeling? Green. Blue. Or yellow. Above the clean edge of the cut her skin was ridged and irregular. She squeezed her fingertip against her thumb.

Six weeks ago, after mass at St John's, she found Desmond standing at the offering table to Saint Agatha. He was lighting a candle in a red glass cup. The small flame flickered merrily, eating up the air around it, making its own small roar, audible if you bent close.

'What is that for?'

He grinned at her, took her elbow and steered her away. 'For us of course, you funny thing.' He squeezed the back of her arm as they walked towards the priest to take their leave.

That night, in the cool darkness, he placed his open hand on the flat of her belly. Immediately, she moved against him, her body a warm shadow, melting like wax, sticking to his skin. It had been like this for her since their first night together, the weight of his hand all it took to win her. Once, early on, she had locked her pelvis to his, had called out loudly, hooked her mouth onto his shoulder. He had pulled away and left their bed, wiping her saliva from his skin.

In their marriage lessons the priest had warned them against excess appetites, 'For it is appetite that leads to sin.' Now she was decorous in her responses, on guard in case her body betrayed her and followed the impulse to curl around him like smoke.

Oh, but his skin was so sweet.

In the months they had been married, he had lit a votive candle at the shrine of St Agatha eleven times. Eleven times he had placed his hand on the flat of her belly.

Last Sunday, Mrs De Brito smiled at her, tapped her with the end of her sandalwood fan, rested it for a moment on her shoulder as the other women whose hats matched their silk dresses watched. 'Children are the smile of God upon a woman,' she said and Winsome felt that watery little stab of fear: the thought of a child.

Holding her finger up near the window in what was left of the light, she could see the lips of her wound, she held them together, squeezing her fingertip with her good hand and as she did, wondered whether those edges would knit back together in misalignment, leaving a small, permanent change in her body, noticeable only to herself. In years to come, she might catch sight of the faint white line and think, *That was the time when I cut myself slicing lemons for our evening drinks.* A line that marked the moment when the heat of the day dissolved into evening, that stood for the sound of spoons tinkling in glasses, an unexplained heaviness in her belly: all that inscribed on the bud of her finger.

'Marriage lessons?' Dr Teresa had bent her head to one side, her fingers resting against her temple as she regarded Winsome. They sat on wicker chairs outside the front of the orange house and Teresa's chair creaked beneath her bulk. 'What sort of marriage lessons?'

'They're teaching us about being married.'

That day, Teresa's clothes were rumpled, her eyelids stuck together when she blinked, and the skin around her eyes folded in on itself as she squinted to see across the garden. When she pushed her glasses up her nose, her fingers were stained yellow. 'I see.'

The wicker creaked again as Teresa stretched out her long legs, bending them to lean forward. 'Well, Winsome, I have something to show you. Something every bride should see.' She stood up and turned towards the house. 'You can call it another marriage lesson.'

In the small hallway Teresa's face was grave even though she used Winsome's pet name. 'It is wise to be prepared, kyi kyi. That is why you have these lessons?'

'Yes, that is what the priest says.'

'Good. Then we are all in agreement.' Teresa paused before she pushed the wooden door open. 'Because love is full of surprises.'

The last light of the day was glowing across the window ledge and the room, Teresa's examination room, was already gloomy. It was a big space, divided in half, with very little furniture—a desk, a cabinet for papers, Teresa's certificates in medicine pinned on the wall, a porcelain basin, three lamps on a high shelf, a green curtain. The air smelled salty and sour.

Teresa lit a lamp and the wick fizzed blue and then white as it caught alight. She pulled back the curtain. Something was laid out on the bed, a large shape beneath the white sheet. Winsome's voice was a whisper. 'What is that?'

The lamp cast deep shadows across the hollows of Teresa's eyes; she placed it on the small ledge above the bed. 'This?' Teresa smiled. 'She was a fool for love.' Her hands were dark against the white sheet as she drew it down.

Winsome knew that the body beneath the sheet would still be warm. The air was still clotted with the girl's struggle. She looked away from the face, focusing instead on the large, distended belly. Dark yellow, smeared with turmeric, bright against the mottled, greying skin. The flesh crumpled and sagged in on itself, the legs

49

were bent and folded outwards, like a little frog. There was a mole on the outside of one knee and, further down, darkness stained the sheet. Winsome turned away.

'Kyi kyi, look a little longer.'

The girl's long black hair flowed off the side of the bed and hung towards the floor, gleaming in the lamplight. Winsome wanted to back away from the body, but she couldn't. 'Who is she?'

'She was a fool. She tried to save herself, but she did not know how. Don't they teach you about love, about loving, in those marriage lessons of yours, kyi kyi? Nha?' Her voice was gentle, but with a tightness.

'Yes.'

'But do they tell you how to love? How he will love you?' Teresa moved towards her, and gripped Winsome's shoulder with one hand. 'Shall I tell you, kyi kyi?'

Winsome thought of the little priest, his tuft of white hair. His red-veined face and dark fingertips. When he took mass or gave communion, he breathed through his mouth and spoke with a lisp, his lips forming a moist oh, connected by a string of saliva. 'Thuth thayeth the lawd.'

'Kyi kyi,' Teresa was very close, 'do you know it all now?'

'They tell us what we need to know.'

Teresa pointed her chin towards the still body. 'Children die. Mothers die. It happens every day.' Winsome had seen their graves in the graveyard in Kalaw. The nuns prayed for the dead. The families gave them money to do it.

'What do you know?'

She knew that a married woman had obligations. That she had to put her girlhood behind her. That she would have to face her duties.

'What do you know?' Her voice was kind and, as she spoke,

Teresa took her hand, held her fingers tight.

'Do you know how he will touch you?'

Teresa guided her hand down under the fabric of her skirt, over the elastic of her underpants, until it was next to her skin, until she could feel the give of her belly and the bristling of her own pubic hair.

'A married woman,' the priest had said, the little string of saliva stretching long then short, 'must bend her body to a greater will.'

She tried to ball her fingers, to hold them away from the stiff hairs, from the beginnings of her sex. But Teresa leaned in closer and Winsome felt the back of her thighs pinned against the side of the day-bed. She could taste the salt smell of blood, the girl's blood. And in her ear there was Teresa's voice.

'He will want to touch you down here.'

Winsome cried out, pulled her fingers free, tried to push against Teresa's shoulder. Instead, she felt the flat of Teresa's hand as it passed along her pubic bone, the fingers tangling in the hair, then sliding between her legs. Teresa touched her in a place where she felt like something would let go, like something in her body would fail. 'He will touch you here.'

Her bladder emptied into Teresa's palm. Still Teresa pushed her fingers deeper.

'He will put himself, his hard self, up in here.'

It stirred her at the edge of herself like a string tied and twisted until it is too tight. She dropped her head against the front of Teresa's shoulder and cried.

'Shh shh shh,' Teresa whispered as she slackened her grip and slipped her fingers from the space between them. She walked to the basin, she washed her hands.

'That was the first lesson, kyi kyi.' She faced the wall as she spoke, as Winsome crumpled to her haunches, arms curled around her knees, crying quietly and wondering if urine had stained the back of her skirt.

The kitchen was dark now and still hot, even though the sun had gone. She could hear Desmond in the next room, clearing his throat, settling into a chair. She held her open hand against her belly, which rounded outwards into her palm, firm and full. She pulled the fabric of the skirt tight against its outline.

If she tapped it, would it sound hollow? Or would something stir and move? Was she the sort of woman who could love a child? She thought of her own mother, the mushroom scent of her scalp, the softness of her arms—but when she tried to picture her face, all she could recall was an oval blur.

The floor of Teresa's examination room had been cool under her body. Hunched on the ground, Winsome had hidden her face in her skirt. She had not moved as Teresa worked around her, straightening the sheet over the girl. Then she bent over Winsome and touched her elbow gently.

'Come, kyi kyi, there is just one more lesson.'

In the garden, Winsome watched as Teresa selected a large sweet lime. She lifted her spectacles and put her nose close to each fruit, checking for small insects, for signs of disease, for a firm and shiny skin. She cupped a lime in her hand and gave a sharp twist so that the stalk relinquished it.

Inside the house, at the low kitchen table, Teresa poured water into an enamel basin and rinsed the lime skin carefully. She dried it with a clean cloth and placed it on a wooden cutting board. Picking up the heavy dah, she sliced off the end of the lime, removed the pulp, then turned it over and over in her hand, a small green cup. A

52

tiny, inverted umbrella. She cocked her head at Winsome.

'This, kyi kyi, is a prevention against the consequences of love.' She took a step closer to Winsome and patted her belly. 'You are still a child yourself. I will show you how to use this. That is marriage lesson number two. Think of it as my wedding present.'

In the close, dark kitchen, Winsome felt a trickle between her legs. She put a finger into her pants and when she pulled it out that finger shone with blood. So there was no baby, not yet, and her fears, Mrs De Brito's tap of the fan, none of these had been warranted. She leaned her hands on the table, a heaviness washing through her that must be relief. *A child*, she thought, *might have loved me.*

The open windows of the small, square drawing room allowed the evening breeze through the house. Winsome carried the mahogany tray and placed it beside Desmond. In two tumblers, lemon juice and sugar swirled like oil against the boiled water, cool from the ceramic jar. She watched as Desmond stirred the liquid with a long-handled spoon until each crystal of sugar was dissolved.

He took a sip and smiled at her. 'Delicious.'

She smiled back.

When Jonathan returned from his first visit to the Victoria Boat Club, he did not immediately climb the stairs to his apartments, but instead took a turn around the garden. The sky was full of stars and it was pleasant to stroll in the night air, which was lavishly cool. Besides, he did not want to meet Khit Tin, who would wake as soon as he came in, padding out to ask if something was required when all Jonathan did require was some quiet, some respite from people and their talk.

He had allowed Ronnie to persuade him to go along to the club as his guest. 'Who knows, Grace, if things go well perhaps we can nominate you.' Jonathan said nothing—he had no wish to join Ronnie's club and no need of it.

And yet, to his surprise, things had gone well. Ronnie introduced him as a new arrival and he discovered that merely being here, swelling their numbers by one, made him a person to be celebrated. Men of affairs, who in London might slide their eyes over his face without even seeing him, wanted to make his acquaintance. He was invited into conversation with a district magistrate and later, on the verandah overlooking Lake Victoria, shook the hand of a man who worked in the Governor's office. Everyone was charming to him and he had to admit that this pleased him.

Despite his pleasure, as he sipped his beer from a tall glass, he felt a curious emptiness. The lake was lovely, reflecting the silver of the moonlight; the people urbane and amiable. But below them the city seethed and it struck him that all this comfort must come with some numbing compromise. As if each man here were a beggar, one hand permanently outstretched from a snowy shirt cuff, reliant upon the native whom they were also obliged to despise. Such a life would destroy even the best of men, would make one less of a man. It was its own kind of scarcity.

Across the room he caught sight of Ronnie's friend, who had not yet come to the hospital for his diagnosis. He turned away from the man, accepted a second drink from the Madrassi waiter, felt himself relax, accepted another, allowed his thoughts to run. So that, when someone asked him what he thought of Rangoon, he obliged them with his opinions, aiming not necessarily for provocation but for honesty. Intending only to air the freshness of his ideas.

'Of course at the hospital I mix almost exclusively with the half-castes and natives and have no compunction about it. As a man of science,' and here he smiled wryly to show that this was not all he was, that he also knew how the world worked, 'how could I possibly mind? I do not believe in prejudice, I believe in evidence. I believe in progress. In fact, I have just employed a half-caste for my clerk, an able man. One should treat *all* the men and women of Burma as one does the men and women of Britain. That is my intention. Fellow feeling, that is all I look for.'

Later he would feel differently, yet when he finally saw that everything here was too intense—the colours too outrageous, the odours too confronting, the heat debilitating, the lushness perverse—even then he would persist in telling himself that he believed in decency, fairness, progress. Above all, progress. But in the cool lake-shore breeze, his voice had been golden.

It was soon after his little speech that Ronnie suggested they take a motor-taxi back down into the city. 'But we'll do it again soon, eh Grace?' Then Ronnie's car glided into the remains of the night.

Jonathan could smell the river, which was not far away, and could even identify the faint reek of the refinery on the breeze as any true Rangoonite could. He turned from the smell, walking the other way, around the side of the building, near where the servants planted their kitchen gardens.

As he strolled, he thought back to his speech with chagrin and quickened his pace across the grass. Down here in the city, his words seemed like an excuse. He knew that he was treated differently from his Burmese and Indian colleagues at the hospital; favoured because he was English-trained, and a white man.

Yet no one seemed to resent it. Some of his superiors were even Indians. He would be serious, he would do important work, but if he was part of a corrupt system, did that make him corrupt too? Or was this a schoolboy's logic? Every day a parade of sick and lame bodies passed before him and he gave his help willingly, no matter who sought it. Was that not enough?

Weary of these thoughts, he stood quite still and gave himself over to the sound of crickets, to the jasmine and another unfamiliar perfume both subtle and delicate. He closed his eyes and sniffed, following its trace through the night air. The scent led him deeper into the block and around the corner of the building, where he was stopped short, his heart squeezing in his chest.

Dead in front of him was a huge man, tall and monstrous, swaying like a drunk in the night breeze. It took a moment before he realised that what he had mistaken for a man was only a vine climbing along an upright bamboo frame, a head fashioned above it to frighten the birds. Bemused by his error, he took a step closer.

The scarecrow—if he could call it that—seemed to be the work of a child; the head was clownish, but cunningly done with blue bottle tops for eyes and coconut-matting hair. He smiled because this 'hair' was not unlike his own, kinked and ginger coloured. Clearly it was a man, for the fruits of the vine swung, long and pendulous, in a repeated parody of tumescent male genitals.

But the mouth of the scarecrow stopped his grin. This was drawn on with a dark red paste, the lips pursed in an uncanny rendition of petulance. It was crude of course, but it was the work of a knowing hand, for in the figure of the scarecrow Jonathan now saw a representation of himself. A white man, alien, yes, but above all demanding and absurd.

On a scrap of paper Desmond wrote:

Mr and Mrs Desmond Goode
request the pleasure of your
company for tea.

He looked up from the copy paper to the thick cream-coloured card in his fingers, then back down at his words in blue ink. He placed his index finger alongside each line, then carefully put the same finger against the length of the card. He looked at his letter 'y'. Was it a little effeminate on the downward stroke? He considered whether he should end the second line at 'of'. Then, with a shout, he picked up his pen and scored through each line.

Desmond sagged back in his chair and let a breath out between his teeth. Outside the air was already beginning to hiss and, beyond the shade of the verandah, the afternoon light was whitening. Soon the heat would shimmer off the walls of his office; even the wooden surface of his desk would feel hot to the touch.

Perhaps a written invitation was too much. It might be better to work it into conversation. He could try it this Wednesday when he met Dr Grace to hand over his notes, figures arranged into neat columns that described a fortnight's worth of deaths. All that would be required was a simple, 'By the way, the wife and I were wondering whether you'd like to come to tea.' Or he could make a joke of it. 'I say, the wife's been badgering me to ask you to join us at ours. Would tea Sunday week suit?' This was how they would do it, the white men, joking and smiling as they discussed business, greasing the wheels of the machine with bonhomie.

If he slipped it into conversation he would avoid another problem, for Desmond was at a loss as to how he should address the invitation. He wanted to write 'Dr Grace', but Dr Grace had insisted on being called Jonathan, like an equal. This was jolly decent, proof that Dr Grace was a first-rate chap, the best of white men. Even so, Desmond could not bring himself to do it on paper.

He smoothed his fingers across the face of the card. He had bought it from the Rowe Brothers department store; it was a display at Rowe Brothers that had given him the idea in the first place. A poster just inside the main entrance off Merchant Street had caught his eye. It was a picture of a tea party. An elegant woman in a blue frock, duck-egg blue, was poised in the act of handing a cup of tea to a man on her right. This man wore a putty-coloured suit with a waistcoat that matched the woman's dress. Beside her, a small table held a teapot, china cups, a tea caddy, spoons and a three-tiered cake plate. The final touch was a tiny yellow rose in a bud vase.

The room was furnished in the style of the English countryside, the armchairs covered in a floral fabric—called chintz, he thought. A diamond-paned window behind the couple opened onto a manicured garden, glimpsed beyond a diaphanous curtain lifted by a pleasant breeze. At the top of the picture were the words 'Tea for Two'.

Everything about the two figures was stylised; the eyes, the mouths; their bodies were described with exaggerated, elongated lines, like a geometric diagram. They had blocks of yellow ink for hair. Yet they seemed more real than a photograph; in fact the whole scene was so tangible, so tantalising, that Desmond could hear the robins singing in the garden, the wind rustling the thatch in the roof, could almost *taste* the cream cakes arranged on the plate.

It was only as he examined the poster closely that he noticed the table in the window before him. He had to touch it to reassure himself that it was real because it was identical in virtually every respect to the picture. He might have been seeing double. The china, the tea caddy, even the bud vase, everything was there. It just needed to be wrapped.

When Desmond enquired about the price, he found it was worth almost exactly three months of his salary, an amount that made his mouth go dry.

'We do have other sets, sir,' the clerk, a dapper Anglo-Indian told him, 'more economical. This one,' he placed his hands at right angles, framing the table, 'is first class. The very top of the range.'

Desmond signed for the lot, then and there. He wanted the poster as well but the clerk told him, with regret, that it was not for sale. Desmond hadn't insisted, instead he'd gone straight to the stationery department for an invitation card.

A knock at the open office door startled Desmond. He dropped the card onto the desk and looked up to see the paper-wallah with a batch of files, tied in a blue ribbon. More bodies delivered, more cases needing attention.

Outside the leaves of the mango trees would be still. The gardener would have retired to his hut to sleep until the evening.

Desmond carefully picked up the card again and slid it into its envelope. He paid special attention to the envelope's sharp creases; so easy to damage if one were not careful. He wrapped the whole thing in a sheet of tissue paper, and slid it into the middle drawer of the desk along with the scrap of paper he'd written on. He would think about it later. He locked the drawer then rolled up his sleeves, ready to spend the afternoon in the cool and silence of the dead.

Winsome was late. She was lost and she was late.

Under the white porticos of the Scott Market, the grids and lines blurred rapidly into fruit, animals, flowers, china plates and back to fruit. Wide cloths bloomed on the ground, covered in goods for sale; they spilled onto the lanes, reshaping straight lines into jagged ones, corners into curves, until she was far too absorbed by the detail to know where she was.

'Kai Tea Shop is at the northern end of the market.' Desmond had drawn her a map. She looked down at it now, in her hand, but the bird's-eye view did not translate to the colour and clutter, the shouts and voices and smells in front of her.

'You will know you are there because there are fabric stalls all around and, at the edges, where the shops are brick, they're all tailors. It is the tailors' district.'

He had drawn little dots, a path for her feet to follow through precisely rendered alleyways. He put names on some of them. He marked an X for the Kai Tea Shop. And another X where the tailor's shop would be. He drew a larger cross with north, south, east and west.

'Don't be late,' he'd warned her, 'I cannot stay away from the office for long.'

Winsome crushed the map in her hands. Under a roof, in a crowd of people, east, west, south and north mean nothing. Nothing at all.

'Please, can you tell me which way to the fabric stalls?' she asked a peanut seller. He pointed. Winsome followed his arm and plunged once again into the sea of buyers and sellers, everyone bargaining for a better price.

It seemed that she had been this way before, until she was drawn to a familiar head bobbing above a newspaper. Desmond appeared. The Kai Tea shop reared up out of the chaos. She looked around; she could even see the tailor's shop—*Walter De Cruz, European-style Tailor. Finest fabrics. Paris patterns.*

She smoothed the map and held it out in front of her just at the moment Desmond looked up. He smiled, picked up his briefcase, and walked over to her. 'I see my map was useful.'

'Yes. Very.'

Walter De Cruz's shop was dark and tiny, light only piercing the front, where the mirror and cutting tables were. There was a small stool for customers to stand on while he measured them, and a counter where he kept his account books and made up the bills. The rest was all dark retreating walls, the grassy smell of linen, vegetable dye and cardamom. Winsome imagined he must use it to spice his tea.

As her eyes adjusted, she saw that every available space was crammed with pattern books, cards of lace, buttons and trim and, of course, fabrics. Bolts of cloth lined the shop walls end to end, muffling sound and shrinking the space further. Silks and calicos, cottons and muslins, even wools for families travelling west, and all in a wild assortment of colours, patterns and textures, like a garden in the night.

Out of this jumble, Walter De Cruz himself emerged. He was small, round and black as a Coringhee. He spoke with an accent sharp as cut glass. 'Mr and Mrs Goode? Delighted to meet you.' If Desmond shook his hand coolly, then Walter De Cruz took no notice.

'Now, my young madam, what have we in mind?'

'Party clothes,' Desmond answered. 'A party frock.'

'Well then, young madam, please.' He took her hand and led her to the low stool. She took a step up.

Party frock. Winsome stood as still as she could, mouthed the words and strained to hear the muffled noises of Scott Market, hoping to calm the excited beating of her own heart. That's what Desmond had said. Party frock.

'Party furnishings,' he had told her when the table, tea service, china and cutlery were delivered. Such beautiful things, wrapped in so much tissue. She had wanted to pick up the bud vase, to examine the delicate cuts in the crystal that made it sparkle so. But Desmond worried she might drop it.

'Party rules,' he explained when he brought home the book on etiquette.

'I have drawn you a diagram.' That evening, over dinner, he produced a small drawing and smoothed it out for her to see. In the centre was a perfect circle with the teapot, caddy, cups, everything mapped out. At the edges of the page, the drawing-room window, the door and each of the chairs, indicated by an X. 'You will need to practise brewing tea properly.'

Walter De Cruz stretched his tape from her wrist to her elbow, ducked underneath her arm and checked the same distance on her right side. He winked as he scratched the measurement into his tailor's book.

Nape to waist, waist to knee. Waist to mid-thigh. Waist to ankle. Breadth of shoulders, length of arms. Inside leg, outside leg. Hips at the broadest point. Hips midway between waist and thigh. Bust. Below the bust. Circumference of neck. Circumference of wrist. This column of figures, this was the approximation of points that made up her own body. She could be a graph, or a plotted curve.

She watched him write down the numbers. His book of measurements was several inches thick and she imagined column after column, person after person, each one a series of points, like stars in a constellation, a collection of heavenly bodies and none of them, not a one, with a head.

'Now, young madam. What have you in mind for this party frock?'

'One moment,' Desmond called out from deep in the shop, his voice sounding distant, muffled by bolts of fabric. 'I have a diagram.'

On Walter's work table, Desmond unfolded his sketch. It was a woman with a long, exaggerated body. She wore a dress that skimmed her contours, flowing across her hips until it ended in a swirl around her legs. The sleeves were short and flounced to midway along the upper arm. The neckline was a deep V. It was a fashionable dress, rendered in meticulous detail.

'Ahh,' exclaimed Walter De Cruz, 'it is exquisite! I have just the fabric.' He trotted to the back of the shop.

'What do you think?' Desmond turned to Winsome.

'I think it is beautiful,' Winsome smiled shyly at him, a honey warmth running through her. Did he know that she had never had a dress like this? Did he know that this dress would make her feel like a woman, that she would feel like a wife?

'No, not that. Do you think he will be able to make it look exactly like this?'

Walter returned before Winsome could reply. He carried a bolt of fabric the colour of sea coral. 'Now, thakin, take a look. Take a look.' He spun Winsome around to face the mirror and unfurled the fabric. It fell nearly to her knees, shimmering softly, floating as if the air were liquid.

Winsome reached out to touch the silky material. It felt slippery and light. It would catch the slightest breeze and whirl about her. She looked at herself in the mirror. A wife looked back.

Desmond sighed audibly. 'No. It should be blue.'

'You like blue?' Walter plucked a bolt of peacock blue silk from a pile nearby and expertly unwound it in front of Winsome. But Desmond was not watching, he was walking through the stacks, fingering the fabrics for himself.

'Not that blue. More refined.'

Walter De Cruz, undeterred, plucked a paler silk from another corner. But from near the back of the tiny shop, Desmond's voice boomed. 'This, this is perfect.' He re-emerged with a roll of heavy cloth in a dull duck-egg blue.

'Mr Goode, you have chosen a quality fabric. The very highest quality. You are clearly a discerning man. But this silk is light. See how it drapes?' Walter swept the bolt through the air.

Desmond awkwardly unrolled a few feet of the blue cloth and held it in front of Winsome.

'I think this drapes just as well. It's the right colour.'

Walter De Cruz re-rolled his silk and faced Desmond. 'Frankly sir, we just bring that in for the English. They insist on the thicker fabrics.' He shrugged. 'They are English.'

'It's the right colour.'

'It is very expensive.'

'I think it looks very well. Don't you, Winsome?' Desmond looked to her and in his handsome face his eyes were almost glutinous, as if he'd been woken suddenly from a dream. The tailor watched her too, a professional smile on his face.

Winsome touched the blue cloth; it was of good quality, but a thick crepe. The fabric creased and folded in upon itself so that it felt spongy between her fingers. Each of these openings would hold the heat. The cloth was handsome, but it would not glide over the skin. It would cling.

In an even voice she said, 'We'll take the blue one.'

'As you wish, thakin.'

Desmond's pleasure in her decision was boyish. He took Winsome's hand and squeezed it, then picked up his case. Before he left the shop he leaned over and kissed her on the cheek. 'You will look lovely.'

As the door swung shut Winsome could hear Walter De Cruz muttering, rolling up the yards of cloth. 'Too bad madam will not be comfortable at her party.'

She watched him put the coral silk up high, out of reach.

At three o'clock the Rangoon heat was at its most crushing. Smells vaporised. Touch burned. Even sound waves seemed flattened, except for the drone of flies.

Most natives, white women and many of the long-time civilians slept until the Rangoon heat abated, but Jonathan could not. Instead, he sat in his bathroom, pouring dipper after dipper of tepid water over himself, wondering if heat could in fact drive you mad.

At six o'clock that morning, on his way to the hospital, he'd found himself shivering in the dawn. Miraculous thing, to shiver. He'd had a new patient, Tommo, a white timber manager with a hopelessly enlarged liver, recently transferred down to Rangoon to die at the company's expense.

'Look at me, Doc,' Tommo had laughed, 'I'm as yellow as a Chinaman.' His eyes watchful despite the familiar manner.

When the water in the dipper reached blood heat, Jonathan rose from the floor of the bathroom and carefully patted himself dry with a white towel. Then, encased, he shuffled to his bedroom.

Khit Tin had set his hairbrushes on the dressing table and his clothes on the valet chair. The sight of his shirt and trousers hanging there nearly made Jonathan groan aloud. He had promised to take tea with Desmond Goode, the funny clerk from the mortuary who took his notes. His invitation card was on the dressing table. Surely it was too hot for tea today?

'Fluids build up in a man, Doc. Look at me. Isn't healthy.' Tommo had rolled on his side, exposing his weeping bedsores for inspection. 'And there's Rangoon, bursting with women. Bursting.'

In the mirror Jonathan checked his skin for prickly heat. He found raised blotches across his chest, through the ginger hair under his arms, along his back. They were an angry pink against the soft white of his belly and hips.

He turned away from his reflection and sat on the bed. Unwrapping the towel around his groin, he opened his legs for inspection. The skin along the inside of his upper thigh was covered with raised lumps. It itched, but he did not scratch. Scratching would tear the skin, further inflaming those red beads of flesh beneath his orange pubic hair. Above this tender mess, his penis and scrotum hung, wrinkled, moist.

'A young man like you, don't want to be going without.' Tommo had turned his head to leer at Jonathan. 'And them Burmese love a ginger.'

Already Jonathan could feel the sweat seeping through his skin. He reached for the tin of talcum on his dressing table, shook a small mound into his palm and slapped it under his armpits, behind his knees, in the small of his back and then, very gently, shook it between his thighs.

'You don't fancy the small talk, them Lal bazaar girls'll do pretty near anything for a rupee.' Tommo had turned painfully onto his belly. 'You a shy man, Doc?'

Jonathan cradled his cock and balls in one powdered hand and smoothed the talcum underneath them. His fingers felt silky, alien, as they slid along his skin.

'Course, if you want a white woman, there's plenty around.' Tommo laughed his wheezing, three-beat laugh. 'The ugly ones might let you.'

Jonathan felt his sweat rolling down his skin, thickened by the powder. Later, in the cool of night, when he undressed, he would find pale chalky streaks, residue of the evening. But now the red hair on his chest was matted to his skin. His scalp prickled. Jonathan took a breath and drew his hand back and forth a little more quickly.

'Or maybe you like them blacky-white ones?' Jonathan had glanced across at the nurse before reaching down to palpate Tommo's liver. 'Aaah!' he screamed. 'Jesus. Ahhh. Jesus. God in heaven!'

Imagine the smell of jasmine. Imagine the coolness of midnight. Imagine the soft, tropical darkness broken by a circle of light. Imagine, imagine. Jonathan drew his hand deftly, quickly along the length of his cock.

When the nurse had left the room, blushing, Tommo caught Jonathan's arm, his grip too strong for a dying man. 'Don't let me go here, not here, please Doc, let me die in the jungle.'

'Thakin?' Jonathan's eyes jerked open and he knocked the tin of talcum onto the floor. Behind him Khit Tin was entering the room. The only warning a chink of ice in the lime water on his tray.

'Thakin?' His voice was soft. 'Are you ready to dress?'

Jonathan snatched the towel and covered his groin then stood up with his back to his servant, at his feet a wide arc of talc across the wooden floor. 'In a few minutes. Just give me a few more minutes.' He heard Khit Tin turn and pad away.

Jonathan looked down at the mess on the floor. His footprints were the colour of teak against the white powder.

*

The house at 56 Inverness Gardens was set back from the road, the gardens shaded by mango and jackfruit trees, a fringe of plumbago bushes beneath them. Jonathan stood at the bottom of the path, his jacket slung over his shoulder. A slight breeze moved the air, but he was damp beneath his clothes and perspiration stood out on his forehead. Wearily, he wiped his face with his handkerchief then sighed before starting up the path.

The building was ugly, a botched attempt at European style; it was squarely built from the local red brick, but the bay windows were already crooked. Mortar had fallen from the brick in patches and there was the inevitable verandah wrapped around the ground floor. Frangipani and yellow lilies, their heads drooping, framed the entrance and red laterite pebbles lined the garden beds.

Someone had repainted the front door red, but this failed to hide a scar in the central panel left by the large round bell that had once hung there. It had been replaced with six smaller buttons. There were six name cards alongside, most traced with mildew, although the name Goode beside number five looked new, and so was clearly legible. Jonathan put on his jacket and rang. Before he'd even taken his finger from the bell, a barefoot and grinning boy no more than eleven years old opened the door. He wore a Burmese-style head wrap, wide-legged pants and a too-big jacket.

'Welcome, Dr Grace.' He followed the child into a hallway that was dingy and close. A fan-wallah flapped his foot, his toe looped in a rope, but the breeze did little more than shift hot air about. Jonathan smelled the cloying scent of damp he had come to recognise as endemic to Rangoon's buildings. There were dark patches of mildew on the cream plaster.

'Please, Dr Grace.'

The boy took Jonathan back along the hall before stopping at a blue door. He knocked twice and then pulled it wide for Jonathan to enter.

The apartment smelled of must and flowers. Three doors opened off the short hallway. The boy beckoned before turning to the right and opening the last door. Jonathan walked through into the drawing room where a slender, dark-haired girl in a blue dress sat in a cane chair. Everything about the girl seemed stylised and exaggerated. Her eyes were very large, her mouth very full and her body curved in elongated lines that were accentuated by the intense blue of her dress. Her skin was the colour of milky tea.

Desmond Goode stood to her right, his waistcoat the same colour as her dress. Before them, a small table was crammed with tea things. A funny little vase threatened to topple to the floor.

Desmond leaped forward and took Jonathan's hand in both of his. 'Welcome, Dr Grace. You do us a great honour.' He held on for a long moment, staring intently, dark eyes shining in his handsome face. Then he let go, leaping backwards like a dancer. 'And may I present my wife?'

The slender girl stood up from her chair and moved towards Jonathan, the underside of her forearms flashing white against the creamy brown of her skin.

'This is Mrs Goode. My Winsome.'

She was tall, this girl, her brown eyes nearly level with his grey ones. She held out her hand. She had a curious scent to her— feral, heady, something he could not name. She did not lower her eyes, or smile as other girls would have done. Her palm was dry and cool as the night air.

'Pleased to meet you.' She let go his hand and turned back to her chair.

'Dr Grace, Jonathan, do sit down.' Desmond gestured to a cane chair beside Winsome. 'We are so very glad you could come.'

Before Jonathan could take a seat, the boy burst into the room carrying a large boiling kettle, his face contorted with the effort. Jonathan stepped back out of his way.

Winsome moved to the edge of the chair and steadied herself, extending an ankle in front of her. With obvious concentration, she took the kettle from the boy and swirled the scalding water around the teapot. Steam beaded on her upper lip; the little yellow rose seemed to wilt. She opened the caddy and spooned loose India tea into the pot, then leaned forward to add more hot water. As she did, her hair fell away at her neck, exposing a small mole at the edge of her hairline. She stirred the tea then looked up at the two men.

Desmond perched on the arm of her chair and squeezed her shoulder approvingly. He turned a broad smile to Jonathan.

'Tell me Jonathan, what do you think about this weather? So unnaturally hot!' He lifted his hand from Winsome's shoulder, the moist indentation of his fingers still evident there. She tugged at the sleeve to release the cloth.

From the kitchen came the murmur of voices, the sound of the boy singing as he boiled up another kettle.

'Well,' said Desmond. 'Here we all are. But where are our manners! Winsome, Dr Grace must be parched.'

'Dr Grace, how do you take your tea?' As she reached for the pot her arm brushed the bud vase. It teetered on the edge of table, then tipped and began to fall.

Before the rains

The notice pinned beside the shop door was written in a dark, looped hand. It read: *Well-spoken lady with excellent handwriting sought to see to things. Apply inside during business hours.* Above this was a brass plate: J H Stihl's Photographic: Portraits and Souvenirs a Speciality. There was a photograph too, taken in the old days. It showed the last Burmese royal couple sitting on a dais in front of a painted backdrop, rich draperies on either side.

But the photograph did not end with this platform; beyond the opulent props and trimmings, the room that contained them was clearly visible. On the floor Winsome could see a European-style coat and satchel and, in the background, other painted backdrops (a riverscape, a ruined stone arch) propped casually against the walls. It was this clumsiness—the awkward proportions, the picture leaking from within the picture—that made the portrait fascinating. Gazing into that room, she felt a molten curiosity, as if she were being drawn to the edge of things, to revelation and intrigue. What would it be like to work in a place that produced objects such as these?

She and Desmond had discussed the possibility of her taking a job. Rangoon was expensive and the lovely tea things, her dress, all of these would have been dear. Most of the other wives at St John's worked; Winsome had often heard them talk, after mass, about their offices or their shops. Pretty girls who wore Max Factor Roseleaf makeup and never left home without hat and gloves, standing in little groups, slim figures silhouetted in the sunlight.

Lily-white Mrs Grass, who sat in a front pew and clipped her vowels carefully, had charge of hiring the counter girls at Steeles Stores. She had made Desmond an offer. 'I have something in the stockroom that would suit Winsome,' she said.

'Not on the sales counter, like the other women?'

'But I don't mind the stockroom,' Winsome said quietly and Mrs Grass smiled, tilting her head to one side. 'Your wife is quite dark,' she said, 'she has quite an Indian chin.'

That was the end of it. 'Steeles Stores,' Desmond told her, 'is second rate.'

But that was weeks ago and she knew that there were bills, that the girl Than Thint had not had her wages. She looked about her. This end of Sule Pagoda Road, outside the shadow of the temple spires, was quiet and seemed very far from the English city that lay just a few blocks away. She pushed the door and went inside.

The studio was large and dark and empty as a cave except that, at its centre, it was lit by Rangoon sunshine pouring through a rectangular skylight. Beyond this light, the corners were shadowy. The air had an astringent quality. As she moved further into the room, her eyes slowly adjusted to the contrasting dark and light.

'Hello,' she called, and her own voice echoed back at her. She took another step. Leaning against a far wall there was a stack of canvas backdrops. She recognised the foremost one with a pleasant shiver; she had seen it in the background of the royal couple's portrait. The riverscape. She crossed the room to examine it.

Close up, the scene was impossible, so startling and perfect she caught her breath. She felt as if she might enter the picture, could almost hear the rushing water, longed to feel the stones beneath her feet. She could not help but stretch her fingers to the canvas; she wanted to touch the sunlight, to feel its heat, although she knew it could not possibly feel warm.

There was the sharp spring of a latch nearby, and a door opened in the wall; a man's face appeared, framed by a strip of yellow light. Winsome jumped back from the painting, her cheeks pink with guilt. His hair was slicked back like an American's and his skin was a smooth caramel. She looked into his face—young and handsome—and felt a trilling along her skin.

He rested one hand against the door jamb, the ruby on his little finger sparkling even in the murk of the studio. He gave a slight smile and looked as though he was about to speak, but before he could, someone else's voice broke the silence.

'Good morning.'

It was a crisp voice, with an Englishwoman's accent. It came from behind her and Winsome turned to see a figure emerge from the gloom beyond the skylight, a tiny woman wreathed in the sweet-scented smoke of a cheroot. As she stepped onto the platform, her broad forehead was bathed in Rangoon sunshine and in that sudden brightness Winsome could see that she was not English, as she had sounded—she had a Burmese face and was wearing a white blouse over an embroidered skirt in the Burmese style.

'I am Daw Sein.' The woman bowed her head courteously and extended her hand to Winsome. Gold bangles chimed at her wrists. 'This is my studio.' Her voice was beautiful and precise.

Now the handsome Burman walked through the door and stood beside the woman, who gave him an affectionate look. 'Aye

Sein,' she said, 'my brother. A student at the university.' She smiled. 'It is I who am the photographer.' And yet Winsome could not associate this immaculate woman with the appealing chaos of the photograph outside. Aye Sein nodded at his sister before turning to leave them. The Burmese woman moved in closer. 'Have you come for a portrait?' she asked in silky tones.

Now that it came to it, Winsome's nerve failed her. She felt small, insubstantial; in compensation her voice was perhaps a bit too loud, maybe even rudely so. 'No, I am not here for a picture. I read your notice outside. I mean the notice about the position. I came in to see if you still needed…' Her voice trailed off.

Daw Sein nodded as if this was what she'd expected to hear all along; she spoke without skipping a beat. 'The work is exacting and dangerous. It requires a certain calibre of mind.' She lifted the cheroot to her lips and drew on it, and as she exhaled a stream of pale smoke, Winsome could feel the Burman taking in her yellow dress, the wave in her hair, her oval face with the painted lips and broad nose. 'And there is another question. If you do prove suitable, then you would be working for me, a native woman. Tell me, would that bother you?'

Daw Sein's eyes were the same inky black as the handwriting on the notice, the beautiful voice just as fluid. Such things mattered, Winsome knew. One had to be sure of oneself. One had to respect a natural line. Choices had to be made.

'No,' she said, 'that would not bother me.'

Briefly, something in Daw Sein's face shifted and her eyes were soft and faraway. But the change was fleeting and her crispness of manner quickly returned.

'Very well then, Miss…'

'Mrs. Mrs Goode.'

'Very well then, Mrs Goode,' Daw Sein crushed the cheroot

beneath the toe of her slipper, 'if you would kindly follow me.'

At the end of a hallway leading off the large open room, Daw Sein stopped before a wooden door. 'We will start with the darkroom.' She led the way into a small space, the air intense with the same astringency Winsome had noticed earlier. There was a high window draped in black and this was the room's only source of light. Beneath it was a work bench. Shelves lined one wall and were filled with glass bottles of various sizes, colours and shapes. Daw Sein closed the wooden door. Immediately the room felt cramped and the acrid air even more oppressive.

'These are the substances we use in photography.' Daw Sein lifted a brown glass bottle from the topmost shelf. 'Lunar caustic. The chemical name is silver nitrate—see the symbol, $AgNO_3$? You would have to learn the proper names. Silver nitrate will turn your skin black on contact. Touch silver nitrate to your eye, and it will blind you in that spot.' She returned the bottle to its space. 'You will also note, Mrs Goode, that each vial has its own position and that this position does not change.' She took down another bottle. 'This is a fixer, it contains cyanide. Cyanide is, of course, deadly.'

One by one, Daw Sein held up the little vials and described them, their uses, their dangers: collodion was volatile and explosive, it could burn your skin; ether would render you insensible. Winsome's head hurt. She feared the harm that one movement of a clumsy arm might bring in this small room; it was as if hate was bottled in those vessels.

When Daw Sein finished, she turned to Winsome. 'Now, Mrs Goode, do you remember which bottle contains the silver nitrate?'

Winsome hesitated. She looked up and found the brown container with $AgNO_3$ inscribed on the side. 'Yes, I do,' she replied, a little throb of pride in her voice.

Daw Sein swept the black curtains across the window, and

the room was instantly, emphatically, dark. 'Very good. Would you be so kind as to pass it to me now?'

Winsome blinked in disbelief. She could feel her palms sweating. Her fingers would be too slippery to handle these murderous bits of glass. She felt the urge to push past Daw Sein, who stood between her and the door, but if she did perhaps she would bring those vials crashing down around them. There were other jobs. All she had to do was say, No, she could not find the silver nitrate, certainly not in the dark.

She could hear Daw Sein's breathing, as measured and precise as her voice. And there was something like triumph emanating from this woman, as if this were a sort of lesson, a test that Daw Sein had known all along she, Winsome, would fail. Let her try, she will only disappoint, a girl like that.

Winsome shifted her weight on her hips as the silent seconds ticked away. She was about to say she could not do it, was about to ask for release when her hand found the edge of the work bench. She felt along its plane until she found the rise of the wall and then, in her mind's eye, could see what was obscured by the dark and knew where her fingers might find the little bottle.

And she realised that she would prefer to have this woman's good opinion. Sliding her hand up the rows, she counted the shelves with her fingers. Silver nitrate. It might blind you.

'I have it,' she said.

Daw Sein swept the curtain open. They both looked at the brown glass bottle in Winsome's hand.

'Silver nitrate,' Daw Sein read aloud, in her crystalline voice.

That evening she was late with their dinner and Desmond was already out of temper before she could even begin to tell him. As if her mortification were the inevitable consequence of opening her mouth. As if it were only a matter of time before there would be some new transgression that he would have to forgive. At the table, pushed against the window in their small apartment, he drank his celery soup in rapid gulps, his cheeks bulging with each mouthful. Winsome waited until he had his main dish in front of him—a piece of mutton beneath a thick white sauce—before she broached the subject of the studio and a possible job there.

'A photographic studio.' He turned the words over in his mouth like a piece of bad fish. He looked down into his plate, sliced into his cutlet. 'What sort of people are they?'

There were sorts of people. Daw Sein had said as much. Winsome returned his meaty stare. 'The proprietor is a woman and...' she thought of Daw Sein's voice, her scented cheroot.

'And?' Desmond's voice was tight with irritation, his knife and fork poised in mid-air.

'And very educated, I think. Photography is a scientific process.'

Desmond swallowed his mouthful and sawed again into the grey meat.

'I would need to learn chemistry.'

He looked up at her, interested. 'Chemistry?'

'Yes. The owner read chemistry at university.'

'She's a university graduate?'

'Yes.'

'Rangoon University?'

'No.' Winsome composed herself before meeting his eyes. 'She took her degree at London University.' There was a white parchment announcing this on the wall of Daw Sein's office.

'London.' He measured out the syllables.

Winsome kept her voice light as she picked up her fork. She speared her cutlet. 'She would like to start my training as soon as possible. If you think the position is suitable, of course.'

Desmond nodded, put his meat into his mouth and chewed slowly.

'Such a queer thing, chemistry. There's a different name for all substances. For example this salt,' she picked up the little wooden bowl from the table and held it in front of her, 'ordinary salt is called sodium chloride.' She put it down again and looked up.

His face was open to hers, his expression fascinated, needy, and her sudden success, the ease of it, needled her. 'And did you know,' she continued, 'that glass is actually a kind of liquid, that it only becomes a solid when it shatters?' Later, much later, she would discover her error, that glass was not a liquid, but something discontinuous, an anomaly like photography itself; like so many other things.

'Glass a liquid!' Desmond murmured as he picked up his water tumbler and held it to the light. He put it up to his face and looked at her through the bottom. He shook his head in delighted disbelief.

At the end of Sunday mass after Winsome's first week at work, she and Desmond boarded the tram for Phayre Street in the centre of the city. Near the back sat Mrs Grass.

'I say,' Desmond called out, walking unsteadily as the tram shook around a corner, 'would you join us for coffee and cakes at the Continental?' He smiled triumphantly. 'We are celebrating.'

Mrs Grass pulled Winsome down beside her. There were damp patches beneath her enormous breasts and she smelled of stale breath and eau de cologne. 'Celebrating?' she asked, her red mouth curving into a knowing smile.

'Yes,' Desmond spoke rapidly, 'Winsome has just obtained a position at J H Stihl's Photographic Studios. A well-established firm.

She is being trained in photography and the development process.' He grinned. 'It is a job that requires knowledge of chemistry. Of science.'

'Oh, the Sein family's studio!' Mrs Grass exclaimed, smiling widely, her yellow teeth flashing at Desmond. 'The Seins are a wonderful family, very rich. Very European in their outlook, for Burmans. All Rangoon knows them.' Winsome felt her stomach lurch. She dared not look at Desmond.

Mrs Grass went on, 'Very much the done thing to work with the Burmese these days.' She lowered her voice. 'It would be a different matter if it were Indians, of course,' she laughed, 'but the Burmese are another thing altogether. It is progress. And I am all for it.'

Winsome kept her eyes on her lap.

'As am I,' Desmond replied, his voice brittle. 'We are all for progress, both Winsome and I.' Then, as the tram gathered speed, he began to laugh a little, standing in the rush of air from the window. Winsome watched his profile as he gazed out. He tapped the thick glass, turned back to Mrs Grass. 'Do you see this?' he announced, turning to face them both. 'Not a solid at all. A liquid. Like water.'

And, as he laughed again, Winsome could see his eyes were bright. He seemed giddy with the smoothness of the tram as it slid over the steel rails, giddy with his progressive attitude, with the sensation of getting somewhere, with the pleasure of being a modern man in a modern city.

His laughter was infectious and when he turned his eyes to hers, she found herself also laughing, Mrs Grass too, all of them joking and talking more and more loudly until they heard the sharp trill of a bell and the tram driver shouted, 'Phayre Street'.

They stepped down into the Rangoon dust, holding their

hands over their mouths, blinking their eyes in the sunlight. On the bottom step Desmond took her elbow, as if he had overbalanced, and for a moment his fingers sank deep into her flesh until he righted himself and let go.

Smart & Mookerdum's bookshop was an old-fashioned place with a counter where clerks took down your order and then parcelled up your books and magazines in blue-and-white paper. There were tables covered with displays of novels, histories and biographies newly arrived from Europe. At the very back of the shop were shelves of older books, written by long-forgotten men and women, their jackets dusty, the pages traced with mildew, a demented marginalia.

Jonathan, who relished books in all their aspects, liked to take his time among these shelves, lingering at the back of the shop before working his way forward. The scent of ink and glue, the texture of a linen cover, the particular weight of a book in his hands, all of these sensations were a prelude to the pleasure of reading—indeed, sometimes these things gave him greater pleasure than was to be had in the words themselves. That was where he was, a book in his hand, when he next saw Winsome Goode.

She was wandering sleepy-eyed along the tables of novels and seemed as bewildered by the display as she had been by the china teapot, the cups and saucers at her husband's tea party. He watched her as she stopped to read a title here, to run a finger along a spine there.

She was not the sort of woman he ordinarily found attractive; a convent girl with skin that looked as if it might bruise at a fingertip's pressure. It had been too easy to imagine her flesh torn by the vicious ruins of the vase that had fallen from their tea table. That was why he had got down on the floor with her.

She had given off a curious odour—at first he thought it was the water from the vase; stale, already algal—but as he bent beneath the table, his fingers probing gently for jagged splinters, he realised that it was her. Not a scent he would have expected to come from a girl like that.

Jonathan replaced his book, took down another. He shifted his weight a little, leaning against the wooden shelves. That day she had hardly spoken at all and he conjectured that her conversation would be unlike that of English girls; she would be untrained in the smooth, predictable discourse they seemed to slip on with their stockings. Hers would be an untutored mind, her thoughts rough-hewn, perhaps original because of it. Sometimes when he was at the hospital, at his desk, full of the desire for *something* to happen, for *progress* to be made, he sensed that he too was, in one way or another, unfinished. That he was a man who lived on one-way conversations. All of this went through his mind as he watched her, lost among the tables of books.

He wondered if he should go and speak to her.

A clerk must have called her name because she went back to the counter. He watched as she paid, collected her things and then turned to leave. He kept his eye lightly upon her as she moved across the front of the shop, inquisitive only; this was the way that men watched women, women who were already other men's wives.

Before she left, Winsome Goode looked back across the shop

and her eyes caught his. Although her glance was brief, cursory, he felt a silvery jolt before she had even turned away, a catch to the lungs; below the taut drum of his abdomen, heat. Avidity. The taste of acid flooded his mouth, and with it the certainty of injury to come. Yet he could not look away.

Far from him, she passed through the door, the hem of her dress swirling about her calves, and was gone. But even then he was not released but stood, incapable of movement, for several minutes more, the book he had been reading heavy in his hand. His fingers had already smudged its cover.

At the end of a dun-coloured afternoon, with his shift nearly over, Desmond was surprised to see Dr Grace step into the mortuary. 'Delighted,' he said, stepping away from the body of a woman. 'Unexpected pleasure.'

He pulled off his vulcanised gloves; he had been removing the pluck—the tongue, larynx, lungs, and heart—in one long piece, clearing the body cavity to expose the organs beneath. He wiped his hands on a cloth. His fingers were sticky with the work—his gloves needed mending.

'I thought I'd collect your data myself, thought I'd save you the trouble of coming over to the hospital.' Jonathan's fingers snaked along his arm as he spoke, scratching at his skin. 'Sorry,' he followed Desmond's glance, 'prickly heat.'

It occurred to Desmond that Dr Grace was one of those white men susceptible to fever. 'Right you are,' he replied, smiling and rubbing his hands together. 'Decent of you to come. I'll just go and get them.'

In his office, a little annexe off the mortuary, Desmond searched his desk and quickly found the sheaf of papers with the records for the fortnight. He gathered these up, then took a moment to collect himself. He had not seen Dr Grace since the tea party at Inverness Gardens and had worried that he had somehow disgraced himself. It had been far too hot a day for tea and cake, and then the wretched business with the vase. Yet here was Dr Grace, presenting himself as if the two of them were more familiar than ordinary colleagues, although not quite friends. He smoothed the top sheet of the papers and turned to leave the room.

Jonathan was standing above the body, arms crossed behind his back, inspecting the cadaver. 'You have good hands, Desmond.'

Desmond joined him and looked down at his own work. He knew it was neatly done. 'I used to assist the police surgeon. When I was a new recruit, they lined us up and called for volunteers, an extra ten rupees a week. I was the only one who lasted.'

He remembered those autopsies, conducted out of doors or in the dirty shack of some village headman. Wooden floors and bamboo walls, pigs nosing at the rubbish, working beneath a kerosene lamp at night. The inconsequentiality of dead flesh. Sometimes the air itself would sigh and everywhere there would be insects, powder splashing from their beating wings, and the sound of malice shifting in the dark.

'It was the smell, you see, they couldn't stand it.' Both of them laughed in easy comradeship, two men unperturbed by the scent of death, men of science, only men.

'Well,' Dr Grace said, 'you would have made a good surgeon.' But the instant the words left his mouth, Desmond saw regret in his face. Fear that he, Desmond, would take this compliment as an opportunity, would seek to profit by it; push for patronage, for advancement at least, possibly training, ascension to the professions, none of which Dr Grace wanted to give. Like any other bazaar beggar with his eyes on a chance.

Desmond handed over the papers. 'There you are. I think

you'll find them all in order.' Dr Grace took them, pulled out his wallet, counted a little pile of notes onto the dissection table. He handed these to Desmond, and Desmond would have liked to refuse them but he could not afford to. Besides, he did not know how Dr Grace might read such a gesture. He felt the old familiar distrust creeping into the room—now he too regretted Dr Grace's compliment.

Desmond put the money in his pocket then pulled his gloves back on. He took up the knife and resumed his work, and all the while Dr Grace lingered beside him, watching as he cut, as if his company were another kind of consolation. 'Do you know the Latin names?' he asked. Desmond did not and so he began to say them aloud, pointing as he did—mylohyoid, hyoid, larynx, trachea, oesophagus—he pronounced each word as if it were an especial gift and, despite himself, Desmond repeated every one; he was a beggar after all.

There would always be this humiliation; he would always be the one in need, the one who wanted what the other had, who had nothing to offer in return. This made friendship, the effortless congeniality that white men shared, impossible. In Kalaw he would scrub his arms three times with carbolic soap, from the tip of the fingers right to the elbow, because there were no gloves to be had. His skin was raw and broken. Eventually he stole a pair from the surgeon's army kit when the man died.

His knowledge, his skill: these too had been stolen. He had filched them as he stood alongside his betters at work, watching, making mental notes. Anything worth having had to be taken— knowledge was will, knowledge was theft, each scrap precious. This was how it had always been for him and he had not minded until now, because he saw that it would be beside the point. No matter what he had, it would never be anything a man like Dr Grace would want.

The nightwatchman—a new man—rapped at the window and gave him a small, respectful salaam. Desmond inclined his head in acknowledgment. They could hear the man as he tapped his way around the building with his bamboo stick, as if he were testing the bricks themselves, making sure each one was sound, reassuring those within earshot that the whole edifice wouldn't come tumbling down around them. In a moment they would smell his cooking fire.

With the thought of the watchman's evening meal, Desmond felt the full force of the day and, briefly, a monumental tiredness. The long heat of the afternoon was only just receding and he still had work to complete. Soon night would fall and he would turn on the electric light—a small comfort that still pleased him. Later he would return home to Winsome and their dispiriting small talk. If he were held up, as he often was, she might even be asleep when he arrived home, her breasts rising and falling beneath the cotton nightgown, her legs indenting the mattress. Sometimes, since the fever, she slept so deeply that he wondered if she dreamed.

'I saw your wife the other day.'

'What?' Desmond's voice was sharp, guilty, as if the doctor had somehow intuited his thoughts.

'Your wife. Mrs Goode,' Dr Grace said. 'I was browsing at Smart & Mookerdum's and she was there.'

'Ah.' Desmond shook himself, once more in control. 'Yes, she collects my periodicals.'

Dr Grace paused. 'She is a very modest woman, your wife.'

'She was brought up in a convent.'

'Well, I admire her delicacy,' Dr Grace continued, 'but I think a married woman might converse in public with a man who is also her husband's employer; I doubt there is much danger in that. Or perhaps she is shy?'

Dr Grace was smiling to show that he was not offended, that

once more he was conferring something, giving something. And yet, and yet; here was a small thing that Desmond *could* offer, his wife's conversation, such as it was.

'Well,' Desmond replied eagerly, 'I shall let her know. I shall instruct her that she must seek you out.' He smiled then, a man again, the talk that men shared coming easily to him now, 'but be warned, doctor, you might regret opening yourself up to a woman's conversation. You know how they can talk!'

Dr Grace smiled and turned for the door. 'Right you are, Desmond.'

On Tuesdays, the day the new books and magazines arrived from London, Jonathan Grace stood at the back of Smart & Mookerdum's bookshop near the shelf of reduced volumes, his head bowed so that the point of his nose and his fair eyelashes were the only parts of his face Winsome could see. He read the orphaned books, broken, dog-eared, mildewed, the pages dusty with black spores—each one in some way spoiled. He read with the weight of his shoulder against the shelves, his side curving beneath him, and every time she saw him she wondered why a white man, an educated white man, one with power, position, money, would prefer these books to the new, perfect copies on display.

Was it economy, perhaps, or something in how he was made, that he was careful with all things, marred or not? Or was it a quality specific to the books themselves, in the way decay made each one distinctive, no longer an exact copy of the original as it had begun? Dr Grace, lost in his books, turning each page with long fingers, sometimes skipping whole chapters, whole slabs of words, those same long, probing fingers that had moved deliberately as, kneeling beside her, he had searched for the pieces of the shattered vase.

One day, not a Tuesday, she made a special trip to Smart &

Mookerdum's just to look over those books for herself. She hoped to find a novel that she could afford, one that wasn't too damaged, but she was disappointed. The books were uniformly corrupt, traced by green blooms of mildew with a slightly riverine smell. Those that were intact were dull. There were no novels, no poetry or histories. Most were biographies of men she'd never heard of, others were manuals of advice surely long out of date. These were bad books, inherently flawed before Rangoon's growths had written over them. Yet on Tuesday mornings when Dr Grace left the shop, sometimes nodding to her as he went, sometimes passing the time of day, it was often with a small battered book on the top of his thick pile of new magazines.

Desmond had insisted that she greet Dr Grace every time she saw him at Smart & Mookerdum's—a married woman, he said, might converse in public with a man who is also her husband's employer, you are in no danger—and she did so obediently. What Desmond did not know was that she had already begun to watch Jonathan and his books soon after the tea party, had noted the suppleness of his body beneath his clothes, his face that was distinctive rather than handsome. She watched him without seeming to look.

At the photographic studio, she showed an eye for detail that impressed Daw Sein; she excelled at picking up flaws in the negative, a dark stain that would mar the print; she checked the sitters, moving a sleeve that blocked a child's face, correcting misaligned buttons, sashes, the minutiae that might spoil a photograph for its subject.

On the rare occasions they worked out of doors, photographing the Rangoon sights for tourist postcards (the roof of a pagoda, a line of novitiate monks, a spill of orchids) it was Daw Sein who lined up the lens and measured the light, but Winsome who cropped the photograph to train the eye on what was important. Because watching was not only about sifting the details; the skill was also in finding their meaning. At the convent, of all the girls, she had been the one able to read the slightest nuance of dress or gesture among the nuns, predicting their moods—how much homework they would give, how vicious their punishments might be—all from the smallest particularity.

A month before her wedding, she had watched Desmond waiting in the ante-room with the other would-be bridegrooms; Desmond was the only one reading a newspaper—perhaps the others were too nervous—and he had folded it cleverly to prevent the ink from smearing on his fingers. As she watched him she had felt a warmth seep through her, a lustre on her skin; it was the possibility of happiness, for she judged him to be intelligent, an independent thinker, a modern man (she had learned more about men since then). Perhaps this was why she still did not understand Dr Grace's interest in the marred books, despite all her looking. She put it down to her ignorance of men.

Once, she found herself walking behind Jonathan in the city as he moved in his decisive way towards some appointed place and time and suddenly his wrists had flashed, his hands flinging outwards. The long fingers splayed as if he were trying to keep his balance, a little wave of panic like a sleepwalker fending off the hand that would shake him awake.

It reminded her of a too-hot night, the air viscous with jasmine. She had been alone and out of doors in the garden beneath their flat, drowsy, dreaming, when the city had paused around her, the air suddenly glassy and silent. Then, as the lights blurred, the ground began to liquefy. An earthquake. The shaking did not last long—she barely had time to feel frightened—but when she tried to move she realised that she was no longer standing. She had been thrown to the ground without any sense of falling.

The earthquake had toppled three tenements and the tidal surge that followed lifted the ocean-going liners where they moored and raced across the eastern edge of Rangoon, backfilling the creeks with brackish water and flooding India Town and the commercial jetties. On the tram a passenger said she had heard the cries of trapped men and then, as the days passed, Winsome heard for herself the plangent tones of funeral rites bound up with the scent of incense and charred flesh. But further north Pegu, the royal capital of antiquity, was shaken to destruction, eaten by rock until not a single pagoda or palace stood. Ghosts of the ancients mingled with the butterfly spirits of the newly dead. And how very many dead there were—hundreds, the papers screamed, thousands. Cholera threatened. A fug of putrefaction hovered above the cracked fields; primaeval dynasties reduced to a smudge across the sky.

The earthquake coincided with the arrest of Gandhi across the Bay of Bengal and the following morning Indian troublemakers of every caste and creed, Burmans too, were all over Rangoon, protesting. Screaming that the earth itself was realigning the affairs of men and that what was to come was nothing less than the changing of kings.

'Change is upon us,' said Aye Sein who, as a law student, was given to speeches. 'We are not children, Mrs Goode. We may rule ourselves. In one moment, an auspicious moment—perhaps this moment—everything shall turn, you will see.' Aye Sein: collector of slang, hummer of popular tunes, a boy still himself. Once, when he had thought himself alone, she heard him speaking into the dark studio as if he were already at Fytche Square before a crowd. 'Self-rule,' he cried, 'for we are men.' And the tone of his voice had frightened her.

But these omens and portents were too solid, too specific, too political. The strangeness and truth of the earthquake had been in that moment of stillness when she reached out just as Jonathan had in the street, when she plunged her arms into what was other than air. What she could not see, what she could not touch, but now knew was there.

That was all she had, after all her observation, all her speculation. Still she watched him until one day as she walked towards the back of the shop he looked up from his ruined book and straight at her. He did not smile or nod to her that day as he ordinarily did. He only gazed, his eyes so steady, so open that she looked back as openly, as steadily, heat rinsing through her body.

Then she felt caught out in her spying, her speculating, and found she had to lower her face, could no longer look at him. Had to turn back towards the counter, to fumble in her bag for a handkerchief, a wrapped sweet, anything. Had to pretend she was waiting for the clerks who were too busy, were not yet ready to hand her Desmond's magazines and the newspaper. She wanted to run for the exit, to run all the way to the studio and close the darkroom door behind her.

Jonathan Grace, lean-hipped, hands swinging at his sides as he came for her (no book now), auburn hair dark against the light-coloured clothes, skin tanned the colour of sand. A man who was not beautiful, but purposeful and considered. Sure of his place in this world. In any world.

Her hands shook, she gripped her bag even tighter. Her heart thudded against her chest. When she dared look up, he was nearly beside her.

'Mrs Goode,' Jonathan said. He waited as she collected Desmond's order, then fell in beside her along Sule Pagoda Road as if it were natural for the two of them to be walking together like this, their feet beating the same rhythm, his profile, his good humour, the whisper of his clothes as much a part of the day as the sepia heat.

They walked in silence for several minutes before he finally spoke. 'What newspaper did you get?'

She unfurled the *Rangoon Times* and he took it from her. The headlines were about the Indian unrest and Gandhi and striking dockers and salt. He sighed. 'Do you feel like you are always living with compromise? In a kind of perpetual uncertainty?'

She was surprised at his words and unsure whether he expected her to reply. 'Yes,' she said, without looking at him. 'I do feel like that. At times.'

Jonathan closed the paper. 'I never feel entirely natural with people here.' He glanced at her. 'I don't mean you, of course.'

They walked on. 'I always think you can only try to do your best. That between people, you and me for example, or with my colleagues—things such as race and religion should hardly matter.'

'You make it sound as if we are all the same. Or capable of the same things.'

He laughed. 'No, I didn't mean it like that exactly. But surely we *are* all capable of kindness?' And now he seemed struck by this idea of a kind world: 'I suppose what I mean is that, if there is fellow feeling, then surely that is all that counts. You and I are friends, we are cordial, that is in our nature, not our birth.' He smiled at her. 'We decide for ourselves. Do you not agree?'

She nodded. Between them was lightness, if not quite understanding. They came to the corner where she knew he would be turning for the hospital and so she stopped, then blushed, heat racing through her again, because she had anticipated his movements when she should have pretended not to know which way he would turn. To her relief, he made no sign that he'd noticed, only stopped too and turned to say goodbye.

He rolled up the newspaper again and, as he handed it back, brushed his hand against hers, allowing his fingers to linger against her skin. In the pressure of his touch was an opening, a glimpse of something other than was possible with words and of a significance that was also outside her understanding. It stilled her. She looked up at him. In his grey eyes, small golden flecks and more. Not friendship. Perhaps that gesture of his, the little flash of his wrists, was other than she had thought too.

'Do you see this?' said Daw Sein. It was a round piece of glass. She held it upright, its smooth face glinting towards Winsome, then turned it ninety degrees so that it caught the light. A flaw, a tiny bead of air, a scratch, distorted the light, making a jewelled shape on the wall. 'It will have to be returned to the factory.'

Turn the glass and see the flaw, turn it again and see the jewel. Put it down to her ignorance of men.

'I hope there is fellow feeling between us, Mrs Goode, I hope that we are friends. I would like to think that we are,' his voice became a little softer, 'and I hope that if you ever do have need of a friend, a kind friend, you'll call on me.' He did not smile, only dropped his fingers. Then he left her, turning the corner and walking on towards the hospital.

On a morning early in the week, Jonathan stepped onto the wooden landing stage outside the Green Dragon Rice Company mill. The worn teak planks sank beneath his weight and he lurched forward, catching himself just in time. Muddy water, sour and sticky-smelling, seeped through the grey slats and oozed into his plimsolls.

Pazundaung Creek was an opaque milky brown, the water impenetrable even by the Rangoon sun, and it flowed faster, more profusely than any English river he had known. Doublet and triplet waves stood up above its ragged surface, a sign of the currents below. Jonathan had heard all about the surging tides and shifting sandbars on the Rangoon River, of which this was a mere tributary. Now he wondered if he would be able to read even this water, so quickly did it move, so complex was its course as it washed past him towards the deeper, wider river downstream. A creek like this that ran into a bigger water was always more dangerous and this moment, like the moment before love, was when you were blind to anything beyond your pleasure. He stole a glance at the old boatman, a gnarled Burman, brown as a walnut, who all of his life had sailed rice lighters—those small, fast native boats—up and down this river. This man sat Asian style, on his haunches, patiently holding Jonathan's boat by the painter. When he caught Jonathan's gaze, he grinned back, his mouth dark red with betel.

Khit Tin hurried over with the last of his kit, a peaked cap, a small towel, a metal canteen of water. The cap smelled of clean cotton warmed by sunshine and as he pulled it on, he glanced back over his shoulder. In the shade of the rice mill, a small group of workers watched him; coolies, their black bodies dusted to a dull grey with rice flour, a trio of truly ugly Burmese girls who sewed up the rice bags. Jonathan stepped farther out. The water that welled around his ankles felt warm and clung like oil.

It was Ronnie who had arranged for him to launch his tub from this private landing, where the rice was unloaded from up river, weighed, milled and then reloaded onto the lighters to be rowed out to the holds of the cargo ships anchored in the middle of the Rangoon River. He and Ronnie had spoken about it at the boat club—Jonathan had cycled up there at the request of a patient.

'I cannot see why you wouldn't row here.' Ronnie gestured towards Royal Lake with his glass, the remnants of ice chinking softly. From the verandah of the club, the lake was a dull, slippery blue, dotted with purple water hyacinths. On the opposite shore, Dalhousie Park, laid out in the English style with just a few of the better native trees for shade, was reflected perfectly on the lake's surface. Everything around them was in the English style; there were English voices of all classes in the air, speaking of English things, wearing English clothes and smelling of English soap, food, tobacco.

Despite the palm trees and the heat, there was little to mar the illusion. There were even some English women there, drinking shandies or lime and tonic, stolid little figures with shrewd eyes that flicked about the room waiting for you to look back, mistaking their allure for power. He preferred another sort of woman altogether, not necessarily beautiful, but with a gift of sweet recklessness, who did not regret her pleasure. Women who were capable of an erotic shiver even in this warm sun; he knew them at a glance, something in the way their skin shifted.

The enclosed lake with its benign water had struck Jonathan as a sham. Why would one row there when the creeks and rivers of the real Burma were just below this ridge? So he spoke of how a British sportsman might like to test himself against an Asiatic river and Ronnie, who really knew nothing about it, was seduced. He had agreed to make his company's landing stage available once the thick of the rice season was over. 'You might row up and down Pazundaung Creek first, though,' he advised, 'before setting out on the Rangoon River itself. Dashed dangerous place, or so I am told.'

The old sailor tightened the painter and brought the tub closer in. Khit Tin, his wide Burmese-style trousers hitched up, offered his arms to steady Jonathan as he lowered himself onto the stretcher. He took up the heavy ash oars and gave one pull, then let the tub drift away from the landing and into the current, his back to the faster water. From the bank, the old man called out in Burmese.

'He says, be sure to stop before Monkey Point,' Khit Tin shouted. 'Look for a stand of toddy palms as the creek broadens. You will hear it from there. Listen for the river's voice.' Jonathan nodded back at the old man who rocked on his heels and smiled his blood-red smile.

It took a few strokes before Jonathan felt the bite of his blades in the water. A breeze played across his back. This was what he had been longing for, the familiar smoothness of ash in his hands, of cutting cleanly through water. He squinted against the brightness and let his mind loosen.

Khit Tin followed him, scrabbling along the bank as far as the end of the rice mill lot, thrashing the grass before him with a stick. When the vegetation became impassably thick, he stood there looking out over the water and Jonathan felt a childish delight at leaving his servant behind. Here was a respite from the awkwardness of life lived continually among others. From the suffocation of people at the hospital, from his own expectations, from the stupefaction of heat, from the visions and nightmares that racked his body with a longing for what he could not name. He dug deep into the water.

Although he was not tall, as many of the best rowers were, Jonathan was powerful and enjoyed testing the strength of his back and shoulders against the fast water. His legs ached deliciously as he pumped back and forth on the stretcher. The rhythm of the boat, the sensation of effort, the raggedness in his chest, the sting of the sun, all of these things gave him pleasure. He adjusted the nose of the tub until he was in the swiftest channel of the creek; his speed increased, he felt himself the equal of this river.

On the banks, a lean-to village stood in the long grass. Tiny market gardens sloped down to the water's edge. He sped past a Burmese fish sauce factory where the stink of putrefaction nearly choked him, but briefly, only briefly. Soon it, too, had passed.

With each stroke the tub lifted a little and he imagined his oar shattering the surface of the creek. Dip-smash. Dip-smash.

Clear beads of water dropped from the edge of the blades; caught by the sun they shone like glass shards. Like that little vase tumbling to the ground. Smash, smash. All those sharp splinters near that smooth skin. Mrs Goode. How neatly his hand might fit into the small of her back, how cool she would be against the heat of his palm. How insistently his fingers might search for that mole hidden at the back of her neck.

Jonathan's chest was bursting, his legs on fire. Doubled over, gasping for breath, he raised his oars from the water, resting them on the thwarts. He was still moving swiftly, drifting. In the slower water near the banks were islands of pink waterlilies, their vines trailing in the current. He glimpsed the back of a crocodile as it rose to the surface. On the far shore a snake swam in the shallows, its head held high and still while its body whipped beneath the surface.

With a start he turned on the stretcher, looked for the widening of the creek and the stand of toddy palms—what were toddy palms? What might they look like? He hadn't even asked. He did not want to be caught up in the confluence of the creek with the Rangoon River. But as he looked around, he saw he was safe. There was time yet. He lifted his chest and went at the water again, this time at a more moderate pace.

He did not consider himself an innocent with women, yet there was a quality to Mrs Goode. She was not like the little Burmese dolls, or the calculating Englishwomen at the club. She reminded him of a gypsy in a story, her shabbiness the perfect frame for her openness, her youth, the strange planes of her face. She was not beautiful but instead reminded him of beauty, and the creaminess of her skin, that skin so easily bruised, raised the points of his teeth. His fingers would make deep dents in that skin, in the plumpness at the tops of her thighs. When he touched her she would groan, her body slackening against his. Her nipples would harden into his palms and her sex, plum-soft and purple, would be glossy with longing.

Jonathan looked up to get his bearings. The creek banks were different now. The godowns, the little dockside factories, the shacks were all gone, there was only a thick screen of vegetation, obliterating all signs of the city. He might have been on some up-country river, emerging from primeval forest. He pulled the tub a little towards a small inlet on the left bank, turning to watch how the current twisted the water. Even in this relative shelter, he had to continually correct his position with the swipe of an oar.

Mrs Goode. Winsome. It was something to do with shame that kept returning her to his thoughts. Another man's wife. Worse, a man over whom he had power.

At medical school there had been an orderly who, for a few bob, used to let gentlemen and their girls into the hospital asylum to watch the simple-minded fornicating at night. The women, shop girls, waitresses, who'd caught a gentleman's eye: one would find them sitting on the back steps of the medical students' residence, a roll of notes held in a small fist, pleading expressions on their faces. Some of them had been quite pretty, dressed in cheap finery, occasionally a new fox fur across their shoulders.

Decent men, men of honour considered where they might do damage. A woman like Mrs Goode would never survive in England, anything beyond this moment was unthinkable—and yet, what if she showed the slightest sign...? She was a Catholic, too.

Jonathan squinted against the brightness on the water. Slowly, he turned upon himself, slid his craft back into the current. That day, on his knees beside her, he'd thought he smelled the water in the vase, old flowers. A smell too rich, so overripe he'd had to catch his breath. But it was her.

Indian, Burman, European, Eurasian. Aryan, Dravidian, Mongolian. Pure bloods, half-castes (crannies, chi chis, yellow-bellies) coolies, peasants. Shans, Karens, Madrassis. Headmen, assistants, sub-assistants, clerks. Separationists, anti-separationists, nationalists. Christians, Mussulmen, Hindus. The intricate net of words like a mildew tracing its way across a page, rewriting, obscuring what was beneath. Rangoon was ordered with a nuance and complexity that baffled him. He struggled to decipher what the most abject street urchin saw at a glance, yet could not help a sneaking admiration for this taxonomy of race and creed. Naming things, seeing them for what they were, surely this was the same impulse that moved him—the impulse behind science and reason, the bringing of order to the anarchy of ignorance, disease and fear.

Before he came to Burma, he had known as a point of science, never mind decency, that all men of brown, white or yellow skin were of the one flesh. This was rational. This was also Christian; a man was a man, only his deeds counted.

But here, flesh was something else and he could not explain this to himself. When skin met skin, something inexplicable took place. He had found himself repelled by the hands of the woman who occasionally came in to cook for him. With a growing revulsion he had watched as she cut onions, pounded turmeric, plucked a bird's feathers until the pink meat glistened against the dirty purple of her dull skin. His gorge had risen and he couldn't bring himself to eat what she cooked. When he went to pay her—adding extra coins—she would not accept the money from his hands, frightened in case their fingers met, shuddering at the thought. Flesh on flesh. Revulsion. Desire. One so like the other.

Above him, the banks rose higher and as he rounded a point of land, he could feel the creek open out onto the river and the miles beyond, to the sea, the idea of it like a coolness, a vastness across his arms. His eye caught a stand of trees on the shore, long fronds in the shape of a fishtail. Toddy palms, slipping by so fast.

At that moment he heard the voice of the conflux, a deadening roar, almost human. Fear ran in an icy trail along his back. Now the skin of the creek folded back over itself. Stiff waves rammed against his scull, shoving him sideways. His heart pumped hard. He pulled wildly, amateurishly at the water. Righted himself only at the point of capsize. Somehow managed to swing the boat out of the current.

With desperate strokes he fought his way to a tiny inlet. Gained the bank and clawed his way onto land. Panting, streaming with perspiration and river water, he hauled his boat up onto mud, then climbed a little further through undergrowth, thrashing at the grass in case of snakes.

Finally, he found a place where it was possible to rest. He threw himself to the ground and waited for Khit Tin to find him.

It was later, some days later, as he strolled in the cool evening breeze at Monkey Point, that Jonathan looked down into the brown conflux of river and creek and saw how close he had come to disaster. In the centre of the river the big ships gently rose and fell, but at his feet the ferocity of the current shook the ground; water tore at the bank, carrying away little doomed islands of grass and scrub, and the air was rich with the scent of crumbling earth. He was not the master of this river, he saw. But he was not its victim either.

It was the first tram of the day but, as the car drew near, Winsome could see it was far from empty. She was not surprised. Who could sleep with this heat, with the monsoon clouds banking thickly above you, a persistent weight in the air? In these clammy nights only the morphia addicts slept, dreaming where they fell, innocent as children. The tram lurched to a stop and she climbed aboard, the air inside already suffocating. She found a seat near a window, rested her head against the cool glass.

In the livid pre-dawn light Rangoon slid past, a city of somnambulists. Private motorcars returned late-night revellers to their homes in the hills; trails of brown men travelled the other way, trudging for the dockyards or railways or rice mills; towards the centre of the city, a queue of Burmans stood bare-chested, waiting their turn in front of an ancient, solemn-faced man who traced dark patterns on their skin. In back streets she could just make out the shadowy outlines of conservancy carts collecting the brimming pails of night soil.

Late in the afternoon the day before, Desmond had called

at the studio. Daw Sein was on the dais, murmuring instructions to a listless Burmese couple, hot and uncomfortable in European clothes. They were not paying attention. Their gaze was instead drawn to the figure at the entrance, a man pacing back and forth, in and out of the shadow, light shining then fading across his broad shoulders. In the sleepy, murky heat of the studio the effect was mesmerising, and she too had stopped to watch for a moment before stepping forward to greet him.

'Desmond?'

He looked up at Winsome and grinned. 'There's a car waiting for me outside,' he announced, his voice loud and theatrical. 'I've been called out to the hospital camps at Pegu. They can't cope with all the dead. No time to waste.'

Winsome could feel Daw Sein and the languid Burmese couple listening. She kept her own voice low. 'How long will you be away?'

He shrugged. 'As long as I am required. A few days. Perhaps more. A week. Who knows?' Then, after shooting a glance at the dais, 'But there is one thing you must do for me, funny thing. My report for Dr Grace, I promised it to him.' He stepped forward, taking her by the hands. 'It is confidential. Can I rely on you to deliver it to him personally?'

'No.' A granite wedge sharp in her belly as she pulled her hands away. Daw Sein's gaze on her. The Burmese couple too. She struggled to compose herself. 'I can't go. Not now.'

Desmond frowned. 'In the morning then? My car is waiting.' And quietly: 'I gave him my word.'

From the dais came Daw Sein's voice. 'Please don't worry, Mrs Goode. If the important man must have his papers, then you must deliver them. Tomorrow morning, I can wait, Mrs Goode.'

Desmond chucked his wife under the chin. 'That's settled

then.' He turned for the door then abruptly looked back. 'Into his own hands, mind, no one else. That is vital.' He left her standing there, still gripped by dank and bitter fear, as Daw Sein translated their conversation into Burmese for the old couple.

The sky was the colour of smoke when she stepped off the tram at the hospital, and the heavy air smelled of dust. Dawn had been subdued, almost insignificant, and the morning remained dismal. Above the hospital's red-brick buildings and thirsty lawns, the clock tower showed nearly six.

As she walked along the pavement, noisily chatting women passed her by, carrying tiffin tins with their luncheon rice—the scent of it made her regret her own hurried breakfast of a cup of tea. She felt in her bag to be sure the thick wedge of papers was still there, then climbed the hospital's stone steps.

She knew it was Jonathan's habit to start work early, he had told her that he preferred the cool of the mornings, and she expected he would be here already, making his rounds. It would be a simple matter to find him, deliver the letters and go. She explained her errand to a nursing sister with a sunburnt face who directed her towards a back wing of the hospital with an offhand wave. 'You may find him in the east ward. You can't miss it, there's a quadrangle with a garden. Wait there.'

It took Winsome a few turns through the vast hospital before she arrived at the garden, a small planting of dwarf palms and crotons in a space bordered by roofed walkways. The garden was quiet, sheltered from the street noise. There was a bench. She sat down to wait.

Heat was already seeping from the earth, the bricks, settling on her skin. The palms, dull green against the grey sky, gave off a cloying scent, sweet and starchy. She could smell the sting of phenol, lye and carbolic, none of which quite masked the lush reek of diseased flesh. There was the scent of smoke, too, from a distant fire.

She shifted on the bench. She waited. She watched for Jonathan. Tiny green birds scrabbled at her feet. A dhobi man dragged a bundle of soiled linen across the brick tiles, *tss tss tss*, then all was silent once more. Above her the tin roofs creaked. Her head fell forward, drooping beneath the weight of torpid air.

Steps rang on the brick walkway and Winsome woke with a start. A nursing sister glanced across as she passed beneath the tin roof, heels rapping against the stone. How long had she slept? What was the time? She would be so very late for the studio.

All over again, Winsome regretted Desmond's loud voice yesterday afternoon, his palpable condescension. She took his papers from her bag, smoothing the ends of the ribbon, and for a moment considered leaving them with someone, that nurse perhaps, then slipping away. After all, in this large and busy hospital, how could she be sure she had found the correct ward, if she was waiting in the right place? Should she go and look for Jonathan?

Her skin shrank at the thought of seeking him out—what if she were in his way, forcing herself on him, an unwelcome distraction from his work? But Desmond had been explicit, and he would ask if she had followed his instructions exactly. At her feet the little green birds scrabbled in the dust.

It was another hour before she finally caught sight of Jonathan, the clock had just struck ten when he came through the door farthest from her bench. He was not alone. Other men followed at his heels and a tall, almond-skinned nurse walked by his side, the two deep in conversation.

He was wearing a long coat, pristine white. He had a quietness about him. As he walked, his wrists flashed at his cuffs.

He seemed warm, straight backed, and she felt a little pang of pride in him, although she had no right to it. When his group paused in the corridor she stood up quickly, and started towards him.

The tall sister was the first to see her, and frowned as she drew closer, her dark eyebrows knitted with such disapproval that Winsome wondered again if perhaps she should just have left the package behind. Daw Sein would not be expecting her to take this long. She slowed her pace, began to turn back towards the hallway to the front desk, but it was too late. Jonathan had already looked up and was moving quickly towards her, his expression anxious.

'Mrs Goode, is everything all right?'

She could feel the sister's eyes running critically over her skirt, the calico bag, her dress creased with waiting. The thin wedding band on her left hand.

'No, nothing at all is wrong.' Winsome pulled the parcel of papers from her bag. 'Desmond sends you his apologies, he's been called away and can't meet you tonight. He asked me to bring you these.' She held out the bundle of papers in its coloured ribbon.

Jonathan looked at the bundle with incomprehension and chill realisation flooded through her; she had been silly to come, to disrupt him, despite Desmond's instructions. Maybe he was thinking that she'd come for reasons of her own. To test his friendship somehow or, worse, extract a declaration of his admiration, of his desire. And had she? Had she come out of obedience to her husband or to show herself to Jonathan? She felt her face colouring.

He took the papers, held the bundle loosely in his hands. 'How did you get here, Mrs Goode?'

'By tram.'

He fixed her with a steady, searching look. His eyes did not move from her face when he asked, 'And how do you propose to get home?'

Winsome felt a coldness grip her scalp; his tone was severe, as though she had somehow erred in coming here. He was embarrassed in front of his colleagues to find her waiting for him like a stray dog. She remembered his voice at the bookshop, the tone: 'Mrs Goode, I hope there is fellow feeling between us, I hope that we are *friends...*'

'I am not going home.' She smoothed her dress. 'I am going to work.'

Jonathan compressed his lips into a thin line before he spoke. 'But the streets—haven't you heard?—the streets are full of armed mobs. Burmans killing Indians, Indians fighting back. You will not be able to get a bus or tram or hail a rickshaw. You cannot possibly travel to work, or home, or anywhere. Not alone.'

Winsome remembered the solemn-faced old Burman, his fingers marking the skin of those men, the acrid smell of smoke. She thought of Daw Sein by herself in the studio—would Aye Sein go to her? Of Desmond in Pegu.

'But I didn't see...' she stammered.

The sister broke in. 'There might be a hospital tonga available, Dr Grace.' Her voice was bland but in her eyes, slate-like resentment.

'I am sure I shall be all right on my own.'

'Would you like me to see to it, Dr Grace?'

'Thank you.' The sister turned to make the arrangements.

'Please don't,' Winsome begged. The tall sister turned again, a withering smile on her face as she waited with exaggerated patience. Winsome appealed directly to Jonathan. 'I don't want to make trouble.'

'There really is no alternative, Mrs Goode. If you would kindly wait here.' He turned to go.

Didn't see: she had said it herself. How typical of her kind not to use, not to *possess*, better judgment. Sitting back on the bench, among the crotons and palms, she could feel Jonathan's disappointment.

By late afternoon she was sick with waiting. Her stomach was rumbling—she had missed lunch now too, but hadn't dared to go to find a food stall or even a cup of tea in case they came for her. Now she need only look around her to be aware of the conflict beyond the solid walls of the hospital: a stream of bodies on stretchers ebbed and flowed, ferried by orderlies whose aprons were no longer so very white. When she took just half a dozen steps along the corridors she could see the injured spilling out of the wards.

From time to time a handful of nurses and orderlies would gather at the edge of the garden to smoke and shake their heads. They talked of men broken, burnt, slashed, drowned. They piled them up with their words, limb by limb, until she imagined a writhing heap. They talked of soldiers, of police—a hundred, two hundred, three hundred of them. And at the end of these lists, like a settling of accounts, one of them would invariably look her way. She could feel them wondering about her, disapproving. Was she harmless? Was she so very helpless? When she could stand it no more, she crept into the centre of the green square until she was hidden by the palmettos and the crotons. She tilted her head towards the thick, roiling sky.

When Jonathan finally returned, his coat was stained at the sleeves and midriff. He looked at her wearily. 'There are no tongas to be had,' he announced. 'I will take you home myself.'

She wanted to say she was sorry, that this was her fault for agreeing to bring the notes. Instead she said, 'Is there no one else?'

'Follow me,' he replied, and she fell into step behind him.

He took her through the back corridors of the hospital, through a ward and past a row of patients. She looked for new signs of the violence, but Jonathan was moving too quickly. He paused before a green door, then opened it out onto a small courtyard where a bicycle rested against a brick wall. He turned to her, his expression a little sheepish. 'Do you think you can balance on the back here?' He pointed to a rack. 'You can hang on to me if you feel unsafe.'

But when they wheeled the bike out to the front of the hospital they were stopped by a small group of Imperial Police. A constable, one of several young, fine-boned Burmese, lanky in his uniform, waved Jonathan over to their officer-in-charge, a squat Eurasian. Around them, Commissioner Road was empty of traffic and eerily quiet. The air smelled strongly of smoke.

With a quick reassuring nod, Jonathan handed the bicycle to Winsome and stepped over to the officer. As they spoke the sergeant glanced across at her, his look appraising, curious. The Burmese boys watched the street.

A sound pierced the air, a howling of voices raised in fear or anger—she could not tell which—and all of them, Winsome, the sergeant, the boy-policemen, Jonathan, stopped to listen. Each one straining to hear. White dust rose in a column that must have been mere blocks away and, above this, pigeons wheeled and arced aimlessly, too frightened to settle. There was the thud of running feet, another cry and then glass shattering before the street was silent once more. The constables nervously passed their bamboo lathis from hand to hand and the sergeant turned his back to Jonathan, waving him away.

Jonathan's face was clouded as he returned to her. 'All the roads out of central Rangoon are cut off, there's a police blockade around the docks. They think the army has been called out. They have orders to shoot at will. I cannot take you to your home.' He paused, uncertain, calculating quickly. 'Perhaps I can arrange for you to stay at the hospital. A bed can be made up…a message might be sent to your husband, to let him know you are safe...'

'No,' the violence of her voice surprised her. Over Jonathan's shoulder, she saw the sergeant look back their way through narrowed eyes. In a calmer voice, she pleaded with Jonathan. 'I feel very much in the way here. Is there nowhere else?'

Jonathan shook his head. He ran his hand through his hair, dark red in the damp heat. 'My rooms are not far...' His voice trailed off as he turned his face away from her. Behind them the massed voices rose again and a sound like metal rain hit the air. The sergeant signalled to his men. They raised their lathis. Jonathan looked back at Winsome. 'You will be safe there. I can at least assure you of that.'

His eyes were a flinty grey, the yellow flecks not so evident now. He was standing close enough for her to smell his warm skin through the clinging odours of the hospital, linen cloth, glycerine soap. It was not too late to resume her vigil on the bench inside; put up with the pursed lips and stares, try to stay out of the way as the wounded and dead piled up.

She was too ashamed to feel gratitude, too small to accept his protection graciously. She thought of him in his white coat, wrists flashing, of his voice in the street outside the bookshop. She felt limp, her body, her head too heavy.

'I don't know what to do,' she said.

He nodded, took the bicycle handlebars from her. 'Then come with me.'

At first the bike veered so violently from side to side that Winsome had to grip Jonathan at the hips to avoid being thrown to the ground. They moved in sharp jerks along Commissioners Road, Jonathan straining so hard to turn the pedals that she felt her own useless weight at the back of the bicycle. Her hands were clumsy against the sides of his body. She feared they might be overtaken by someone, something, a target because of her ungainliness. But as they gathered speed, the bicycle wheels began to whirr with a sweet, mechanical music and the air shifted across her skin until it was a breeze, a caress on her bare arms and legs.

'Hold on, we're turning,' he shouted over his shoulder. Her reply was lost to his back, but she gripped him more tightly as the bicycle, moving briskly, banked left and then dipped into Godwin Road, spinning downhill towards the river.

She smelled honey and spice in the rush of air. Godwin Road, lined with padauk trees, was a deep green tunnel, thick foliage blocking out the cries from the wounded city. All about them yellow blooms lay in drifts along the street, dotted throughout the leaf canopy above. Padauk flowers. Late blooming, these, lasting no more than a day. A sign that the rains were close.

Winsome tilted her head back and inhaled until she was dizzy with the scent, the hum of the wheels, the blur of yellow against a green and grey sky. Faster and faster down Godwin Road they flew. She could not see where they were going, only trust in Jonathan. She moved as he moved, leaned as he leaned until, quite naturally she began to feel that they were not in counterbalance, but rather in sympathy.

There was a pleasure in their momentum, and a relief. The riot, the rioters, the injured, the dying, the hospital, the police, the Anglo-Indian sister, the gossiping nurses and orderlies, the Eurasian sergeant, Desmond, fear, anger, shame, all of these were behind her.

Ahead was the river, a metallic tang on her tongue. But now, at this moment, there was only this harmony between movement and the comfort of Jonathan's body; the rise and fall of his broad back, the salty damp of his white shirt.

She slid her hands forward until they rested gently against the ridge of his pelvis. Through the length of his flanks she felt the bicycle shudder and vibrate, and the smooth sureness of his movement in answer. Beneath her fingers, the luscious give of his flesh, the heat of him rising to her touch. Muscle, bone, hair, breath, all of him in her hands and her own heart beat faster because now she felt she was steadying him. Holding him up, this kind man, this decent man. A man so different from Desmond, from Aye Sein, from all the other men she saw in the streets of Rangoon. And with this realisation she felt tenderness towards him rather than gratitude, and thought that if he should fall she would try to catch him. Catch him, hold him, steady him, protect him.

Jonathan shifted his weight onto one leg, preparing to turn and she leaned into him, laying her cheek flat against his shirt as they swept into Dalhousie Road and then into Crisp Street. As they emerged from the avenue of trees, the sounds of fighting could again be heard clearly and the air was charged once more. They were close enough to the tenements in India Town to hear a roar that must be fire. But Winsome, protected by Jonathan's back, still dreamed. It was only the sound of a distant boom that roused her. Thunder? Faraway guns? The collapse of a building, the wooden beams glowing red beneath grey ash?

As she listened, a coldness gripped her so that, when they swept sharply left into the curved drive of a building, the bicycle's brakes squealing, she panicked and jumped, falling heavily onto the gravel. Quickly she scrambled to her feet, palms and knees stinging.

In the road, three men with painted chests watched them, their heavy dahs hanging at one side. She stared back, unable to move, terror condensing on her skin. Jonathan shouted at her from the portico. She ran to cover.

His rooms were on the top floor and as they climbed the stairs she stumbled, falling again onto her skinned hands. He unlocked his door and stood aside to let her pass. The room was large and silent, the blinds drawn. She gagged a little on the stale air, on the dregs of her fear. When he shut the door behind her, it felt final.

For she knew what was to come. She had always known it. From his salt scent the day he came to tea. From the long shape of him as he held those ruined books. From her own heaty dreams. The night of the earthquake, when she had plunged her hands into nothing, what she found was this.

'Khit Tin!' Jonathan's voice reverberated loudly off the walls.

'I'll fetch him,' he mumbled before disappearing into a low hall opposite the door. Soon he was nothing but the sound of footsteps, of doors opening and shutting. Only then did Winsome move from the threshold and into Jonathan's apartment.

The furnishings were simple. An electric fan stood in the far corner and there were electric lights too—but these were the only luxuries. At the centre of the room, two cane club chairs faced one another across a low teak table. A dining table and chair were pushed against a wall next to a small sideboard. On the facing wall, between floor-to-ceiling windows, were a desk and a bookshelf, half-full—with those marred books perhaps. She crossed to a window and pulled up the blind.

Outside, the murky sky was a dirty yellow, as it often was before a storm. From this height the human cries were muffled, then masked by another low boom that crossed and recrossed the sky. It came from no direction that she could discern and seemed to go nowhere at all. She turned from the window. Her hands were burning. She raised them into the light and found a flap of skin lifting from her right palm, oozing blood. She ran her tongue over it and the rank, mineral taste made her wonder if something rotten was welling up from deep inside her.

'He's not here.'

She jumped and turned. Jonathan stood at the door jamb,

his pale trousers, his rumpled linen shirt glowing in the gloom. He walked towards her at the window, narrow hipped, clear eyed. 'Khit Tin. I don't know where he is.' His face was creased and he avoided her eyes, kept his gaze elsewhere. He saw the blood on her hands. 'You're hurt?' Taking her hand, he opened her palm, exposing the torn skin.

His breath was honey, padauk flowers, his skin sharp sweat. The scent of him made her shiver.

I hope that there is fellow feeling between us, I hope that we are friends.

Outside the boom resounded once again across the sky. She turned towards it. She turned back.

'Please.' Her voice was a rasp.

He looked at her now and she could no longer think; was only dimly aware that she was shaking, that she could not stop. 'Shh, shh,' he said, 'shh shh.' Then he put her torn palm to his lips, placed his hand on the small of her back until she felt the flat of her belly touching his, the softness of her breasts sharpening against his chest. She started to cry. 'Shh shh.'

He led her to the cane chair. He fetched a cloth and some water and then, kneeling before her, took her hand in his and washed her wound. He folded the same cloth over and gently wiped her face. When his hands changed, when his fingertips trailed along the length of her throat and his eyes grew dark, she guided his fingers to the buttons of her dress. She ran her own hands along his belly, over his hips, looked for his softness, found his firm sex. Pushed herself against him, hooked herself into his skin. Through the window came the boom of thunder, or guns or fire.

Later that evening, as Winsome and Jonathan slept, the sky finally broke and for a few moments rain raised the dust all across Rangoon. The shower did not last long—they never did at that time of year—but it was heavy enough to strip the last of the padauk flowers from the trees and to sweep the golden drifts into rivulets that streamed down Godwin Road, into the open drains and out onto the Rangoon River, where they floated on the ebbing tide.

In her studio, Daw Sein opened the shutters to watch water spray off the road, the letter she'd been writing half-finished on her desk. Up country, near the hospital camp's makeshift morgue, Desmond paused to listen to the drumming rain. The brief downpour subdued the fires in what was left of the Coringhee tenements, and wet the tongues of the coolies taking refuge in the old lunatic asylum. The showers cleared the air, but only briefly. These were not the true monsoon rains, those would come later.

Rain

On that first night, the first night of the rioting, Jonathan woke abruptly. He had been dreaming of plums, the yellow plums his mother used to put out for show in a blue bowl. Something of their sweet perfume, their sticky softness stayed with him so that he was adrift in the velvet darkness of the tropical night, the click of a gecko connected with the suppleness of flesh, the salt licked from his fingers with the brine of another's skin, the rush and gurgle of his own body with the steady rise and fall of breathing beside him. Her back curving away from him, and beneath, the swelling of her buttocks and the bud of her anus, smooth thighs parted to a bent knee, still smelling, still smeared with his semen. He touched his tongue to his teeth and raised himself from the bedclothes. He would wake her with his fingers, with his mouth.

Beneath him, she slept on, her legs extending down the bed in an echo of his own sleeping shape, her face half-turned from him, half in shadow, and the way her arms were thrown about her head, like a child, touched him so that he felt a tenderness for her. She slept with abandon. She had abandoned herself to him. But even as he gathered his body across hers, he heard the scrape of a foot at the door. It was unmistakable, Khit Tin, padding closer on bare feet. Bringing tea—no doubt as an appeasement for his absence, but Jonathan also suspected prurience. He had learned to listen for the sly chink of cup against sugar bowl on a tray held in steady hands. Khit Tin's Burmese way of creeping about like a spy when there was a woman in the apartment, on his face a blameless expression so like insolence.

Jonathan sat upright, his body tight with rage at Khit Tin's incursion. Behaviour that would ordinarily irritate him tonight had consequences beyond himself alone. His servant must not see Winsome. Silently, Jonathan eased himself from the bed and moved towards the door, his body taut. He found the handle and turned it quickly, flinging the door open to surprise Khit Tin, perhaps even to upset his tray of tea things.

There was no dim shape looming from the darkness. It was not morning; it was not even dawn. There was no Khit Tin with his tray. The narrow hallway opened out onto the sodium-blue light of the empty living room. The air was cool on his face. He was thirsty. He moved through the hall to the kitchen to find some water.

The little kitchen was close and hot; the window overlooking the back of the building, with its mess of servants' lean-tos and cooking huts, was shut tight, insects thudding softly against the glass slats. The electric light did not work. Instead, he had to search for matches, a candle. He found tumblers too; a tray, a cloth to line it, a steel jug, which he positioned beneath the ceramic chatty before opening the spigot. Tepid water trickled out.

As he performed these small tasks, his hands looked strange, as if the water, the tray, were nothing to do with him at all. A large moth hit the window with a solid thud and set his heart beating fast. It left a splash of iridescent dust.

He was still unnerved by the force of his reaction to Khit Tin's imagined presence, the defensive reflex. He did not wish for Winsome to be compromised in any way, was aware that it was yesterday's violence that had led to the intensity of feeling between them, their appetite for one another honed by the heightened emotion of the riots. People behaved differently in dangerous times, or so he had read. Now he knew it to be true. Yet his own fury at Khit Tin he did not understand—it was more than protectiveness towards Winsome, it was a *feeling*—not honour, or decency or delicacy. More than the simple wish not to be an agent of harm.

The jug was almost overflowing. He snapped the spigot shut, then looked about for lemons, or limes. But there were none to be had, no ice in the box either, in fact; no sign that Khit Tin had been there at all the previous day. Jonathan blew out the candle and carried the metal tray back through the apartment.

After the stale air of the kitchen, the openness of the living room soothed and distracted him. A breeze, scented with rain, came through the tall windows; careless of him to leave them open. He set his tray on his desk and walked towards them.

The night was still dark but, from the freshness of that breeze, Jonathan judged dawn to be no more than a few hours away. On the very hottest nights, nights such as this one, he often slept at the foot of these windows, cooled by these same night winds. He knew that the natives made a habit of sleeping outside on their balconies, sometimes without nets despite the mosquitoes. The movement across his skin was pleasant and he thought that perhaps he could have made a makeshift bed right here for himself and Winsome, for both of them—it would have heightened his pleasure. Outside the wind sighed a little, and he stepped over the low sill and onto the balcony.

Rain had washed away the smoke and the tropical foetidness.

The air was clean and the city still. He could smell trees, the river; he was briefly, powerfully reminded of an English midsummer's night. Looking out over the city, he could see the gleam of the water and the Lewis Street Jetty, where the trouble was rumoured to have begun. Further still were the narrow streets of East Rangoon and a little to the north the cream-coloured government buildings— the courthouse, the customs house, Lloyds, the Imperial Bank, the European Surety.

Despite the riots, the grounds of the secretariat building were still lit up, the brightness showing through the thick fringe of palms and banyan trees. Above the city, in the Pegu Yoma, rose the grand houses around the Shwe Dagon Pagoda, the Golden Valley where excellent little men and their excellent wives looked out over the lakes. He had taken lovers from that set; had gone with women like that.

Those women. Winsome was so unlike them he couldn't imagine her in their company. She was not schooled in the social mores of the Golden Valley, she would be defenceless against its cruelties. She was not sharp, she had the dust of the convent about her. She was not chic, she was not even beautiful, not in their way. Not of his world. Not free. Not his.

As if in empathy, a low groan reached his ears. Some poor devil lying injured in the street below. The groan came again, but this time he was able to locate it in the apartment, his apartment. It had come from behind him.

Jonathan climbed back over the threshold, heart beating solidly, rapidly against his ribs, and peered into the greyness of the room. 'Winsome?' he called, his throat very dry because he was almost certain that what he had heard was a man's groan. And now he was equally certain that he had not left the windows open. He strained to hear what he could. There was only silence. But he felt the presence of the other, the groaning man, injured and desperate.

He wiped his mouth, took another step and called out again, louder this time, 'Someone there?' The same voice moaned in the dark; with it, the creak of a cane chair. Peering into the murk, Jonathan caught a movement in the half-light and the sheen of sweat on skin.

'Who is that?' Slipping further into the room; his fingers brushing the tray on his desk. He picked up the box of matches, struck one and held it up.

Khit Tin stared back at him from across the room, as if conjured by thought alone. His eyes were bright and glittering. He cradled one arm with the other, and Jonathan could just make out a slick raggedness beneath the shoulder where the skin should have been smooth. Khit Tin moaned once more. The match went out.

Jonathan crossed the room and knelt beside his servant. There was the rust smell of blood and fear. Another stench he couldn't identify, too foul and vegetal, sweet like decay. In the flare of another match, Khit Tin's belly shone black. His skin was febrile and when Jonathan prodded at the edges of the wound, his servant gasped. Something had pierced his flank, leaving a wound that was deep and torn, but did not mean death.

'This needs suturing,' Jonathan stated, surprised that his voice sounded cool, authoritative—like a white man's—when he still felt shaken by his earlier fear. He turned back to the desk for the jug of water, the cloth from the tray. He found the stub of a candle, a half bottle of gin and all the while reminded himself that Winsome was asleep in his bed.

He tried the electric light and, wondrously, it came on, but threw only a dim glow—an effect of the riot, no doubt—so that it was difficult to see the wound; he needed more light. Instead, he felt for the edges of skin. Slowly, methodically, as gently as he was able, he cleaned the area with the rag and the alcohol. Khit Tin was silent and almost still, never once acknowledging the pain; and it would be painful, Jonathan knew that. As he worked, he thought that he could feel his servant's fear, but perhaps it was loathing, for on that yellow skin, in the dark of the night, Khit Tin's blood was as black as ink.

He thought back to the men, his patients, who had come into the hospital that morning. On the bellies of those Burmans who had suffered the most violent wounds were designs of some ancient and native origin, painted onto the skin with a thick dark substance.

The muck he was wiping off Khit Tin's skin was black and grainy as well as gluey. Not just blood, then, or soot, or grease from some leaking machine. He understood these patterns marked men as warriors; they were signs of power and commitment. He imagined a knife molten in the air, then his servant's ragged steps as he staggered through the shadows, eluding the patrols of police, slipping up the back stairs to this flat, returning to his master and the pretence that characterised their relationship—which, for the moment, they seemed to have laid aside.

Jonathan put down the cloth and wiped the heat from his own face before going to fetch his bag from beside the desk. Sitting beside his servant once more, he laid out his suture scissors, his needles, the black silk.

Servants talked. That was the way of things. Even servants who slipped through the night, holding their guts inside their belly with one limp hand. The number of Europeans, even counting the Eurasians, was small. Rumours and half-truths were constantly being circulated through the clubs, the hospital, the European restaurants and assembly halls. He would have to make things clear, despite the humiliation of explaining oneself to a servant (but perhaps he and Khit Tin were past that now). He was obliged. He could not take his actions back. And so, for Winsome and also for Desmond, he must make sure he was understood.

When Jonathan pierced his skin with the needle Khit Tin didn't flinch or look away. Bending over the wound, Jonathan drew the silk through the skin, looped the thread to make a knot and tied off the stitch before pushing the needle into flesh once more. He wondered how messy this could possibly become.

'There is someone else here, Khit Tin.' His servant was used to unexpected visitors, and yet Jonathan felt rather than saw those black eyes flick upward, then down again. This was his only reaction. Jonathan's fingers slipped against the needle and he paused to wipe them before continuing. 'This person is a woman. It was not safe for her anywhere else, with the fighting in Rangoon.'

Khit Tin's neck strained forward—the stitch was too tight, Jonathan could feel how it bit into the flesh. He slid his scissors under the black thread, easing it loose. He preferred not to leave a scar. 'So I brought her here to protect her.' Khit Tin drew a long slow breath. 'She is still sleeping. We won't wake her, will we?' Beneath his fingers, the edges of the wound met evenly. It was a neat job that should heal perfectly, barring infection—God knew what was in that black muck. He was about to ask Khit Tin whether it was still painful but instead, placed his fingers against the wound and pressed down hard. Khit Tin gasped. He covered Jonathan's fingers with his own hand.

For a short moment, they looked steadily at one another, Khit Tin's eyes as dark and opaque as the paint Jonathan had cleaned from his skin. His servant gently lifted Jonathan's fingers from his then he pointed with his chin at the room behind them. Jonathan turned. Winsome was standing there.

Grunting with the effort, Khit Tin hauled himself from the chair. For a moment he teetered on his feet, then seemed to sag.

Jonathan wondered if he would fall, or if perhaps he was going to confide in them, explain his absence and beg forgiveness, promising his silence as compensation. Perhaps he had misjudged his servant. Blood always looked black in the night.

Khit Tin righted himself then turned his gaze towards Jonathan. 'I will make breakfast,' he said, his English, as always, so careful, such a delicate morsel in his mouth. He shuffled through the apartment towards the kitchen.

Winsome walked over to the cane chairs. The grey light that pierced the windows made the lines of her face, her jaw, her full lips, the curve of her cheek, exquisite. Soon day would fill the room. He watched her take in the needle, the black silk, the crumpled rags—stained, but not with blood—the room around her, the light outside. She reached for the switch and turned off the lamp.

Rain did not always fall during the monsoon and when the sun came out, it seemed to Winsome that it shone with a searching brilliance, with the quality of truth, of revelation. In those first few days of just-rinsed mornings and pellucid afternoons, the sky always seemed too bright. She had to shade her eyes.

At dawn on the King's Birthday a soaking rain fell. The paddy husks that had been scattered only days earlier to absorb spilt blood slowly expanded into a slimy mass while the detritus of a week's riotous slaughter (torn clothes, shoes, hanks of hair, scalp still attached) bobbed along the surface of drains. Rain washed away the overflow from pails of stale urine and shit, as yet uncollected by the conservancy workers.

By the time Winsome stood waiting near the secretariat gardens for the parade to begin, the sun was out and steam rose in patches from the tarmacadam. She saw that this morning light had a treacherous clarity: turn one way and you saw bunting along Fraser Street, British civil officers in morning dress, Anglo-Indians waving flags, the best Indian and Burmese families drinking sherbet and eating biscuits made from real butter; turn in the other direction and you could still make out the rectangular outlines from the Cameron Highlanders' gun placements. She too was doubled; deceitful and guilty, yet in love with, entranced by, the shine of the day. Beside her, Desmond stood with a Union Jack in his hand. The street was already lined with people, ready for wooing, two and three deep in places. On such a morning, one might forgive anything. Should she turn to him and beg?

'I can't see,' Desmond sighed. 'We should have come earlier. Why didn't we come earlier?' She knew he was itching to push past the man in front of him, a stocky Burman happily spitting pumpkin-seed husks at his feet. She touched his arm gently.

But he was not to be mollified. He sighed and shifted in his dark suit ('all civilian officers will attend the parade and shall appear in morning dress or dark lounge suits'—he had read the instruction to her). 'Well, something must be done,' he said. She dropped her hand from his arm and pulled at her sleeve. The blue dress was already too warm.

'Ah,' Desmond cried, pointing to the other side of the street. Right at the front of the facing crowd, not more than a foot or two from where the parade would pass, was Jonathan. He looked up, eyes slate grey in a pale face, and a surge of desire sluiced through her, followed by shame.

Immediately she started to shake. She told herself that she wanted to turn and run, to lose herself in the crowd. Yet she knew that she would not and that this was a lie because, despite her shame and her guilt, she felt joy at seeing him. Standing there silently, a dissembler, she did not know herself—there was a looseness in her joints, the resurrection of his touch along the backs of her thighs. With an effort, she stilled her trembling. 'Why, isn't that Dr Grace?' Desmond turned to her, cheerful now, eager. 'We should go and say hello, we must thank him for protecting you during the insurgency.' He plunged into the crowd, in a moment already a pace or two ahead of her. He pushed aside the man with the pumpkin seeds and waved away the marshal who was patrolling the lines of spectators.

And now blood and reason drained away, leaving her empty, yet improbably upright. She had to will herself to breathe, she had to force herself to move, because what choice did she have but to follow in his wake, to take the complaints, the insults, the angry glares as her due. It was the least she could offer.

'Hai, Dr Grace,' Desmond called as he marched across the road and straight up to Jonathan. She saw him tip his hat, hold out his hand, plant his feet, each movement jerky, false, like the sitters in Daw Sein's studio. Her own body felt mechanical, movement some kind of miracle, as she struggled past men and women, as she made her way to his side.

Adulterer. Lover.

'...and so I find that I am in your debt, for what would I do without her?'

The clear air was white, the light blinding.

Desmond turned to find her standing there beside him, just as he would always expect her to be. Smiling, he chucked her under the chin, a gesture of public affection, the kind of thing one offered one's wife as a token of benevolence, an adequate replacement for love: there you are, helpmeet. His touch was a humiliation, an accusation burning her skin, and all the while Jonathan looked on.

Eyes on the ground, blinking, blinking. She wiped them with her fingers.

So she stood listening to Desmond fill the space between the three of them with his talk of the weather and the parade and how, no matter how ill events seemed, order had a way of reasserting

133

itself, for that was the way of things. *If I look at him*, she thought, *Desmond will know*, but this too was untrue. What she meant was, *If I look him in the eye and there is nothing returned, how shall I live?*

On that first morning in Jonathan's apartment, in that still-dark room, she had been stirred by voices—half-heard, half-dreamed—it was Desmond and Teresa in a room close by and they were talking about her, she was back at her convent school, a bride again on the morning of her wedding. But the profanity of her dream woke her properly. She smelled Jonathan all around her, on the sheets, in the air, on her skin and she remembered where she was and what she had done. As soon as she did, guilt and shame pressed down on her so that she was unable to move, so that all she wanted was to drown in the darkness of the room.

Yet guilt was also love, shame was met equally by desire, by the warm satisfaction of his body, by her own astonishing pleasure. Nothing in her convent-school training could have prepared her for it. She knew about sin, she knew about confession and forgiveness. But love—she had not known about love. Love fused the soul with the flesh; it made her whole; it felt like a blessing. 'Deus caritas est.' This was different. How was she to make sense of it?

They stood there in the crowded street, while Desmond talked and talked, a small cloud passing, a shaft of strong sunlight breaking it up, and then, as if on cue, from the western edge of town came the shrill of the pipes. The crowd pushed in closer. 'Capital,' cried Desmond, his voice exultant, 'it is the Cameron Highlanders who will kick us off.'

And now she was feeling ill, as though she might faint. Her head hurt and the day, with the sudden bright heat of the sun, was already too close, the people around them hemming them in.

'You are fond of martial music, Dr Grace?'

'Yes, I am.' Jonathan's voice was quiet and even. His face was turned towards Desmond, who licked up his words, greedy for his attention.

'Myself, I love it. I never missed a performance of the police band, no matter where I was stationed.'

'And what about you, Mrs Goode?'

'She loves military music too.' Desmond turned briefly to her. 'In fact, you will enjoy this, Winsome.' He turned back to Jonathan. 'Pipes, drums. So stirring.'

'I have a headache, Desmond,' her voice was brittle, rough-edged. 'My head hurts, I am unwell, I can't stay here.'

'What?' He didn't even try to hide his annoyance as he looked around. 'But of course you would like to watch the Highlanders pass, would you not?'

And now she found that what she felt was a prick of jealousy. 'No,' she said peevishly, 'I would not.'

Desmond's face hardened. 'Nonsense,' he retorted and she felt a sting of fear. 'Besides, it will only make you worse if we try and move through this crowd. I think you'd better just lean on me, at least until the Highlanders have passed.'

'I dare say I'll be all right on my own.' She turned away from them and pushed into the crowd.

Behind her the sound of the band drifted along Fraser Street as heads stretched forward and voices were raised. *God Save the King*. In the sky, the sun shone upon them all—a good omen for the King's Birthday—that light made the air shimmer until she was dazzled, nearly tripping as she fought her way free of the spectators. She rested against the brick wall of a building, slowly breathing in the warm air with her eyes closed.

When she opened them again, she saw Jonathan following. He was coming to tell her that she was behaving badly, that he had made a mistake, that he was sorry about what had taken place between them, that he did not love her, could not love her, regretted it if she, in fact, loved him, but could not help it. He would remind her that she was married, that she was young (too young). That she was churlish and foolish and poor—poor of spirit, ignorant and backward. That she was a small person destined to live a small life.

Words welled up in her throat and she felt she must speak or choke; if he was coming to tell her these things, then she would answer them, she would not be silent no matter what she risked. She would tell him everything. First, she would tell him that she loved him.

But when he finally arrived in front of her, he only had breath for one word. 'Winsome.' His voice so low only she could hear it, but it was all she needed. She took his hand and pulled him around the corner. Then she touched his face, kissed him.

Arm in arm they walked along the streets—deserted now that the parade had begun—up to Montgomery Street, past the railway station. She was elated, filled with delight that she might look at him openly, that she might have him close to her, feel the nearness of his body, the supple flesh and muscle, the bone and hair, the smell of sunshine on his clothes and his scalp, all of him pulsing with life that seemed to push back against her hand, along her thigh, her shoulder, wherever their bodies touched and this was enough, she would be content just to be near him in this way. But with this happiness, a counterpoint of fear. She might so easily prove a disappointment; she already was to one man.

She knew she had lived a small life compared with his, a mean little existence with not very much in it. There was a word for it, a word like poverty. Paucity. That was it. She would have said it out loud if he had not been beside her. It meant not enough, never enough, and in her mind's eye she saw the world divided into the things she could have, those small sufficiencies, and those she never could. As she thought this, she pulled her hand loose from his and walked a little bit away from him.

The sun was higher in the hazy sky. Music from the parade had died off and there was a steady trickle of people walking along Montgomery Street. How much time had passed? Minutes, an hour, hours? Jonathan took back her hand, held it between both of his. 'I told Desmond that you were probably in shock, after the riots, the crowd, I said that I would find you and bring you to him. He will be waiting.' It sounded like an apology. They turned back towards the noise and tumult of the crowds at Fraser Street and went together to the observation tent in the secretariat gardens.

Several Indians were clearing the centre of the floor in preparation for dancing, one of them lighting a string of little coloured lamps despite the brightness of the afternoon. A band tuned up at one end of the tent and she felt a tiny surge of pleasure at the sound. Frowning as they did on public touching between the sexes, the more devout Buddhists among the Burmese had politely taken their leave and so it was mainly the Europeans, the half-castes, the anglicised natives and Indians who remained, a jubilant group, noisily seating themselves around the dance floor, handing round drinks, laughing loudly.

As she passed each little knot of revellers with Jonathan at her side, she too felt jubilant, carefree. As if all those men and women shared in her feelings; they watched her, they watched them together because even though Jonathan was walking apart from her, he was so clearly hers. Curious looks. Admiring glances. Jonathan touched his hand to the small of her back and she turned her face to smile at him, warm and pretty. This, she thought, was what it felt like to be lovely. (But you are no beauty. You are something else altogether.)

In a corner across the room, Desmond sat alone at a table with four chairs. There were three drinks waiting in front of him, the ice already melted. (The day was hot after all—but how long had he been sitting there?) He scanned the crowd with a bitumen gaze. When he finally saw them, his eyes fixed on hers and remained there, his face rigid.

'Are you feeling better, funny thing?' he asked, pulling back a chair for her, his voice like the scrape of metal. 'You still seem a little flushed. How lucky we are that Dr Grace was there to take care of you again.'

She willed herself not to glance at Jonathan. 'I'm fine now,' she said. They sat down. The band started up a new tune.

Desmond's eyes did not move from her; she smoothed her dress, took a sip of her drink. Light glinted on his glass as he raised it to his lips. He had bought some cigarettes and lit one now. The tobacco crackled as he inhaled. Jonathan talked about the hospital, asked him about the highland pipers, but his eyes continually slid away to rest once more on her face.

She turned away and studied the couples dancing on the wooden floor; men and women, their bodies soft-skinned beneath their clothes, blurring and gliding, like skaters. She blinked away her tears.

When the first tune ended and another had begun, a faster song, Desmond stood up abruptly. He leaned over her. 'Dance?' His voice loud. 'Are you—is she well enough?' Jonathan protested, half rising from his chair. Desmond ignored him and held his hand out towards her. 'Well?'

All around them, beneath the hot canvas and the fairy lights, eyes, ears and mouths set the air alight with signals. Jonathan's face, uncertain. (He said he loves you; if that is true, then nothing else counts.)

But other things did count. A tawdry little scene played out beneath these fairy lights. Would he forgive her that? She turned her face to Desmond. She put her hand in his and stood up to dance.

Desmond held her tightly by the wrist as he led her amongst the moving couples. When they reached the floor, he pulled her in close. As they began to sway and catch the beat of the music, he clamped his hand to her back. His breath was sour from the drinks and felt hot on her cheek. He knew all the steps and, because she did not, she looked down at their feet, away from his eyes. Trying to follow but of course unable to match him.

He whirled her faster, smiling if she missed a step. Around them the music blared, an intricate, syncopated beat, stopping when she least expected it, starting up again, quicker and quicker. He moved smoothly, anticipating the music, pushing her back and forward again, skilfully, in time with the band. He was a good dancer, a nimble dancer but still she faltered, tripping and falling heavily against a blonde woman with an orchid on a band around her wrist. The woman's partner shouted at them.

She could see Jonathan at their table, up on his feet watching, while beyond him men in lounge suits sat at the bar, white men and their white women, their eyes also on the dancers, tapping their sandalwood fans in time with the music. Curious looks. Knowing glances. Jonathan waiting for it to end. She turned back to Desmond, apologised again to the blonde woman, held her arms up.

Round and round they went, each turn tighter until she was close enough to feel the heat of Desmond's body, to feel the top of his leg as he thrust his knee deep between hers, pushing at the inside of her thighs with each beat of the music. With a hand at the back of her head, he clamped her skull to his so that their lips were almost touching, their eyes nearly level. 'Stop,' she hissed. His grip was too firm, she could not pull away.

And now they were dancing blindly, unable to see anything but one another. He held her up as the room, colours, faces, lights smeared around her and she felt dizzy and sick. She pushed against him with both hands, harder this time until he stopped. Her breath came in gasps, her eyes hot with tears.

'Some damn fools cannot hold their drink.' It was the little man again with his blonde partner. Desmond took no notice. Instead, he lurched away from her, off the dance floor.

'Forgive me,' she said, then she followed him, past the chairs and tables, past Jonathan, catching up with him just outside the marquee. She put a hand on his arm. 'Do you love me?' she asked. 'Do you even like me?'

He looked back at her, surprised, and briefly she saw another man emerge, younger, less sure, a bruised face. Then his eyes closed over. 'None of that matters,' he said, before turning and walking back inside.

It was the flat end of a sultry afternoon when Winsome left the studio on Sule Pagoda Road, the key borrowed from Daw Sein in her pocket. Instead of turning west for home she turned east, towards the part of the city that hugged Pazundaung Creek.

Rain had threatened all afternoon and now the sky opened, sending down a fierce torrent. In the moment it took to raise her umbrella, pedestrians and rickshaws had rushed from the street to shelter beneath the eaves of buildings; only the motorcars continued to slide through the rain, mica storm windows shining, exhaust dissolving in the air. Her umbrella was useless against the downpour, but she did not mind the rain, the warmth of it creeping steadily up her dress.

Rangoon was a city cradled in the arms of rivers. In the monsoon those rivers found again the old grooves, the dried-up channels. In the past few weeks it had become common to see shop doors thrown open, brown streams coursing across the steps. Once, in the middle of the city, she had had to wade through water that was thigh-deep and rising. The moist air thickened her hair, her hips, and her breasts felt full against her clothes. In the newspapers there were daily reports of drownings.

Beyond Dufferin Gardens, where the tarmacadam ended, Winsome turned into a muddy lane without a signpost. The air had a slippery smell. Lanmadaw Grove was one of those forgotten East Rangoon backstreets, a relic of the Burmese village that used to squat on the creek flats, now the home of criminals and anarchists, morphia addicts and failed rice farmers, its rotting thatched roofs and woven walls in archaic contrast with the brick shop-houses going up nearby. Once, she'd seen Aye Sein at this corner, hunkered down among a knot of Burmans, talking earnestly. But most people hurried past to the wharves upstream and did not even know it was here, this street where the conservancy carts rarely passed before noon, where it was impossible to keep your shoes clean.

She stopped at a house set back in an earth compound and raised above the ground on stilts, native style. It was of a simple design, one narrow room on top of another. The walls were made of meshed bamboo to catch the breeze, and at low tide that breeze brought the smell of river-weed and mud.

The house was empty. She knew that immediately. In the weeks she had been meeting Jonathan here, it had become her habit to listen for him (fearing that he would not come, that he didn't want her any longer, joyful at the sound of the door latch, which meant that he did).

Winsome shed her shoes and climbed the narrow teak staircase to the upper room. Rain hissed against the thatch and the wind, which sent occasional gusts through the room, drowned out all sound from the lane below. She shivered as she unbuttoned her dress and hung it across the chair to dry as best it might. Then, shivering again, this time with pleasure, she pushed back the mosquito net and crawled under the sheets.

Those rough, smoky sheets reminded her of love, of Jonathan. She rubbed her legs against their papery coarseness, felt them scratch against her hips and shoulders. She liked it that he didn't have a name for her, didn't call her his heart or love or dear or darling. Liked the way he spoke gravely, lay still while listening. She liked to put her ear to his chest, the way his heartbeat resonated like a deep-toned bell, how he was just as lost, just as hungry as she was. She told him of the convent, of Teresa, and how she had helped her in the infirmary, of the stinging scent of lye in the laundry rooms in the summer, the picture books in the library she had coveted. How all she remembered of her mother was the taste of rice eaten from her fingers.

At a creak on the stair she sat up, instantly alert, appetite rising in her. But it was just the house shifting. She turned and wound herself in the sheets again, touched a hand to her thigh.

Lover.

She drew her hand along the moist skin on the inside, slid her fingers upwards and half-closed her eyes. Her fingers tangled in her pubic hair.

(You should feel shame. You should feel guilt.)

She pulled back her hand, there was no longer any pleasure in it. Across the room, water from her dress dripped onto the floor, leaving a small puddle. Lover. It had a different ring now. She threw back the sheet, snatched up her dress and pulled it over her head. Her skin itched from the starch in the bed-linen. She crossed to the window. Rangoon was a blur, the creek would be rising. She might be trapped here. Perhaps she should light a lamp. Was there a lamp in this little house?

Under the bed she found a candle stub in a cracked drinking glass and some matches. She lit one, but the wind took it so she lit another, cupping her fingers around the yellow flame as Desmond had taught her. His hands were always steady when he lit the lamps at Inverness Gardens. She had been afraid when he closed them into fists and shook them at her, but that had been nothing compared to his face, ugly, bewildered (and yet he hadn't said a thing, did not charge her with his words). She recognised the look, had watched accusation grow behind his eyes. Love has made you shameless. More: love has left you without the need for shame.

Shame, they had that in common. It was the stone in the rice, the mud in the well water, the violence in Assumpta's fingers, the way Mrs De Brito tapped your shoulder with her fan. An old weakness peculiar to their kind, a sensitivity that permeated the body like oxygen and corroded the tissues so that you might flinch at just the thought of disgrace, as if it were a blow. And when the blow did fall? Perhaps what you felt was relief. This was what she saw in Desmond's face when he looked at her and thought to accuse her—the inevitability of her moral failure, of his humiliation.

Winsome squirmed beneath the wet fabric of her dress. She scratched at her forearms, where the chalky residue from the sheets caked on her flesh. She tore at the small of her back, between her shoulder blades, at the back of her legs, but it gave her no relief. She paced back and forth across the room, setting the candle flame guttering.

On the bed those sheets, too starched, too stiff, twisted over the indentation she had left in the kapok mattress so that it looked substantial, as if a body (her body) lay just beneath. Sometimes Jonathan touched her not gently, but warily. If he came now, at this moment, he might put out his hand to this sheet and find nothing, as if she had never been here at all. If he came.

Late one afternoon, early in their affair, Jonathan had sent word that he couldn't meet her. That there was a fever on the wards. Dizzy with the fear he no longer loved her, she slumped on the rough teak steps, cradled her head in her hands. Then, wanting only air, forced herself to stand, to take a step, and another. Out of the house, down the stairs, along the muddy road, walking towards the smell of the river, following its scent until at last she found Monkey Point.

Beneath a heavy silver sky, as portentous as a photograph, a large ship picked its way along the deep central channel of the river. Grey smoke billowed from its funnel and before her the light peeled back to reveal something true. For a moment, with the logic of a dream, it seemed as if the sweeping clouds, the bands of rain, the docks, the city, all of Rangoon were *conjured* by the boat itself.

But she recognised this was only an illusion, a temporary flattening of weight and matter. Before her was a ship; in her damp hair, only the wind.

Winsome quit her pacing and stood still, blinking in the middle of the room. Her arms stung from where she'd scratched them, the wet dress was heavy against her hips. Desmond was wrong about her. She was not beyond shame or guilt. In fact disgrace was her offering, a gift, the measure of her love. And so? She remembered the sharp little tap on her shoulder from Mrs De Brito's fan.

Well then. Let them think that this was her hunger, appetite, thirst—they would have names for it. She would face them; she would face Desmond (wake with him, eat with him, submit to her duty). She would face anything. What else was possible? She sat down on the bed to wait.

Rain drummed on Jonathan's metal roof, as urgent as his own pulse. It drowned out all other noise, washed out all thought, all other sensation so that he was overwhelmed, drowned, swept away. In the first few weeks of the monsoon, that drumming had felt like a release; he had roared aloud with it. But now he knew that while a shower might end, the rain was never really over. Pressure would build, the air would darken until he could hardly breathe and then the drumming would begin again until he wanted to scream aloud, demented in his empty apartment. Rain then, that was his excuse.

With the rain came fever. Fever with its ripe, sticky sweetness that was also the scent of desire (and why had he not noticed this before?). That morning during his hospital rounds, all he could smell was longing, seeping from the sheets and blankets, the skin and hair, spilling over bedpans until every ward seemed saturated with it. Until he was coated in it.

The smell was thick on him as he walked out of the hospital, still in his white coat, his shift not yet over, and turned into Commissioners Road towards Monkey Point, towards Winsome. He didn't send word. He knew she would be working and that perhaps she would not even be able to see him. But that did not matter against his need for her, against the fear that he might burst, like a leaden sky, if he did not at least see her. This, ineluctably, was the way of things. Rain—fever—desire.

It had been dry when he left but by the time he reached the Sule Pagoda Road large drops had begun to fall and because he had left with nothing—not a coat, not an umbrella—he had to sprint the last few hundred yards, finally taking shelter beneath an ancient banyan tree opposite the studio. Water fell all about him in silvery ropes and he felt trapped, not just by rain but by his longing too; already wet, yet afraid of becoming more so.

He was about to turn back and run home through the rain when he saw a glimmer of white in the windows of the studio, a small but telling movement. Hair rose on the back of his neck and with that familiar, electric jolt, he realised that Winsome was there, she had seen him. Now she would show herself. He was prepared to wait.

146

When the door of the studio opened it was not Winsome who emerged, but a minuscule figure. She wore a Burmese blouse so white it seemed to glow in the shade of her umbrella as she stepped down onto the street. With an elegant movement, she twisted her skirt so that it did not trail in the water coursing along the road. In a few steps her red velvet slippers darkened to maroon, while beyond her, through the doorway, he sensed Winsome, detecting her scent even in the rain.

The tiny woman stopped in front of him. Her fingers, closed around the stem of the umbrella, were no thicker than a child's, yet her face was that of a woman, her dark eyes shrewd and intelligent. When she spoke it was as if she were addressing him from behind a window, as if she were still indoors, such was her poise. 'Would you care to come inside?' she asked, her voice clear against the noise of the rain.

'Yes please,' he replied, and splashed back across the road behind her.

The studio was large, open and surprisingly quiet despite the roar of the rain outside. A single grey shaft of light fell from an opening in the roof, but did not penetrate the entire space, so it was impossible to tell how far the room extended. A darker rectangle indicated a recess—perhaps a hallway—that must lead to the darkroom. Against one wall, tall canvas backdrops like paintings were stacked haphazardly. To his left, a screen with a pearly finish gleamed in the dim light. Winsome was nowhere to be seen.

'I am Daw Sein,' the woman announced, extending her hand. 'This is my photographic studio.' She spoke English flawlessly, with only the slightest trace of music to her accent.

'Dr Jonathan Grace.' As he shook her hand, she inclined her head towards him respectfully, an echo of the Burmese shiko.

Her umbrella made a steady drip, drip against the cement floor and he began to feel the dampness of his own clothes, their clamminess against his skin, even though he was not cold but quite warm.

'Aye Sein will fetch a towel for you,' she said. Then, as if in afterthought, 'Would you drink a hot cup of coffee, Dr Grace?'

'I would,' he said, 'thank you.'

She called out into the darkness and a handsome sullen-faced youth loomed forward out of the gloom. In rapid Burmese—too rapid for Jonathan to understand—she issued her instructions. He waited for a sign of Winsome, sniffed the air for her. He pictured how it would happen—how she would appear suddenly and her face would change; how she too would dissolve with love.

'Now, Dr Grace, please do come and sit down.'

Daw Sein led him behind the pearlescent screen to a small room with Burmese-style mats on the floor, a pair of European chairs in red damask and a desk with Limoges china cups set to one side. He was relieved when she waved him to the chairs and then sat down at the desk, opposite him. Opening a drawer she pulled out a lacquered box and offered him a cigarette. 'English tobacco?' He declined. 'Have you been in Burma long, Dr Grace?'

'Several months.'

She would be a good talker, this little doll of a woman, he could tell she was one of those talking women, with her beautifully modulated voice, those appraising eyes. She was like a mother entertaining her daughter's beau until the girl herself appeared, beautifully dressed, making her entrance.

'They say, Dr Grace, that England's famous rain seems nothing at all once you've experienced the Burmese monsoon. Do you find this to be the case?'

He wanted to laugh—the Burmese woman's tinny poise, the

absurdity of sitting in wet clothes talking to her about the weather, the imminent appearance of Winsome, all of these things made him euphoric, unguarded as she watched him, her head cocked to one side, waiting for his answer. In this spirit of generosity he told her the truth.

'Like so many things in Burma, I find it...' he searched for the words, 'strange, rather wonderful.'

But these weren't quite the right words. They sounded hollow somehow. Daw Sein raised her eyebrows (such a perfect arch to them, they might have been painted on) and nodded seriously before continuing. 'I'm told our rains can have quite a deleterious effect, can drive some Europeans quite mad.' She leaned a little forward, her smile showed small teeth. 'I believe white men call monsoon the scandal season.'

No, no. This was all wrong. He was suddenly wary, on the verge of anger. He wondered if Winsome had confided in this Burmese woman who talked and talked? Surely she would have better judgment than that.

On the boat, some of the men, commercial travellers of the old school, had issued dire warnings of monsoon brides. Honey-skinned girls foisted upon white men by their clever mammas; a child concocted. And you, duped, paying to support the girl, then her family, then a whole clan of brown layabouts. He had laughed at them, but their talk came back to him as he watched Daw Sein, her perfect English from her doll's mouth, like a puppet, like a creature in a play.

He stood abruptly. 'I must go.'

Opposite him, Daw Sein watched without surprise, her blankness so like impertinence. (His mother's word, and what would she make of this woman in her silks, her jewels, with her French china and her dark, shrewd eyes?)

The scent of coffee filled the air. The sullen youth had returned, hair plastered to his head. He had a dry linen towel over one arm and, on a tray, a metal pot. Daw Sein gave Jonathan a nod. This time it felt like mockery. She reached behind her desk.

'It is still raining, you will need this.' She handed him her umbrella.

She was right. In the street rain was falling with a redoubled ferocity as he strode along Sule Pagoda Road. Beneath the borrowed umbrella he was still damp. He dropped the umbrella into the lap of a blind beggar and walked on past the whitewashed brick buildings, past the British food shops, the tailors, the cinemas, past men like anyone you might see in any London street. But this was not London rain. Daw Sein was correct—after the monsoon, nothing seemed the same.

What had he done? What was he really doing? He had not thought beyond this rain, beyond his own appetite. He started to run.

Everything here was too intense, colours too outrageous, smells overpowering, heat debilitating, sound and sky all vast, all rendering him insensible, unable to think. Rain soaking him more deeply when he was already wet through. All that moisture, the perverse fecundity it brought; mildew, mould, fungus, an efflorescence on every surface. Like dark cancers, deadly spurts and globules of flesh in the sealed world of the body.

He would behave honourably; he was not in the business of destroying women. He understood that his loyalty was required now. He would be decent, courteous, all these things and more.

But dear God, please let it stop raining.

When Desmond came home that night he was greeted by the servant girl, Than Thint. She followed him through the flat, her slippers striking the sole of her foot with an irritating slap. *Slap slap* as he emptied damp papers from his cardboard briefcase, *slap slap* as she told him, her voice ludicrously grave, 'Mistress ill, mistress sleeping.' *Slap slap slap* as she ran to keep up with him, striding down the hall. He hoped she would trip and fall on her face.

Mistress ill. Mistress sleeping. Her headaches. Her silences. Did she think he hadn't noticed? Going to bed early, coming to breakfast late. Meals a silent penance. The way she had of sliding out from under his eyes. So far he had said nothing, only watched and waited. But already tonight was different.

He opened the bedroom door, Than Thint at his shoulder.

The curtains were drawn tight against the daylight and Winsome was nothing more than the outline of sheet. He couldn't even see the rise and fall of her breathing.

'See, thakin?' the girl whispered. He thought about walking into the room to see if Winsome was in fact asleep. But the girl was watching. Still Winsome did not stir. He pulled the door shut, the latch clicked.

And if this was a genuine womanly ailment, a presence growing within her, what then?

'You can go now,' he told Than Thint, but she continued to hover about him, avid, self-important, following him to the living room, fussing at the little table set for one. He had to shout at her.

He found his dinner on the kitchen sideboard, one blue plate covered by another. When he lifted the rim his stomach curled; it was the most frightful muck—a fish cooked until it was in pieces, the skin a brownish grey and all of it swimming in some dirty yellow sauce. To one side there was a large spoon of cold rice. The smell of garlic rose from the flesh and there was a slick of oil shining on top of it all.

This was the girl's work, not Winsome's. It was native food

when he craved something plain and nutritious and substantial. Something that would fill him up, that he could chew.

He tipped the whole ruddy mess into the bin and then dropped both plates into the sink. He heard the china crack. He searched the cupboards for a loaf of bread and the jam jar.

Through the window and across the back garden the day was fading, bathing the kitchen in a sickly yellow light. Cooking smells drifted across the sweet wet grass. From somewhere not too far he could hear discordant music, the shrieking of birds.

It was a few minutes before he noticed the ants swarming in a ragged line over the window sill, a line that thickened at every passing moment with more bodies until the frenzied searching of individuals became an orderly chain, a single will. He followed them to the sink.

Ants massed over the greasy remains of his dinner, their bodies dark against the yellow turmeric stain. His stomach turned again with revulsion, yet he could not take his eyes from them. They were so consumed by their hunt for food. They swept across the plate like a clock hand, their antennae twitching.

Had he not worked hard? Had he not taken opportunities that others were too fastidious to consider? Been careful, so careful his head ached with it? He had worked to unravel the codes and gestures of men like Sawyer, like Dr Grace, like the civilians—those men of the secretariat, the heaven-born men of position. And yet here he was, standing over the sink eating bread and jam for supper while Madam slept. Slept it off. Slept and dreamed.

He put his palm flat on the draining board, blocking the ants' path with his wrist. Disturbed, they crawled in all directions. But it only took a moment before they were once again marshalled into a ragged line, again purposeful, searching as one for the congealing patches of rice and fish and oil on the ruined plate.

Their small bodies tickled the skin under his wrist and when he shook his arm they bit him, raising red marks. The small sting of it made him blink, fascinated. Here was the evidence of being: sensation. He crushed a few of the ants with his thumbnail. Their bodies released a scent that clung to the base of his wrist. A scent alien to his body, but familiar.

Upstairs she was lying in his bed, his sheets tucked around her. She would have him think she was consumed by heat, insensible with fever. A woman suffering. She did not know what suffering meant.

He shook the ants from his arm.

The hallway was already lit by a kerosene lamp, the girl must have put it there before she left. There would be another in the bedroom, turned down low so as not to disturb the sleeper. It would throw a golden light across the bed, giving a copper tone to the hair. There would be the scent of warm skin.

He turned the handle. The latch clicked on its spring. He closed the door behind him.

She was already awake, sitting up with her back against the headboard.

Fever? We shall see about that. He sat on the edge of the bed without speaking.

'I was sleeping,' she said, reproachful. He smiled, leaned forward and twisted the sheets from her. She was still wearing her dress, the yellow fabric balled up between her legs.

'I was sleeping,' she repeated, in her voice that little waver of panic. Her eyes were wide, her breath rapid, her fear so like arousal. He stood up. He ran his fingers through her hair. The sound of it like a trance. He felt a little thrill in himself, something familiar about it, something rehearsed, like stepping outside himself.

'I am ill,' she said. Then stop then please then stop again. But who would hear her? The girl? Dr Grace? The important white men of the secretariat?

She pushed at him and leapt up from the bed, she ran. But where was there to go, except to the wall?

He walked around to her. Why would you run from me? Are you not yourself? And it took no effort, almost no strength at all, to pin her there with his body, her struggles and cries as insignificant as the ant stings on his wrist.

Her hair. There was a scent to it, something caught there that was not hers—tobacco smoke, English soap, coal fires, semen. The same scent at her throat, he made a V there with his hand, but she clawed at that hand, turned her face away from him, turned her body too.

Fine. He pinned her shoulders to the wall, pushed his face into that hair, then into the back of the neck, found the little hidden mole; it was there, too, that scent. She was infused with it.

He ran his hand along the shoulder, the length of back, along the buttock, the back of the thigh, he sighed into the hair as he rucked up the yellow skirt, found the cleft of the buttocks, his fingers searching. Yes. He would make a space for himself there.

'For God's sake,' she whimpered, then for god, for god, for god. And she pushed and fought against him, pushed back so hard that he had to put his hand to the back of her skull and hold her face against the wall. A shudder passed through her and she sagged against his shoulder.

He leaned into her with all his weight, catching his own breath, gathering himself once more. Fear like arousal. Hatred like arousal. Her obligation, an arousal. Again the room juddered, there was that little shake in the walls, he could feel his own fingers touching her, her skin touching him back. Inevitable, all of it. Beneath his weight her ribs flexed. Please, she begged, and please again, gasping. Then she was silent. Weeping perhaps, quietly and to herself, the way women sometimes did. He shifted his weight a little, caught again at that scent.

The scent. His arms stinging, he pushed his groin against the cleft between the buttocks, felt the tightened muscle beneath him, heard himself moan aloud as the scent led him beyond her.

And then she began to laugh. It shook him, that low, mean sound. He pulled away from her.

'You think you can smell him on me,' and she laughed again.

Stung, shocked, he staggered backwards and when she turned around and faced him, he pushed her harshly, back against the wall, away from him.

Her face was hard, and her voice was that of an old whore. 'Or is it me you want?' She began to unbutton her dress. 'Come on,' she whispered. 'You can still smell him here.' As she moved towards him, she threw a long shadow against the wall and the lamplight was reflected on her face, in her eyes.

He sank onto the bed. Was it a trick of the light? Standing before him, she had a singularity, a capacity he could only glimpse, and not name. He thought back to the day of their wedding, to the tea party, but could not summon her face as it had been, not with this woman's face, this woman's body in front of him. He looked away. In his mouth he could taste the old familiar bile.

He shook himself. Anger rose in him once more. Bitch. Whore. He stood up. He fastened his trousers. 'Dress yourself, for God's sake.' He crossed the room to his armoire, pulled his shirt over his head, changed into a fresh one. He dressed slowly and deliberately. And all the while she watched him. When she spoke, her voice was flat.

'What are you going to do?'

He fastened the links at his sleeves and knotted a new tie.

'I don't need to do anything.' He forced himself to walk, not run from the room. He turned to her before he left. 'Take it from me, you already disgust him.'

He washed and dried his hands before leaving the house. Rain was falling and the night was oppressively hot. He caught a tonga.

He had intended to return to his own office, to sleep in his chair if need be—sleep like the dead—but, as the hospital buildings came into view, he changed his mind.

There was fever on the wards and, in the mortuary, a growing number of corpses. Men would be preparing pits for the soon-to-be dead. They would be erecting oilskins and digging drainage trenches by firelight to keep the carcasses dry. Lime dissolved bodies quickly, but you had to keep the water off for it to work and that was nearly impossible—in the wet, the dead took their leave grudgingly.

He had always thought of himself as a man able to rise above his circumstances. His climb through the ranks, his status as a man of science, all his achievements he credited to this quality. But he was wrong. Worse, he had deluded himself. He had not risen above anything. He had not risen at all.

'Driver,' he leaned forward and tapped the man on the shoulder—but where was he to go? The words were out of his mouth before he could think about them, names he had heard other men call to tonga drivers. 'Strand Hotel,' he said. The driver gathered the reins and turned towards town.

Daw Sein was already in position when the doors of the secretariat opened, her camera trained on the space as Joseph Augustus Maung Gyi emerged, the first Burman to be appointed Governor (Acting). As she released the shutter and light flooded the aperture, the roar of the crowd rose. Black-coated men rushed the steps. Maung Gyi raised his arms above his head in a brief, celebratory gesture. Again and again, with a rapid succession of mechanical clicks, she exposed the film as Maung Gyi was bundled into the landau, his wife a step behind, the driver pulling up the canvas hood to shield them from the drizzle, the horses surging forward, men scrambling out of their path. Then the landau was gone, next stop Jubilee Hall.

She lowered the camera and took a breath, the crowd's adulation curdling the air. In every newspaper were pages and pages of congratulations with almost nothing else in between. On the secretariat steps the important white men remained, watching it all from beneath their black umbrellas. They would come out white in the negatives, those umbrellas—a symbol of Burmese royalty whose irony was not lost on her. She took three shots of them before she put the camera back in her satchel and hurried to her motorbike.

She had to nose the bike through the back lanes, nursing the little engine, which was running hot. Rangoon's main streets were impassable, cordoned off for the Governor's triumphal procession, but even these small, winding alleys were congested with celebrations. Men sat in the drizzle, drinking toddy wine, shouting at women passing by, overcome by this Governor with his Burmese name and his Jermyn Street suits.

The motorbike was German, and old. It had been going cheap when her stepfather bought it—along with a Berliner phonograph, a pair of ugly red drawing-room chairs and a Luger pistol—from a business contact in Germantown. There had been a Germantown in Rangoon once, where you had Kaffee und Kuchen at 4 pm, listening to their dyspeptic music. The Great War was coming and the businessman had to go. She rode home behind her stepfather pillion-style, schoolgirl braids jumping on her back.

It was not more than two years later that she sat upright beside him in the pony trap, hair no longer plaited but pinned up, a book of French verbs in her lap. Her stepfather's glance across the reins—he was one of the new-style Burmans; a speculator who bought and sold property, who saw angles, who made deals and believed in possibilities. Her mother's rice warehouses and his rice ships; their young son, a boy who would inherit it all; and this older girl, Dolly, precocious, luminously clever.

'There is a hillock on a bend not far from here, and from that point all that you will see belongs to me.'

She nodded, took up her book: 'Je m'appelle Dolly Sein. Tu t'appelles, il s'appelle, nous nous appellons, vous vous appellez, ils s'appellent.' He would send her to Europe, to London. University was not out of the question for a girl like her. In his gaze she felt her own worth.

It took her nearly half an hour through the traffic before she finally arrived at Jubilee Hall. The crowd was already so thick she had to leave the bike around the corner. A half-caste clerk was trying to keep order but the people kept coming, cramming themselves into the meanest of spaces.

She hadn't a hope of getting a clear shot of the Governor when he arrived, not with all those people between her and the portico at Jubilee Hall, so she climbed a wall, hitching her skirt up around her knees. From this vantage point she could see clear across the tops of those dark heads. A fine mist of rain fell, water beading in her hair and on her clothes. In the air she could feel the vibration that was the breath of men along the processional route, of all Rangoon gasping as one.

On the delta that day, she and her stepfather had spotted a lone Indian soldier, a Sikh, standing on the raised lip of a paddy field long before they reached the famous hillock. It was an unusual sight, a soldier in that part of the delta, and her stepfather had let the reins drop. He turned to her. 'Shall we have a look?'

The Sikh soldier was broad shouldered and tall. As she picked her way along the mounded mud, deep ochre against the grey kid of her boots, she imagined herself as une petite demoiselle, une vraie mignonne. But he was not watching her. Nor were the gangs of paddy workers, although they had paused in their work. All eyes were bent across the plane of water, fixed on a gang, eight men strong, their backs burnt dark but their hair blond, brown, red—German boys. Europeans. Prisoners of the English now, their heads bent over the green shoots of paddy, water stirring around their ankles.

Later, when she finally did go to university in London, when she had travelled to Paris and Baden Baden and Belgium and Dublin, and had learned to dream in English and French, then she would know that men were only ever men. But that morning, the sight of those eight boys had made the world of wars and newspapers, leather boots and French verbs, spin. In that paddy field the eyes of the workers, the Indian soldier, even her stepfather, all of them had blinked against the same light, monstrous and sublime. The air had seemed gelatinous, quivering with particles that formed and collapsed beneath the weight of moment.

And now the landau pulled up, the Governor descended and the sound of the crowd's joy washed through her all over again, and they too were deceived by what they saw. The Governor walked among the people and, despite her good vantage point, she could no longer see him because he was lost in that crowd. She took the photographs anyway. She shot and shot again.

There was one fair-haired boy among the German prisoners, his skin burnt brown like the others, but when he stood, a gap of silvery flesh showed at the waist of his dhoti. He had a child's face, soft and appealing, and his dirty skin was streaked with sweat in the same way that a child's face might be streaked with tears. All over his smooth body, pale hairs caught the sun and flared with light like a corona, like a sign. She saw him often in those weeks, as she rode in the pony trap beside her stepfather or walked along his fields. Guten Tag, Reismeister. The silver-fleshed boy gazed up at her, his eyes unashamed.

It was only when Maung Gyi had been inside Jubilee Hall for half an hour that the crowd began to disperse. Daw Sein dropped from the wall. She mounted the bike and kicked at the throttle, slipping out the clutch. Around the city, she took more photos, working until dusk. Then she roared back to the studio to develop and print her film overnight. On the way home her back wheel skidded against something soft in a gutter. There was a groan. She did not stop to look.

The boy was found dead, buried up to his neck in the shade of a rice godown, in the same way that the old kings used to bury a boy or an old woman outside a building to fix their ghost to that spot as an eternal guardian, bound over for all time. She would have wept for him, only he had looked like he was dreaming.

The English authorities had not known quite what to do or how to behave. The boy had been a prisoner, but a white man as well. They removed the German gang from the valley and sent more police. They never found the culprits and, until the European war ended, the District Commissioner refused to tour without at least half a dozen stout constables in attendance. Everyone called it a senseless act.

But little Dolly Sein had seen the sense of it. It was a message to *all* white men that there were cold and eternal things as yet beyond them. A boy could be denied death. They, too, were capable of loss.

In her darkroom, Daw Sein put her satchel with the exposed cylinders of film on the bench. She unwound the first roll and watched patiently as Joseph Maung Gyi emerged in triumph all over again, the important men standing behind him, their protective umbrellas now white as she had anticipated—each figure announcing itself with a little ring of darkness or light, a corona like the young German soldier's.

Years after the Great War had ended, when she was a student travelling though Europe—her grand tour—it was not awe that she felt among those much lauded icons of their civilisations, not jealousy either, but something worse; it was as if she had lived through a famine and could never again have enough to eat. Standing before their grand palaces, beneath their great arches, walking through gardens and piazzas, it grew on her that she was without things that might have given her comfort, and in their place longing had calcified, deeply mortifying and much worse than any fear.

She knew that men like Maung Gyi, men like her stepfather, would never deliver Burma. They sheltered beneath those black/white umbrellas just as surely as these important white men who now swam beneath her fingers in the chemical bath. She remembered her stepfather as he stood on his hillock, looking across the sodden delta at all the land that was his, each chaung, each spilling drift of paddy a gift, and on his face an expression of such tenderness.

Up and down the country bridges failed, railway bolts were loosened. From the delta there were whispers of political gatherings. But these were actions too rational in their nature. They were bloodless, when she knew if there was to be liberation, there must also be bloodshed.

'My Dear Comrades,' began Aye Sein's letters to their political friends overseas. 'The Burmese are called the Irish of the Empire. Like you, we shall earn our Independence with our Blood.'

But what was their blood actually worth? Another Burmese student dead, who among the English would care?

It was late and the studio was quiet, the blankness of the hour accentuated by small stray sounds as the day, this historic day, passed over into night. A gecko clicked behind the wall, a beam creaked and settled and with these sounds, Daw Sein felt coldness steal over her. She paused in her work. Her Burma would be for children she would not bear. It would be a place beyond what she, or anyone, could imagine. The face of the German boy came to her with the force of a blow, he had looked as though he was dreaming. She too dreamed.

In the hallway outside the darkroom, Winsome Goode's footsteps clicked against the teak floor and something of that human, rhythmic sound infused Daw Sein's reverie, for she had entered the boy's dream. Actions, gestures were no longer real, but part of the evening's texture. The air itself was possibility (point yourself, launch yourself) as it had been once before. Love, he whispered in her ear, I died for love, a Burmese martyr. And she knew this was true, for the boy had stirred the desire, the fear and imagination, of white men.

The steps stopped and Winsome Goode must have paused outside the wooden door, her hand brushing the panel with the smallest of sounds; she would be leaving for the day but before she left, she wondered whether she should knock and say goodnight, so she stood there, uncertain. Daw Sein waited and when the sound of steps echoed once more along the corridor, felt her blood run again.

Love, then. This was what must be coaxed from the chemical bath. It should be like choosing a lover. Winsome Goode, with her fine, fair skin. Winsome Goode, who had gone with a white man, a powerful white man.

Daw Sein took the next roll of film from her satchel and began again.

When Jonathan woke that morning, the gumminess of sleep left him almost instantly. Outside the day was clear, the air crisp and dry, and there was none of that dismal dripping he often woke to. He stretched in the early-morning light.

Cycling to the hospital after breakfast, he was astonished at the delicacy of the morning; all the months of wet had washed the dust from the Rangoon air and instead of that hazy bronze light he remembered, this morning had a pink and blue clarity. The buildings, the people, the trees, even the sky were sharply illuminated so that he could see them as they actually were.

All about him were the smells of plants, jasmine, buddleia, lime and for once the stink of cooking from the breakfast carts did not assault him, but instead swept past on the morning breeze. Even the ragged palms looked whole and fresh. His mind, too, felt at ease, thoughts slotting comfortably into place without any of that dark uncertainty. He felt as if he had sloughed off the unnerving effects of a bad dream.

He took his time wheeling through the hospital forecourt so that he could linger in the fresh morning. He knew that this was only a temporary respite from the rains; the old hands had warned him of these false dawns. Rangoon would be sodden for weeks to come. And yet he also knew that soon there would be whole stretches of days just like this; when the cool, dry months arrived, this sort of weather would be ordinary. Today was merely a taste, a promise of what would be, and he was reminded of his boyhood, the long-anticipated summers when he climbed, rowed, read, and thought as he liked.

He paused at the green door to the staff quarters. Reluctant to go inside to the electric light and clammy air sealed within the thick stone walls, he savoured the warmth of the sun on his shoulders for just a moment longer, the same sun that only a few months ago had felt like a lash across his skin.

All morning he enjoyed this smoothness of mind. He executed his duties crisply, with an insight and ease that gave him pleasure and, as he went about the hospital, he considered what Rangoon would be like if the climate were more temperate and less extreme; how much more rational and considered people would be, how much more might be achieved (he would never again overlook the importance of small things, like the comfort of dry clothes).

Absorbed by the work, he forgot about the months of damp heat, the endless drumming rain; what was in front of him was all there was. He finished his rounds quickly—fever season was almost over and there were fewer patients in the infirmary—and completed his charts and pharmacy orders well before time. With an hour or two in hand, he stole back to his desk and took out his research papers, tied with a coloured ribbon, still in the top drawer.

It had been months since he'd opened up this stack of jotted notes, reports and figures. Remarkably, the files were untouched by mildew, a miracle he put down to the phenyl in the hospital atmosphere; it was all one could smell today. He flipped lightly through the pages, conscious of a rising excitement, an impatience to get back to the work; his purpose here *was* work, after all. It was important.

He came across a note in Desmond Goode's hand (Deaths from Respiratory Ailments Organised by Race) and stopped. He pushed the files away and surrendered to a withering rush of self-loathing, anger and pity. During these months of monsoon he had never really considered Desmond. Competent, a little obsequious, a man who never seemed to mind what was asked of him; with his long limbs and his slightly protuberant eyes, he resembled the frogs Jonathan used to catch as a schoolboy and sometimes, in the rough and tumble of exploration, destroyed. But now this limited man was testing him. For with dismay he realised the real reason he had let his work slip.

Jonathan stood up abruptly, took a step from his desk. His promising ideas, his intellectual dedication—all of it had been corrupted, irredeemably compromised. How could he look at these words and figures again when all he saw were his personal failings? A lack of discipline. His own moral dishonesty. For the first time that morning, he felt the old monsoon stickiness creeping along his skin.

When he was a student he had sometimes become so absorbed in a case or experiment that he went for days without sleeping or eating. He gave himself over wholly to his intellectual effort. At the time it had felt good and right.

Yet those impassioned, abstemious efforts, those periods of monk-like devotion hadn't always resulted in work that was any good. The mind resided in a body. That was a fact. The body had needs that must be met. That was another fact. He dealt in facts— for what else was there? This truth settled over him like a fine dust.

One made mistakes, but mightn't one atone for them, mightn't one forgive them?

Jonathan ran his fingers through his hair and took up Desmond's paper again. He forced himself to look down at it once more, to look objectively. It was neatly presented, the figures clearly broken down. Beneath this page was another sheaf of notes in the same hand. Some were dated from before the rains. When had these little bundles of notes stopped arriving on his desk? Weeks ago, or months? He hadn't noticed. He shuffled through them. Each pile was as tidy as the first, all of them impeccably done. If he wrote these up now he need never refer to them again. He could put them in the back of a drawer and forget them.

Jonathan sat down, took up a clean sheet of paper and began to organise Desmond's figures into tables.

By the time he had finished, the morning was truly spent and it was past the hour for lunch, his groaning belly told him so despite the sparkling air that made it seem like morning still. He gathered the papers and charts, separating the old data from his new work before tying them up in discrete bundles and putting them away. Then he strode through the hospital and out onto the street.

The afternoon was warm, the light clear and sharp. He was starving, his hunger voluptuous, the kind one experienced after a long illness. Later he would meet Winsome at Lanmadaw Grove, but now he would eat. The thought of the food at the Indian coffee houses was an insult to this lavish appetite; the hospital mess was also out of the question. He wanted steak and butter and white bread, he wanted strawberries and apple tart with fresh cream, and cheese. There was only one place that would do: the Angus Restaurant. Expensive, but a hunger like this was not to be wasted. And it was such a fine day—he would walk to Sparks Street.

The Angus was near the row of cream-coloured, square-shouldered buildings that housed the Bank of Bengal, the Standard

Chartered, the National Bank. He enjoyed the clean lines of these buildings, splendid in this pinky-blue day. Behind black double doors, the restaurant dining room was brightly lit with electric light and cooled by electric fans. The tables were covered with thick white linen. The room smelled of grilling meat and brown butter. Someone had put little posies of paper-white narcissus into the tiny china vases on the tables so that the scent of spring mingled with that of cooking. He imagined banks of modern Frigidaires in the kitchens, overflowing with cheese, butter and kippers, all of it just days ago in England. A waiter saw him to a table and he ordered the sirloin, bounced his teeth together in anticipation. There was a shout from the bar.

'Grace, I say.'

It was Ronnie, who had arranged for Jonathan to use the landing stage at his firm's rice mill. He was dressed in a beige linen suit and school tie, a ridiculous pretension in a city like Rangoon. In front of him was a tall glass and, beside that, a large bucket of ice. 'The very fellow I was thinking of.' He held up his glass in a mock salute as he climbed off his barstool.

'Good afternoon, Ronnie.' Jonathan hoped he wouldn't ask to share his table; men like Ronnie made him feel as if he had picked up the wrong fork.

Ronnie sat down. 'Rum thing, Grace. You'll appreciate this. Just at the minute I find myself in want of an oarsman: funny thing, then, to see you walk into this place. Are you lunching?' he asked as the waiter brought water jug, glass, serrated knife. 'Perfect.' He spoke loudly to the waiter, 'Hai, you there, bring my ice over here, would you?' then grinned at Jonathan, asking with mock politeness, 'You don't mind, do you?'

'Of course not.'

Ronnie leaned forward in his chair, stirring his drink

absently. The gin drifted in diffuse patterns through the melting ice-water. 'I am trying to avoid the office this afternoon. The rice market's shot.' He roused himself. 'But never mind that, we haven't been seeing you at the club.'

'Fever season.' Jonathan realised as he said it how sallow Ronnie looked; not from the sun either. Another sort of monsoon feverishness perhaps? He knew the effect; the flesh seemed to fold in upon itself. His own body was thinner, lacking in fibre. He had let things go and perhaps it was the same with Ronnie. But that dull skin. He began to wonder what might be concealed behind Ronnie's blurred face, his amiable expression. 'How are you keeping, Ronnie? Didn't make it up to the hills?'

Ronnie shrugged. 'Commercial men never do.' Then, with an incisive look, 'Still rowing are you, Grace?' and Jonathan felt his own loss of flesh as a kind of moral diminishment, further evidence of his weakness, his willingness to compromise everything that might be worthwhile.

'No, not so very much. Fever season.' This time it sounded like an excuse. Ronnie nodded as if he understood.

The waiter brought pale yellow butter in a blue dish and little white rolls, softly dusted with flour. 'Don't mind me,' Ronnie said, waving his arm vaguely as Jonathan fell upon the bread, spreading the butter in thick slabs, its salty creaminess filling his mouth.

While he ate, Ronnie talked. 'I'm helping with the big regatta—the All-Rangoon Regatta. Heard of it? We're down on men in the fours and the eights. Short of coaching too.' Jonathan reached for the second roll and spread the remaining butter to its very edges before licking the greasy remnants from his fingers. The rolls barely touched his hunger.

'Rangoon University is rather keen to field a squad in the rowing. Young, students; Burmans all of them I'd say. Pretty keen to test themselves. It seems no matter what the arena, we cannot run from the Burman's braggadocio.' He gave the ghost of a grin. Jonathan knew the sort Ronnie meant; there were Burmese students at the hospital, earnest types. He had publicly applauded their application. 'We wouldn't want to let those chaps in without a scrap,' Ronnie continued. 'And the old rivals of course—the Yachting Club, the Oriental.'

The steak came, caramel brown with dark marks from the grill, its surface glistening with fat. Jonathan's knife slid easily through the flesh, revealing a pink interior that oozed clear juice with oily little bubbles. In his mouth the meat was sweet, salty, with a bitter toasted edge. He had to force himself to eat it slowly, to savour each morsel. 'I haven't been on the water for a few months. I'm not sure I'd be of much use.'

'Not at all, Grace, not at all.' Ronnie signalled for another drink. His face brightened. 'I know, why not come up and see the tubs on the lake? There'll be a few chaps about this afternoon, the weather is perfect. Unless you're busy?' Ronnie smiled again. 'It really is quite remarkable I've caught you here. I never see you up in town, never see you on the lake or at the club or anywhere. I don't mind telling you, some people have wondered aloud whether you'd gone native.' The smile became a grin. 'Or if there was some woman in it.'

Jonathan felt a chill at the back of his neck. He chewed mechanically through the steak in his mouth, now as flavourless as rice pish-pash. He looked into Ronnie's smooth, bland face. Ronnie who worked in a rice firm. A man who organised games, theatricals; amusements to divert his fellow passengers. A mild and trivial man, one of those commercial sahibs who knew nothing of things beyond the centre of town, of the hollowed-out morphia fiends and fever epidemics, of infant deaths and syphilitic peasants, of places like

Lanmadaw Grove. There was nothing sharp about Ronnie. So he had thought.

Ronnie leaned forward now, his tone almost intimate. 'I would consider it a great favour, Grace, if you would come up to the lake again. At least think the thing over.'

He disliked the club—the rituals of Englishness that he did not recognise, the women, their exposed flesh intended as enticement, the man-made lake with its planted fringe. Their hypocrisy, the admittance of natives only as servants. But how could he decently refuse? He thought about the suffocating little house in its dirty little street. Perhaps his whole life would be lived like this, in the company of men with whom he would be forever out of step.

'I have an engagement later on.'

'We won't keep you long. I give you my word. Car's parked around the corner.'

He thought about Winsome, and waited for sexual desire to lick over him. Instead he felt a sick churn of fear. Ronnie smiled expectantly.

'All right.' Jonathan raised a hand for the bill.

The club was busy, even though cocktails were hours away. In a corner of the billiards room, half a dozen men and women were rehearsing a play and had marked out a stage using four chairs. As some recited lines in the centre, others lounged beyond this perimeter. Ronnie stopped for a moment to watch them. 'It's *Audrey Ambrose's Adventure*,' he whispered in Jonathan's ear.

The name meant nothing. There was a woman with short, fair hair—the ingénue, he thought—who wore slacks underneath a sleeveless top, showing off a boyish figure. She cast a curious glance at Jonathan before pulling her cardigan over her shoulders (all that white skin) in dismissal or invitation. He imagined her in moonlight. She would sniff the air like an animal, smile her white smile. 'Direct from the London stage,' Ronnie murmured as they turned away. 'I understand it is rather good.'

Jonathan was surprised to find the bar empty. Beyond the verandah, the lake was a pale, benign blue in the sunshine. What was it about water that made it so relaxing? He followed Ronnie across the lawns to the squat boatshed and found himself calculating, as he walked, how the thing might be managed—dry rowing for the timing, training with weights too. It would depend on what level of skill they had. There was plenty of water, the rivers and lakes were full; in a few weeks conditions would be near perfect.

In the shed, a thickset man was selecting a tub. 'Wombit,' Ronnie called out. 'What luck. Wombit, this is Jonathan Grace. Might be of use to us against the Varsity.'

Wombit turned to him, took in his spare form, raised an eyebrow. 'Do you have any kit? I was just about to go out.'

'Afraid not. I'm meant to be elsewhere later this afternoon.'

Wombit shrugged. 'I was only planning a once around the lake—fifteen minutes. Twenty if you're out of condition.'

The lake was smooth but behind Wombit, in his undershirt with trousers rolled up, Jonathan's legs already burned, his chest was near to bursting. He suffered, but he would not stop. He was weaker than he had thought, his stroke no longer fluid, his body lacking condition. How had he let this happen? But he would not stop. He thought he might vomit, acid was already rising in his throat, when Wombit suddenly slumped forward and let go of the water. As he turned towards Jonathan, his mouth was still gaping and he could barely speak. 'Your timing's out,' he gasped between breaths. 'But you'll do.' Jonathan almost grinned.

In the bar afterwards, they talked about the shape a regatta might take. The beer was very cold and the afternoon pleasant and they talked on about the rivers they'd rowed, their old crews. It was only when the sun was low that Jonathan remembered Winsome and his appointment in Lanmadaw Grove. He stood up abruptly and took his leave.

As he walked out of the club, he realised that his bicycle was still at the hospital. He cast about for a rickshaw or gharry, but there were none to be had. He would have to walk and it was a long way. At the edge of the city, clouds were already beginning to boil and the air was stickier—the pink and blue morning seemed a long time ago now. He finally found a gharry down the hill, but by the time he arrived at Lanmadaw Grove Winsome was not there. There was nothing but the hint of her scent, her taste in the air. He waited; but he knew she had already gone.

When he retraced his steps down the stairs and into the street, he reminded himself that these were simple appetites. Sensual habits formed in the grip of the monsoon fevers. He regretted not having seen Winsome but he was not entirely sorry. He wondered if what he felt at her absence might possibly be relief.

Each morning Winsome took the bus to work at the studio. On Tuesdays she stopped at Smart & Mookerdum's to collect the magazines. In the evenings if Desmond was home, she sat with her head over a book or her sewing. Once a fortnight she ran up the steps to the house at Lanmadaw Grove.

Nothing happened; everything changed.

Jonathan was standing at the window, a dark silhouette in the bright afternoon light. 'What do you hope for, Winsome? What do you hope for between us?'

'This.'

'Only this?'

Now that the weather was dry and cool, she wore the blue dress to St John's on Sundays. If it did rain, it was only ever a shower. 'Like English rain,' Mrs De Brito said, her voice brimming over. It was a voice just like hers that had floated across the church aisle one Sunday. 'She has someone, you know. An Englishman.' It was bad enough to have a man like that. It would be worse still if you could not keep him.

Jonathan was fumbling with the buttons of his shirt. 'I've

been asked to row for the club's first four. It will take up a lot of my time. I couldn't very well say no.'

Sometimes, walking out along the wooden gangplank at Monkey Point, she could pick out the crews training in their sleek craft while beneath her the ground trembled as the current shifted and hammered against the bank. There at the very edge of Rangoon, in the deepest part of the river, the big ships dragged at their moorings. If she closed her eyes, she could feel the rise and fall of water until it was the sea that swelled beneath her and the taste on her tongue was salt.

Most evenings Desmond arrived home late. In the mornings he was gone before dawn. He took comfort in the taste of Indian whisky, prolonged silences, aggrieved indifference; in mockery and small, childish cruelties (salt in your tea? How clumsy of me). He did not raise his voice. Why would he bother?

She wrote a note: *Late in the afternoons I touch my arm, my breast, to remind myself I was once touched by you,* and tore it up.

On the evenings when Desmond was not at home she read the newspaper aloud to the girl Than Thint. She read about parties, regattas and amateur theatricals. Rice prices were plummeting, an up-country train had been derailed and sabotage was suspected. In a northern monastery, a boothi vine had produced a dragon-shaped blossom.

Daw Sein asked, 'How is your English friend?'

Alone at the Lanmadaw Grove house, Winsome stripped the bed, folded the stale sheets and left them on a cane chair.

And then one morning, as she hurried to work, she saw Jonathan a few blocks ahead of her on Sule Pagoda Road. He was looking into the window at Barnet's Emporium—wasn't that his way of leaning on his right hip, his way of showing the whites of his wrists? She walked, almost ran, half a block towards him before she saw the woman. A white woman standing close beside him, hatless, her fair hair cropped like a boy's. She wore trousers and her shoulders were bare.

Before she could catch her breath, the two of them climbed into a car waiting at the kerb, the man putting his hand into the small of the woman's back. He turned his face, the man, as the car moved off, looking back through the window. Surely those were Jonathan's grey eyes.

That evening she sat outside with Desmond, who watched her through the thick glass of his whisky tumbler. She kept her head bent over her mending. As she pushed a needle through the heel of a sock, the point sank into her thumb. A tear fell onto the wool. Then another.

'What is wrong, memsahib?' His voice the mocking singsong he used only with her.

'Nothing.'

Desmond sucked at his drink. 'And yet there are tears. Tears for a pricked finger.' He paused. A bat skimmed the tops of the plumbago bushes. 'Tell me, how is Dr Grace these days? I never seem to run into him at the hospital anymore.'

She swallowed the evening air. It tasted of bitterness itself.

'Of course one does hear of him, a big important man like that. We all talk about him; about his patients, his clever diagnoses, his choice of collar, the cut of his shirts. Even his private life is discussed.' He swirled the whisky in his glass. 'Some say he has quite an eye for the ladies, your Dr Grace.'

Grey eyes looking back at her through the car window.

'More tears, memsahib?' Desmond clicked his tongue. 'He has tired of you then? I knew he would. I admit I didn't think it would be so soon.' She stood abruptly, upsetting the mending basket. Needles and pins spilled out onto the lawn.

'Really, Winsome, your behaviour tonight is quite extra-ordinary, even by your standards…' The antiseptic scent of whisky hung in the air between them. 'You stand up, you sit down, you sew, you cry…'

She bent to the ground, her fingers searching for the sharp little points hidden among the grass blades. She dropped the pins into her open palm.

'…whatever will you do next?'

'I hate this.'

He laughed. 'You made this.'

She closed her fist around the pins. 'Have I hurt you then? Really? I doubt that anything I do touches you.' She dropped the pins into the basket and turned for the house.

He followed her, his voice loud now, harsh. 'You think he loves you. Well what do you suppose it is that he loves? Your dirty yellow skin? The charming way your legs peel open? *Listen* to me.'

She kept walking. He shouted and tried to catch her sleeve but she pulled away sharply so that he stumbled. He sank onto the grass but his voice, his urgent tone, stopped her. 'It is not you he loves at all. How can he? You are something he devised, a creature he imagined. A dream. An Englishman's dream.'

'You've had too much whisky.'

'No,' he said, 'nowhere near enough.'

They looked at one another through the fading light. Bats swooped in clusters of two and three through the scented air.

'You've quarrelled with him, haven't you?'

'No.'

'He's left you?'

'I don't know.'

Desmond nodded as if something had been made clear to him. He leaned heavily onto his hands, pushing up onto his feet, and brushed down his clothes. 'Why do you suppose the English come here? I've always wondered why one would leave a cool, green land, an Eden, for this.' He waved an arm, taking in the city, the river, the delta, the sea beyond. He gave her a frank look. 'Well, memsahib?'

All the next morning in the studio darkroom, she plunged exposed film into watery baths of solution and waited for images, shapes, to reveal themselves.

Had Jonathan tired of her? He had not answered any of her letters. But on paper, her words look meagre.

She remembered an afternoon at Lanmadaw Grove when rain had swollen the creek and threatened to cut the house off from the rest of the city. They had been delighted by the prospect, she and Jonathan, lying in the string bed, listening to the rain, smelling the tide. Eating the air as they remade Rangoon in their own image—a floating city, adrift. That had felt honest to her, as if how you lived was simply a matter of will. Now she saw it was Rangoon that shaped *them*. Rangoon, corrupted and corrupting. Jonathan, the girl with the bared shoulders, Desmond; the city dreamed them all.

In the dank air of the darkroom, discovery sprang along her skin, made her jump, made her move. Tears pricked behind her eyes as she snatched up her bag. She would explain this to Jonathan and make everything clear. She left the studio, mumbling something to Daw Sein about illness. Outside the afternoon light blared down at her and for a moment she lost her bearings. As she turned this way and that, she realised that Jonathan might be anywhere. The hospital. His apartment. A street, a shop.

In the hills above the city, the dome of the Shwe Dagon flared white. She knew exactly where she would find him. He would be at the club, his English rowing club. She stepped into the street and hailed a gharry.

The clubhouse was set back from the road on a plateau in the hills and surrounded by a lurid green lawn. Beyond this, the soft blue of the lake. She paid her cab fare and got down.

At the centre of the club's facade was a portico and inside stood a porter, a massive Dravidian in pink livery with a pair of wire spectacles on his nose. Past him, the club doors were open and up a few steps she could see a hallway, brightly lit. The porter nodded politely. 'Yes, miss?'

He was mild, this porter, and behind him the building was still except for the quiet drone of the electric lights. In the lenses of his spectacles she saw her own vaporous reflection.

A door opened in the hallway behind the porter and two women passed through the hall. Their faces were coated with thick colours that exaggerated their eyes, their lips and cheeks, the blush on their skin, and they had folded tissues over the necklines of their dresses. One of them threw Winsome an appraising glance.

This is mine. This. And this.

'Yes, miss?'

Fear ran along the nape of her neck. 'It's nothing,' she said and shrank away from the porter. She turned back along the drive. She walked fast. As a motorcar with several passengers came towards her, she ducked across the lawn and headed for the lake.

Winsome skirted the side of the building and came to an open area beneath the verandah where tables and chairs had been set out on the grass. Paper lanterns hung from bamboo poles and drinks were already being served.

She turned away, walking in the opposite direction, towards the blue water. A group of men were moving towards her, their bodies damp with sweat.

'Winsome?' Jonathan's voice. A look of displeasure he did not hide.

The men around him looked at her with curiosity and she could not meet their gaze. He spoke quietly to these others then took her arm, leading her along the lake shore, back the way he'd come. As they walked, their feet sank into the soft ground.

There had been days, weeks, stretched and frayed with longing to be near him but now, instead of the old avidity she felt only awkwardness. She had intended, had felt it imperative, to explain about Rangoon. But: 'I saw you with that girl outside Barnet's,' was all she said, and her voice was raw from all the hectic weeks of waiting. He didn't reply. She stopped and looked into his face. 'Are you tired of me?'

'No,' he said, 'I am not tired of you.' But his voice was heavy and he would not look at her.

'I don't care about that girl. I know what men are, Jonathan. I know if it wasn't me there would be someone else.'

In the rosy light his hair glowed and his skin was golden. Soon that sun would burn down to red, the sky would flash green and night would come quickly, as it always did. She saw a softness to him that she hadn't noticed before. Jonathan, smooth as a boy, wanting only comfort. She took his hand.

'But would just anyone do?'

'No,' he said, 'not anyone.' His voice grew fond and fierce. 'Never just anyone.'

There it was, the familiar hunger; they might lie down in the reeds together right here, they might love each other. She touched his face. 'Come back,' she whispered. 'Come to the house again.'

He pulled away from her. He tensed inside his clothes, writhed as if his skin were suddenly too tight. It made her itch to see it, it made her eyes ache.

'That foul house,' he wiped his hand over his face, 'I hate it, you know. I hate the stink of the creek, I hate the lizards in the roof, the mosquitoes. I hate walking past the opium smokers, the madmen, the dregs of Rangoon, all of them watching me.' His face was ugly with revulsion. 'This city,' he spat, 'it is too hot, too close, the sky is too low. It is too much. All of it is too much.'

He glanced at her, his face unguarded, furtive, guilty—he was no longer talking about the city.

'Too much,' she echoed. She had felt that she was never enough.

'I've asked too much of you.'

'You haven't.'

'You aren't made for deceit.'

'But I love you.'

He looked down at his hands. 'Winsome,' his voice was gentle now, or patient. 'I am a coward, I know it.' He continued quickly, in case she stopped him, as if she could stop him. 'But this city pushes in on a man until everything is ruined.'

'Not everything.' Her voice running rough over the words.

'I'm sorry.'

She reached for him, but he took a step back and would not let her touch him. It was not comfort that he wanted, then. At least, not hers.

'If things had been different, Winsome, maybe then...' he took a step away, turning over his private thoughts. Then he turned back and shrugged, his voice changed. 'You must have known that this would happen eventually. What did you expect?'

His words sounded like someone else's.

And then she knew they were someone else's words, a woman's words—his woman's, the girl with the white shoulders. When she spoke, in front of Barnet's, she had waved her little white hand in the air as if she were clearing something away.

'You have somebody else.' As she said it, she knew it couldn't be true.

But he wouldn't look at her. 'You'll see that this is for the best.'

On the way back down through the hills, in the back of an open pony trap, she felt as if she were in some tawdry dream—one of those small dreams of Englishmen that Desmond had warned her of. The sky dimmed to purple while over her shoulder the dome of the Shwe Dagon Pagoda glowed the same coral she'd seen the morning they first arrived in Rangoon.

Below her, in the darkening city, lights were coming out like displaced stars. When she reached the bottom of the hills and the streets of the town, she realised she could not go home to Desmond, to the flat at Inverness Gardens. She headed for the river, for Lanmadaw Grove.

It was dark when she arrived and the house smelled of must and disuse. She could not find a lamp or candle and there was no light from the street. She half-fell, half-stumbled towards the teak stairs and as she climbed, pain overtook her and she had to stop and lie right there, across the steps, unable to move, unable even to cry.

She lay in a kind of stupor, alive only to the vibrations of the night—the croaking frogs, the ship bells, the lapping of water. Up through the teak boards came the rumble of trams and trains and motorcars, the creak of buildings as they settled into the earth—and, as if in answer to the night, she felt the plunges and leaps of her own body. She gave herself over to these pulses, rushes of air, liquid movements, contractions of the flesh.

She was stiff and cold when the moon rose a few hours later, but the light stirred her and she climbed up to the top room, to their bed. She found the sheets folded on the chair, just as she'd left them days and days ago. Shivering in the blue light, she wrapped one around her shoulders. She lay on the bed.

And if she had not gone up the hill to the English club? If instead she had waited for him here in this foul house that he loathed?

Too much, too much.

He meant you.

You are the finger that probes the spot already too tender. You are the strained silence. You are too much because in the end you are not any one thing. That was what he'd meant, it was in his face. And now he had that girl with white shoulders. He had betrayed her, she knew it, yet she still could not believe it of a man like him.

Everything, he said, is ruined, and then he had shown her that there was truth in ruin; that certain truths were only possible at the point when someone failed you.

He would be back in his apartment by now, the pale stone buildings and echoing streets spread between them. The woman would be there too. The murmur of her dress as she walked between the rooms. Her smile as he placed his hands lightly across those slender shoulders. The sigh of silk dropping to the ground.

She closed her eyes and fell asleep.

When she woke it was to the whine of mosquitoes. The sky was light, but she could not tell the hour. She pulled the sheet over her face and slept on. When she woke again it was to another familiar sound, the latch of the door. She sat up. Below her, the floorboards creaked with the weight of a man's tread.

She had to wipe her eyes on the sheet before she could stand up. She gathered the sheet around her and hurried to the landing.

Gazing down the stairwell through a joyful, grateful blur, she called out, 'I'm here, Jonathan, I am here.'

The man on the stairs looked up. Aye Sein's handsome face held hers. 'Mrs Goode. My sister said I would find you here.'

Dry

It struck Desmond as rather a good joke. In fact, he'd almost laughed aloud in the man's face—a Mr Partington, who sat directly in front of the Commissioner's office, where Desmond had been summoned to receive the news. A man with a white collar and clean nails and an odd habit of patting the papers in front of him, a man nearly as fastidious as Desmond himself had once been.

'Congratulations on your promotion,' Mr Partington said as he handed over an envelope with the details confirmed in writing. It was clear from his tone, as he took in the frayed collar, sour breath and evil-hued skin, that he doubted very much whether Desmond deserved it. Desmond wasn't sure which he'd enjoyed more, that pale-eyed disapproval or the unexpectedness of the news. Together they were deliciously droll.

He hadn't bothered to open the letter. He knew the job would be some distance from Rangoon in a large and moderately unpleasant regional town. Toungoo, perhaps, the big railway junction where the engines were turned and recoupled, or Moulmein, a few days down river by paddle steamer. This promotion would be conditional upon him taking up the position urgently, no doubt within a matter of weeks. He knew these things without being told. It had been his life's work to observe men who worked in buildings like this one, for his ambition was to be such a man himself. Now it seemed that with this letter, his study was complete—knowing was like breathing. He held the envelope lightly in his hands. Yes, the news was unexpected, but it did not surprise him.

He walked into the foyer where a coolie was polishing the floor with a coir pad. The man murmured three words in English (or not English) 'not a leg, not a leg, not a leg' so that it had become a song. The shine of the floor spread from his hands. Desmond moved around him, then took the steps out of the building two at a time before walking briskly across the lawn. At the street, he stopped and debated whether to take a rickshaw or an omnibus. No, he would walk. The day was cool. He put the envelope in the pocket of his jacket and turned right to take the road north.

So. What had once seemed like deep and mysterious ties possible only through a common birth, education, religion or technology was nothing more than a two-tiered system. Unravelled it was only an 'us' and a 'them' maintained by a small set of superficial, tangible rules. The rest, all of it, just sidelong glances and second-guesses. The way you knotted a tie. Code words and jargon. 'Sound'. Or 'unsound'. As if they were plumbing the depths of man.

So. He had mastered the way of white men, and all because he could not master his wife. This was funny too, because he had married her for exactly this; to present a better prospect for promotion: a married man, substantial, capable of a life. He started to giggle.

And then he had a brainwave. He would tell her at the regatta, after Dr Grace's race. He would insist that they go and when they were there, as she was looking out over the lake at her former lover, perhaps even as Grace's boat crossed the finish line, he would tell her that he had been promoted and that they would be leaving Rangoon. Ha! He laughed aloud to himself, startling a passer-by. He laughed so hard that he had to stop and sit down on the kerb. He could not stop laughing, because funnier still was his realisation that this promotion, this unspoken settling of accounts, might actually take him to a role as a district assistant or something even higher. Perhaps even a full officer one day.

The thought of it sent a fresh wave of hilarity juddering through him, rattling his teeth and shaking him to his kidneys. They would describe him as a man who knew when to keep not only his head but also his own counsel. Oh, he was helpless with it. And throughout his rise she would be there, it would be just him and Winsome, no other witnesses on those lonely nights in distant jungle towns, bitterness their only nourishment, his success a reproach.

He had to hold himself to stop his violent shuddering. His breath came in gasps, his body convulsed. Still he could not stop. He staggered to his feet and gathered himself, walking again, but his sides were in spasm and he could not catch his breath. He hobbled to a tram stop, hung onto the post and slowly calmed himself until the tram came. Then he heaved himself aboard, his stomach sore.

The conductor—jumped-up squirt of a man—gave him an impertinent stare as he held out his hand for the fare. Desmond had a good mind not to pay, but when he had settled himself into a seat his breathing began to come more naturally and he felt a little better. Through the window, Rangoon's big shops, glass-fronted tea rooms, lime-washed banks and merchant houses.

He put his palm to the glass. Flies, a grasshopper, a grey moth were trapped in the wooden frame. Dead, all of them, but when the tram moved forward the breeze made their wings flutter. The sight of them combined with the ache in his ribs made him nauseous.

Already he could taste the futility of the life he had been imagining. No sense of humour, that woman. Like some sort of ghost in his bed, at his table. Well, perhaps it wasn't that funny. Perhaps it wasn't funny at all.

He tried to flick the moth out the window, but it disintegrated in his fingers. The touch of it, the little powdery explosion that coated his skin, made him gasp as his stomach lurched.

He minded, he had always minded, the slights and smiling cruelties inflicted upon him; in the Imperial Police, at the hospital, in church, on streets, in shops, outside the District Commissioner's Office by the man named Partington. He had thought himself the master of it, had schooled himself in not minding. Believed he could overcome it by understanding how things worked, by teaching himself through objective scientific observation what really mattered. But this was how things were.

He wiped the residue of the moth onto his handkerchief then replaced it in his pocket next to the letter. Should he open it here? He took it out and smoothed the envelope between his palms.

For the first time, it occurred to him that he might refuse. He could turn down the appointment and slip into some other life. One that he had not anticipated, that even now he could not imagine. Between here and that other life, like the space between one heartbeat and the next, was the difference between who you were and who you might become.

And what might that be? Where would he work? What would he eat? What might his name be? What kind of place would he live in? Whom would he know? A void, an abyss, opened before him and he felt dizzy with it. He needed air.

He got to his feet and stood in the tram's open doorway, then lurched forward, dropping onto the running board as the wind caught the envelope still in his hand and made it flap. He could feel it tearing from his grasp. But before it slipped free, he launched himself out into space of the road and landed heavily in the brown dust.

Jonathan slid his arms into the sleeves of the navy twill jacket. He was due at the club and because the evening promised a chill, Khit Tin had brushed this woollen jacket and left it out on the bed. It was one he used to wear in England, and he was fond of it, fond enough to bring it to Rangoon, where it mostly hung at the back of the wardrobe. As he shrugged it on he was pleased to find that the serge was tight across his shoulders and snug around his arms when only a few months ago it would have hung from his frame. This reassuring bulk, this hard-won flesh was a sign that he was returning to himself, like an invalid emerging at last from a long convalescence.

He pulled off the jacket and walked to the wardrobe to find another. Rummaged in his stud box for a different pair of cufflinks, then took a moment in the mirror over his tie.

It was not only his body that was stronger. Experience too had fortified him, lending him strength of another kind. Yes, he had made mistakes and he had acted without due consideration for the consequences. The words of Ronnie's syphilitic friend came back to him, 'Boredom, loneliness, the scourge of Rangoon.'

Well, he would be the first to admit that he had done harm, and that perhaps it was out of boredom and loneliness; of course he felt bad, but in no way a lesser man. In fact, one might even say that he was a rather better one. He had recognised his errors and had worked to make amends at some cost to himself and his own reputation. He had taken his blows. Now he could rightly consider himself inoculated against the fever-dreams of the rainy season, a man proof against waterlogged days to come. (He might think of her with a pang, but he had slipped those past months into—not memory exactly, nothing so solid as that. Call them impressions, a familiar scent, a snatch of a popular tune.) As he stood in front of the mirror, his reflection looking back, wrapping one end of a silk tie around the other, none of it seemed real.

Behind him the jacket lay dark against the cream counterpane. It would need letting out. This he could leave to Khit Tin but it was tricky job, easy to make a mess of it. Perhaps he would ask Ivy to recommend a tailor, she would know someone clever.

How was it that no one else had noticed the ironic tilt to Ivy's ingénue smile? Her eyes, as she sat in the bar among the rest of the cast of *Audrey Ambrose's Adventure*, had not flicked around the room, trawling for admiration. Instead she returned his gaze openly before standing up to walk over to him.

Would she like to take a row on the lake? (He had to say something and he was still in his rowing kit.)

'Why don't we?' she replied, that same dipping smile playing about her lips. Ivy, for whom the point of abandon was always slightly further away than he would have guessed.

Later, their first night together, she was luminous with pleasure in the act of love and that mouth, its smile white in the moonlight, whispered again and again, 'Why don't we? Why don't we?'

Jonathan left the flat without speaking to Khit Tin and ran down the stairs into the street. He decided against cycling; he would walk until he saw a taxi. A breeze that smelled of river water played across his face, the evening, like his days, like these past weeks, already unfolding with an effortless rhythm.

With a shrug of her slim shoulders Ivy dismissed all difficulties. She wrote for the fashion pages, she adored Chanel and Patou, was a *slave* to modernity for its clean lines, its clarity. She moved season by season, like an animal, and this, it turned out, was the knack to progress. She recognised things, people, places for what they were. She outstripped him, she left him trailing in her wake and what might wrong-foot him was invariably clear to her. 'What else did you expect?' she would ask, when he complained about Ronnie, or the club, or his servant, Khit Tin, that white smile an enticement.

On Sparks Street he found a motor-taxi, a big black Daimler and, hang the expense, he got in. The car slipped through the golden light, turned right and began to climb the hill. The engine barely registered the effort.

In his work, too, he was making progress. This was also Ivy's gift. He saw now how he had been slow, distracted, naïve about so many things. For example, the park-like pastel gardens surrounding the big houses that dotted the Pegu Yoma, these had appeared to him as so many forced displays of ostentatious Englishness. Now, as the car glided past, they seemed rather a kind of parallel, a balance to the city below. He had learned that Rangoon, with its chaotic streets, its occult strangeness, was not necessarily his concern.

Except for Winsome, of course. For her he would always reserve a sweet regret. He had loved her. In a way, loved her still, of course he did. But where was the sense in continuing? The undeniable fact that there was no future to it had stifled love just as surely as guilt killed it. He could not take back any of the events of the monsoon. He had thought himself a man who did no harm to women; he was wrong. He had to live with that.

But had he hurt her, really? Ivy might point out that some men would not have made a choice. Some men would have strung her along, kept her on the go rather than breaking with her. His mistake had been to involve himself with a woman too young, perhaps, to know how the world worked. But what else did she expect? This was what Ivy would say, if he had felt he could ask her about it.

For Ivy came to love as a man might. Principles, misgivings—she saw that these were ideas frequently cut off from the way the world actually was, from love itself. He had no answer for her pragmatism, for her whispered 'Why don't we?'

With her, everything was possible, there was not that turning and turning forever within the same moment. She steadied him. They could have a life.

The road suddenly bent back upon itself, hugging a red laterite outcrop, and the car seemed briefly to swing out into space. The city's rivers and creeks and narrow, snaking chaungs glinted beneath him, winding their way towards the horizon, across the delta and south towards the Andaman Sea; to the west, the Bay of Bengal. He hung above it all for a moment and then, the engine revving, the car powered on, rounding the curve and hugging once more the line of the road.

'Why don't we have a life?' He said it aloud into the back of the cab. He imagined his hand cupped around one of Ivy's slender shoulders, pictured her face, the familiar tilt of her lips, the life they would lead, their home together. All he had to do was ask.

Aye Sein led Winsome from the house at Lanmadaw Grove into a golden morning. He took her to the studio and left her sitting on a wooden chair, waiting for Daw Sein to find her. He had things to do.

Daw Sein's face bending over hers, light pouring through the pane of glass in the roof, reflected from her broad forehead with a vitreous shine. Her palms were cool on Winsome's skin.

'Courage, Mrs Goode.'

It was Daw Sein who cleaned her up, made her eat, made her drink, made her sit calmly before sending her home to her husband, for where else was she to go?

In the middle pews at St John's, hymnal in his hands, Desmond's voice soared to the roof, right to the rafters as she stood at his side and she wondered if the first instant of every morning would feel like the moment when she first woke in Jonathan's bed, the smell of him on her, the tang of their lovemaking still coating her tongue. She was not in the mood to be forgiven.

Her body was stiff, her hips ached when she sat in a chair, her feet were rigid when she walked. At night she hobbled from their bed, urine tickling the tops of her thighs. Sleep. Eat. Dress. Cook. Speak. Walk. Sleep. She blinked in the daylight while Rangoon dreamed around her. She walked up close to buildings just in case, deep in their shadow, her fingers trailing along the stone, finding the fissures and cracks. She tiptoed.

'Take heart, my friend.' Daw Sein's clever fingers were busy with the camera aperture, measuring the light; was there not always some hope in love? She had been young once. She had known men. 'He may yet come back, your white man. You must only give him the opportunity. Find him a reason.'

'Do you really think so?' She could hear herself, greedy for seduction all over again.

But she was not listening hard enough, otherwise she, of all people, would have heard in Daw Sein's voice a woman also in thrall, an appetite as voracious as her own, fed by rumours from the delta, by Burmese pipe dreams, by a hope long repressed.

A pathway opened. A thought presented itself, like one of those fine cracks her fingers found in the Rangoon stone.

You know an important white man. Why would you let him go?

Hope. Without it, how would the story go on? Where would be the sense in it?

Winsome was wearing the blue frock, the one he'd had made for her. Desmond remembered the day they chose the fabric, how he had made the final selection himself from among the jumbled bolts in that dark little shop, and he had chosen well; the dress looked smart and the colour suited her. Watching her standing in the pale morning as they waited for the special coach up to the Royal Lake, one might even imagine that she had worn it to please him, as if today were an anniversary or some other private celebration; that her gaze was actually a trance of memory, reliving a moment shared only by the two of them.

There was the sound of an engine, and she looked up. The bus had arrived. She moved forward to the kerb.

He handed her up onto the bus and through her blue sleeve felt the pulse and quiver of her flesh. At home, smooth in the drawer of his desk, was the Commissioner's letter; beneath it, his own formal reply (a humble and delighted acceptance), signed and sealed in its envelope, waiting only to be posted. They took their seats, the driver engaged the gears and the bus moved off for the brief climb up to the lake and the All-Rangoon Regatta.

There were chairs and benches set up along the lake shore. Desmond chose a spot that was not too close to the water's edge, but from which they could still see the races. Close to the landing stage where the crews would return afterwards. She sat down beside him, silent and separate. He flattened the program against his lap and tapped his foot on the grass as he waited for the races to begin.

It was remarkable how quickly one became caught up in the drama of the racing, falling in with the tempo of the crowd despite oneself. Desmond exclaimed as they exclaimed, settled as they relaxed and so, as the morning passed, from time to time quite forgot the reason he had brought her here, his announcement, his little coup (except that the letter was still in its drawer).

He found himself exhilarated by the strategies of the oarsmen, which he quickly learned to identify. What pleased him best was when a crew held their strength in reserve, waiting until the very last moment—when their enemies were already spent—to attack. For those capable of such a bold move (and he knew from his own experience that it was always a gamble to withhold one's strength) victory was certain. One could see it in the attitudes of dismay and desperation among the lesser oarsmen well before they even reached the finish line—the realisation that they had tried too hard too early and, as a result, their hopes had been overturned. When one eight came roaring home from a position that had seemed unwinnable, he forgot himself and stood up, roaring and applauding despite the censorious looks around him. When he sat down again, he laughed aloud. Never mind the rest of them. He was enjoying himself. Beside him, Winsome shifted in her seat.

It wasn't until the afternoon that the first fours swarmed along the pontoon at the eastern edge of the lake. He watched Dr Grace's boat glide towards the starting line.

There were four boats in this race, all of them from the old

English clubs with the exception of a team from the university, all Burman, all students and quite green. Already Desmond could feel a different sort of tension in the crowd, people bunching close to the shore so that he had to stand up to see. He watched as the crews shifted their oars in the water, then that moment of absolute stillness before the gun sounded and the race began.

Desmond pushed forward to get a better look. By the halfway point Dr Grace's boat was level with the rival Royal Yacht Club but by the third line, with a quarter of the distance to go, the Royals had fallen off and it seemed as if the thing was won. He felt the spectators around him relax. Then from the farthest lane there came an unexpected challenge as the University crew began their charge. They had been biding their time in just the way Desmond had admired in earlier races. Now the four of them were pulling faster, their timing so sharp it seemed as if they were automatons, not men. Their boat was like a wing, rising up out of the water, glancing across its surface, and they surged inexorably nearer to Dr Grace.

Around him the crowd rushed close to the water's edge, but Desmond could not move. With every breath he could feel the University men gaining, his own heart beating faster as they drew alongside, now man for man, stroke for stroke, in the same way that he had once stood up with some poor bastard in a police boxing ring. This gentlemen's sport was in fact a gladiatorial contest, the two boats squared, close as an embrace. 'Go!' he shouted, 'go on.'

Ten yards from the line and surely University had won a famous victory, he felt the joy of it. Then one man missed his beat and they were no longer a single will, but four men floundering. Disappointment flooded through Desmond. In the final yards, it was Dr Grace's crew that nosed home first.

It was another quarter of an hour or more before the first four crews arrived back at the landing stage. Oarsmen stringy with exhaustion stumbled from their boats, the stewards handing them back onto land. Dr Grace's crew was surrounded by a little knot of men and women offering congratulations. Desmond watched him standing at their centre, shivering in the drenched wool singlet that clung to his torso, his red hair dark with sweat. A spasm of anger clutched at his belly.

He looked down at Winsome. He wanted to feel her flesh cringe, he wanted to feel her apprehension. He tugged at her arm. 'Come on, I have something to tell you,' he murmured the words in her ear. 'I have some news.' He looked about the grassy lake shore and pointed to a neem tree apart from the crowd. 'Let's go over there where it is a little quieter.'

He stopped beneath the tree, its branches bending low around them so that they stood half hidden in the green-grey light, shadows shifting and the antiseptic smell of neem bark strong in the air. Now that the moment had come, he felt a flutter of anticipation.

He turned to her. 'I have been offered a promotion. Modest, but encouraging all the same. So you see, I am also due congratulations.'

He couldn't quite keep the acidity from his tone, but she did not seem to notice. She didn't even speak, and he wondered briefly whether she had heard him, then realised she was only waiting for more. How well she knew him. But of course—a relationship like theirs, spoiled and sour, created a particular kind of intimacy.

'Naturally it will mean some changes,' he paused, relishing the effect, 'the job is in Toungoo. We will have to leave Rangoon, quite early in the new year.' She couldn't hide her shock, and he smirked. 'But I understand Toungoo is a nice place. Quiet. With an enthusiastic church congregation. I'm certain you will like it.'

She was silent. When she finally spoke, her voice was even. 'I won't be going with you.' It was such a childish defiance, he almost laughed. But then her face changed, became more set, and when she spoke again her voice was stronger. 'I will stay here.'

He felt that nausea again, the same pinching of his sides he'd felt on the tram, and he knew his face was comic with surprise. 'What do you mean?'

She looked steadily at him. 'I won't go. I will stay here. In Rangoon.'

'Alone?' So easily she had him. She too was contemplating that void, the emptiness between who you are and who you might become—what he had been too weak to withstand. He wanted to spin her back to him, to shout in her face, 'What do you think will become of you? How do you think you will live? What will people think of you? Of me?' But this would not make any difference, he knew that, it would only show her that she had bested him. He stopped himself with an effort of will. He needed to think.

At the shore, crews were still hauling their boats from the shallows, tilting them until the water streamed out, splashing their legs and feet, while at the centre of the lake four more boats had already taken up their positions side by side. Another race was about to begin. The spectators bunched forward, mesmerised by the prospect of a new struggle, the winner and losers of the previous race quite forgotten.

She spoke again, just as quietly. 'I know I've wronged you Desmond and I am sorry for it. You shouldn't have married me. I know I owe you something, that perhaps I should come with you to Toungoo, but we make each other so unhappy. It seems the wrong choice.'

'So you are to decide what's best for both of us? For *me*? Your decisions have not turned out well so far.' He took several steps, snatched at a low branch, turned back. 'I will not allow it. You will come with me.' Her defiance—for it was defiance—unnerved him and now his voice was too loud, his hands clenching into fists. He needed to think. The letter in the drawer he would post in the morning; he would act—he would choose. He took a breath and mastered his voice. 'We will discuss this at home. We will leave now.'

'If you wish. But there is nothing to discuss.' He stared at her; he almost admired her. At the convent she had been such an awkward girl, not quite pretty, not experienced, only hopeful that limited cleverness and a willingness to please would make up for what she lacked. He had judged her a harmless creature, blank to her fingertips.

Well, perhaps misery suited her. She had become another sort of woman, lit by what she wanted, which was Dr Grace. What he thought had ended badly had not ended at all, not for her. Yet he had been certain it was over. There was talk around the hospital of some other woman, a blonde, a real memsahib. Perhaps Winsome's resistance was a tactic—maybe she thought that if she stayed here in Rangoon alone she would attract his pity.

And then it occurred to him what he ought to do. It was so obvious he was surprised he hadn't seen it sooner. From a certain vantage point, it might even seem like an act of love rather than outrage or bitterness. He softened his voice. 'You say we make each other miserable, well then, we won't spoil this day with further disagreements. We can discuss Toungoo later.' She nodded, wary now, watching him, moving in a measured fashion. The little fool.

He took a deep breath. 'There are still several races to come. I propose we stay and watch them. But perhaps we should first offer our congratulations to Dr Grace?'

*

The grass was thick along this part of the lake shore, beneath it the mud gripped and clung. Winsome lifted one foot and then the other, deliberately sinking a little further with each step. As she did she remembered the sensation of walking in this grass, in this mud, before. Memory was like a second skin; repeat any action, any gesture and the body recognised it so that you might see yourself as you once were and as you were now. This was how you remembered, walked simultaneously here and there, between grief and hope. Her love for him, her shame at his rejection, these familiar responses sprang along her skin, raising the hairs, quickening her blood. She could not stop it, just as she could not stop the mud from coating her feet. At any moment he might appear. She did not know what would happen then.

They found him on his own in the grassy space between the club and the boat sheds, sitting on a lawn chair in the sunshine with a glass of beer in his hand.

'Ah, Dr Grace. Here you are!' Jonathan started at the sound of Desmond's voice. 'And you are alone, but perhaps not for long,' Desmond continued. 'I think we catch you at a propitious moment.' He took Winsome's hand in his own and led her forward. 'I hope we are not disturbing...'

Jonathan's face was tight and blank. He rested his glass on the arm of his chair as if postponing his pleasure in the beer. She could see where his fingers had smudged the glass. Silence settled over the three of them; against it, the sound of the crowd further down the lake shore, the clatter of crockery on trays in the clubhouse, servants' voices murmuring and indistinct, the slap of the door as waiters came and went, the breeze in the trees, the lapping of water.

'Congratulations on your victory,' Desmond began, 'it really was a thrilling race, wasn't it, Winsome?'

Jonathan nodded his thanks.

'Yes,' Desmond continued, 'a famous race. I particularly admired how you were able to fend them off at the very last. From where we stood, it looked like they had the better of you, but we were quite wrong. A question of perspective, perhaps? Or is it simply that one can never entirely predict the outcome of…well, anything.'

Jonathan kept his gaze fixed on Desmond, his expression unreadable. He refused to look at her, even to glance her way, so that she felt superfluous; that properly, she ought to keep silent. It didn't matter, because the faint scent of him, the long look of his thighs in the chair made her ache to touch him, desire crawling along her flesh. She was silent because she could not speak.

'We have news of our own, Dr Grace.' Here Desmond turned to her, smiling his cat's smile as she felt her skin shrink. *Don't*, she thought, *please don't, not in front of him.*

But Desmond continued. 'I have been promoted.'

'Congratulations, Mr Goode, I'm sure you will fulfil your new role admirably.' Desmond gave a little bow as she searched Jonathan's face for a trace of ridicule.

'Ah, but that is not all, Dr Grace.' Desmond slipped an arm around her waist; she stiffened at his touch but did not pull away. 'You see, the job is in Toungoo and so we are shortly to be leaving Rangoon.' He turned to her. 'But I doubt our news is of any real surprise to Dr Grace. I suspect we have Dr Grace to thank for his intervention in our affairs. I suspect it was he who recommended me for this promotion, although he is too modest to admit it.' Desmond turned back towards Jonathan, 'Look at him, he will not confess. But I am of the opinion that he has done more than recommend my services, I believe he has gone so far as to secure the job for me.' He smiled. 'So you should thank Dr Grace, we owe him our good fortune; if we are leaving Rangoon, then it is due to him.'

Jonathan gave a little sardonic exhalation and then picked

up his beer. He sipped at it before settling back against his chair. 'I don't understand.' She pulled herself from Desmond's embrace. 'Jonathan, is it true?'

'Don't press Dr Grace—nobody likes to advertise their good deeds.'

She ignored Desmond and took a step forward, standing between the two men. 'It can't be true,' she said. But she looked at Jonathan and was not sure. 'Have you arranged for us to leave Rangoon?' She couldn't help the entreaty in her voice.

He compressed his mouth, annoyed. His eyes flicked past her, rested on Desmond's, flicked back again. 'I don't understand what you are asking.'

'Did you arrange for us to go?'

Another glance between them.

'That's enough, Winsome, you mustn't cross-question Dr Grace.'

She stepped away from Desmond and around to the bottom of Jonathan's chair. Now she faced both of them and Jonathan had to lean back in the lounger, had to raise a hand to his eyes and shade them from the sun.

'I must apologise for my wife...'

'Did you do this to send me away?'

The two of them spoke at once. 'Don't be ridiculous. Things happen, better not to read too much into them.' 'Hardly your place to ask.'

From the clubhouse there came the slam of a door. Jonathan and Desmond turned towards the sound. It was a waiter with a laden tray and it occurred to Winsome that they would seem an odd little tableau, badly arranged. The waiter stepped carefully through the muddy grass.

'It is true that I gave Desmond a reference, I did that months ago. He is my employee, his work is more than satisfactory, I owe him that. Did I recommend him for a job? Why would I not?'

'But what about me, what happens to me?'

Desmond took a step forward and his voice was sharp. 'You are my wife, Winsome, what happens to you is for me to decide.'

Conversations in which she did not take part, decisions that did not take her into account, only silence required of her. Suddenly she was numb with fury.

'That is not what I want.' As she heard herself, she realised her voice was a woman's voice—tangled, impotent. She spoke directly to Jonathan. 'I love you,' she said.

He looked away, his mouth twisting, a brief grimace distorting his face.

'That is enough, Winsome, we are leaving.'

Jonathan picked up his glass and pointedly turned his gaze back to the lake. It was this last gesture that felt like a violation: as if he had blotted her out of existence, as if he could expunge the past few minutes from his memory, the past few months, as if none of it could possibly have taken place.

When Desmond took her by the wrist and led her away she did not resist. 'Goodbye, Dr Grace,' he said.

She stumbled back along the lake shore, through the mud behind Desmond. 'You are like a child,' he observed as they walked, his voice without rancour; the man of science, the husband, the teacher. 'You do not understand the world. Perhaps it is your pride, but you do not know when enough is enough.' He paused. 'It may be painful to face this now, but you must learn how things really are. Toungoo will be good for you.'

He meant it. As she listened to him she felt no guilt, no sadness, no shame. Not even loathing.

All those weeks ago, when she had run to Jonathan at the

club and he dismissed her here, on this very shore, she told herself she wanted to die. It had not been true. It was not true now: she wanted to live. Desmond was right—her husband, that observer of the world, that natural philosopher—she did not know when enough was enough. Even now, betrayed, discarded, laughed at, her own humiliation thick in the air, she found that she still wanted Jonathan; it was in the arc of her movements, in the connection of her flesh to her bones. With him, there would be sadness and grief. But without him, the land was bare. None of it, not any of it, made her want him any less.

Immediately the race finished, Jonathan felt an extravagant exhaustion. His body completely spent, he was incapable of thought for whole seconds, unable even to parse the world around him. Wood, sky, water. That was all he knew and everything else in that moment seemed superfluous. He relished the sensation, but it was too brief. Here sweat was never the purge it was in England, he was used to that, but the mental quiet—the cleansing emptiness, the pleasant drifting after hard physical work—that was gone almost as quickly as it came; too soon his brain was jumbled again, thoughts crowding in upon one another, disorderly, irrational, as if the rains had never ended.

And he was suddenly, catastrophically bored. Of the hospital, of his own stupid research, of this ridiculous club. Oh God. At the party after the regatta, washed, shaved and changed, he found himself almost instantly unable to endure the social niceties, the phatic phrases and toasts: how long was he required to stand here at the bar, being stood drinks for his part in the victory? How long was he meant to talk about sport and the state of empire, a topic on which his opinions were at best perfunctory? He quarrelled with Ivy, who lost patience with his complaints and said he was impossible.

When he looked around the room he saw only men in whose company he had always chafed; men who continued to congratulate him, but to whom, he knew, he offered little prospect of a decent conversation. He was in their estimation perennially unsound, a person to be tolerated, cadging their indulgent attention in the same way a native might cadge a few extra rupees off you in the bazaar.

Ivy had told him before this was rubbish, and he supposed he must have believed her on some level because he continued to come here, continued to stand at the bar, continued to talk nonsense, his malaise always in the background, as persistent as his prickly heat. Once again Rangoon had got the better of him.

Now it was Christmas Eve and the club bar had been transformed. Dark green clumps of holly bent the slender stalks of the ornamental palms that stood in brass pots along the walls. It looked as though some belligerent pathogen had taken hold and was proliferating unchecked among them. There were wilting paper chains and the reek of burning suet and sugar, the pudding for tomorrow's lunch, an overpowering stench in the sudden heat (for the weather had hotted up, a reminder of what was to come in the months ahead).

At the bar he ordered a beer and found himself offended by the barman's ostentatious bustle, his fiddling about for a glass, a cloth, a small plate of short eats. All about him the noise of conversation, the laughter, grated on his nerves. Across the room he saw Ronnie, but did not even give him a nod. He took his glass from the bar and found a table in a far corner. A sprig of holly sagged beside his ear and he pushed it away.

Ivy was up in Maymyo for a few weeks with the rest of the *Audrey Ambrose* cast.

'The play is sure to be hit with the army crowd up in the hills.

You don't mind do you darling? Say you don't. I'll be back for the New Year.'

He did not mind, but he said he did. As he watched her make up her face, her slender shoulders bent forward, she no longer looked the ingénue but was instead someone briskly competent, a modern woman, her skin without flaw. Her eyes met his in the mirror and she gave him her best smile. A new season was upon them. 'And when I get back,' she said, 'why don't we do something about your manservant?'

The beer tasted cool and bitter, a good taste that soothed him. He ordered another and a whisky too as the place filled up. There were more women than men in the bar tonight, daughters, god-daughters and nieces alongside their mothers, godmothers and aunts—their presence somehow connected with Christmas.

A young man with a cigarette in his mouth sat down at the piano by the French doors and began to play a carol, a girl tucked in beside him on the bench. He was trying to jump the rhythm, attempting a syncopated version of 'Good King Wenceslas', his left hand bounding up and down the keys. The result was unsuccessful and a porter was despatched to stop him. The girl glanced at her mother/godmother/aunt, then shrugged her shoulders in a pretty show of sympathy. She was a pretty girl.

There were other lovely girls all around the room, decorous smiles beneath their clever eyes. He signalled for another beer, another whisky, and as he watched them, ate a few of the salted nuts from the barman's little dish.

The day he'd seen Winsome Goode at Smart & Mookerdum's, or rather, she'd seen him, she had been among the shelves at the far end of the shop, half hidden from view. Perhaps she had been watching for him, perhaps she had been waiting for him and the meeting was some sort of clumsy seduction. As he caught sight of her, he was shot through all over again with the pain of that scene at the regatta, even though a month—no, longer—had passed. He braced himself for her hurt but, although her eyes were sad, in the bookshop it was a gentle 'Hello, Dr Grace'. She had even smiled.

Having her so close, it was as if his fingers were once again tangled in her hair, searching for the hidden mole, trailing along her throat. He had done the right thing to stop what had been between them, he knew that. He had not wanted to see her suffer. At the regatta, it was only Desmond who had seemed to know how to behave. Jonathan himself had been exhausted, unthinking. He regretted this, but could not see how it might have been different.

Something in her had shifted now, he felt it immediately, but could not put his finger on what had changed. She had taken pains with her hair, her voice was lower, more private than he remembered. But there was another quality, perhaps it was in the directness of her gaze or the fullness of her mouth, the way it curved, the corners cutting into creamy flesh.

In those brief weeks after the rains, he'd watched her fade—it was well known that they did sometimes, these girls, despite their youth—but at this moment, with the scent of linen and ink about them, she was lovelier than he'd ever seen her. As she spoke, she touched her fingers to her arm, and he wondered all over again why even such a fluttering touch didn't leave a mark, so finely grained, so translucent did her skin seem to him.

One more meeting, she said. She was leaving in a few days with her husband and everything else was behind them. One last time to say goodbye. Only that. What harm could it do?

He could see plenty of harm.

She looked at him gravely with a child's wide eyes but spoke with her woman's mouth: I do not want what you would not give freely. You once promised me friendship. That would be enough.

She smiled again and he found himself wondering what it would be like to unwrap her once more, to put his hands on what lay behind her new manner. He wondered if she still smelled like river water, like the stems of flowers too long in the vase.

She would meet him, she said, at the house in Lanmadaw Grove.

He said what was done was done, that he would not be able to see her, that he was sorry, but it would be best that way.

She said she would wait anyway. They were leaving Rangoon after Christmas. There was a leaving party for Desmond at the mortuary. She would wait for him then, on Christmas Eve.

She would be waiting there now.

That silvery jolt along his skin, in his viscera.

He had thought he was done with the Goodes.

The young jazz hooligan was back at the piano, two or three girls shimmering around him, preparing to sing. They looked out over the room, gauging their effect.

Watching them, their alluring little movements, Jonathan felt heavy, blunted, as if this were the end of days, and only he remained, sclerotic, ossified, to witness these clockwork lovers as they chattered and kissed. Who among them was even capable of love? Love was harm. He had not been able to stand it.

Jonathan pushed his glass away and stood up. He found Ronnie, who was sitting with the friend from across the Rangoon River. The rest of the table was made up of people he didn't know. He slapped Ronnie on the back. 'Happy Christmas.'

'Plenty of tasty creatures here tonight, Grace, and Ivy is away—you might be in danger yet.'

Jonathan made his excuses.

'What?' Ronnie protested, but he was already in his cups. 'Happy Christmas then, you old relic.'

Jonathan walked out of the bar and along the wide corridor to the front steps of the club. He nodded to the porter before looking out onto the evening. A clear sky; there would be stars later on.

In a few days Winsome and Desmond Goode would be gone, that was true. She had asked for his friendship, and he had once promised her that he would always be her friend. That was also true. If he went to her now, there would be harm in it. But there would also be love.

He walked out onto the club's circular drive and hailed a rickshaw.

Winsome turned the key and stepped into a russet darkness. The late afternoon light pierced the weave of the bamboo walls and made deep red patterns that shifted across her skirt, her arms and face. Tonight she would wait for him in that corner where it was darkest. She turned towards the teak staircase and climbed to their room at the top of the house.

The linen was gone, but she found the little candle stub in its cracked glass under the leg of the bed. She picked it up and wiped the greasy rim with her finger. The wick was burnt away to almost nothing but she replaced it on top of the table all the same, and then walked around the string bed with slow steps. From the window came a breeze and the briny scent of creek water, all of it saturating her in sensations as familiar as sleep.

She knew now that she was capable of a clinical turn of mind, but that was not enough. Reason took you only so far; the body would always have what it wanted. This was not madness but truth. Already she had surprised herself with her relentless patience—she had begun to think of this as a womanly quality, the woman in her.

Earlier, as she walked towards the house, she had half expected it to be covered in vines so that, when she opened the door, it would be to a tunnel of green with little creatures sliding through the walls. But it was just as she remembered it; only the linen was gone.

For a moment she stood quite still and listened to the sounds coming through the window: the wind, the call of birds, the sand shifting with the tide as it took the big ships out to sea.

Wanting, not-having, the city whispered its dreams to her, they drifted across her skin and raised her sweat. Rangoon: that was what kept you going. She stood up and took a final glance around her.

The news came from a man so ordinary his only distinguishing feature was a pink rag tied around his forearm to cover a festering wound. He refused a chair, sat on the floor instead and, when they brought him rice, fell on it, wolfed it down.

Between mouthfuls he confirmed the whispers. He had come from up country, where their father's land had been; there were others like him, scores more, hundreds, perhaps thousands. An army. Men of the delta. They had already attacked a forestry encampment and had killed a white officer and three villagers, including the headman.

As he spoke, his eyes flicked across the room, lingering on her French china, the lacquer screen inlaid with mother-of-pearl, the German chairs.

Daw Sein took up a cheroot from the box on her desk, her hands shaking so that the match died and she had to light another. She left Aye Sein to finish questioning the man and walked out beyond the screen separating her office from the studio.

Night had fallen and the studio was murky. The only light

came from the lamp on her desk and the burning tip of her cheroot. She stepped silently onto the dais, white smoke trailing over her shoulder, an orange glow reflected in the skylight.

At the end of their meetings, Aye's nationalists stood together and chanted, 'Run out and meet the onslaught of danger!' These were students and lawyers; scholars, even men of influence. Now here was a man to whom European chairs were a mystery, and yet he and his brothers had taken on the British with bronze spears and steel dahs—for, as he confessed, his army had few guns.

A terrible excitement ran through Daw Sein; once more the air was possibility. The whispered rumours had substance. The seditious predictions in the Burmese press of a rebellion had come true. For two, three days now, these men—these peasants—had controlled delta towns no more than a few hours north of Rangoon. She turned these facts over and over in her head, trying to make them real as she paced across the dais.

Killed a white man. Cut him up for good measure. And the murder of that white forestry officer had inspired others to join them. They showed that they would not falter and that the tide of affairs was with them. She imagined the wide-eyed terror of the white men behind the doors of the secretariat here in Rangoon; fear would be squeezing their bowels, would already have ruined their peace of mind with bloody visions of dismemberment.

From across the studio the murmur of the men's voices rose and fell. She dropped her cheroot and ground it out beneath her toe. She wiped her hands along her hips, took a few angry steps forward, turned.

What would it take to move the students and lawyers from their protests and strikes, from *talk* to action? What did violence cost? You set your revulsion aside. You raised your hand. You struck out. Wasn't it as simple as that?

She remembered the German boy, his sagging head, his luxuriant white-blond hair lifting in the wind, a vision at once sumptuous and strange; she had thought she understood it.

Daw Sein lifted her gaze to the skylight. A few stars glinted beyond the glass. One might also be seduced by violence. It was important not to be sentimental. It was important to be certain of one's actions, of their outcome, of how they would be read.

'Dolly?' It was Aye's voice calling into the dark, his body a silhouette beside the edge of the screen. 'Have you got whisky? His wound hurts. And he is tired.'

For the moment all that her Burma required was this: a soldier fed, a bedroll procured. She walked back into her office. She took a bottle of Indian whisky from the cupboard and handed it to Aye; moved behind her desk as he poured the tawny liquid into two glasses.

The man would need a safe place to sleep tonight. Not here, of course—they were far too close to the English quarter of town and the streets were busy with Europeans celebrating Christmas Eve. She would take him to the house at Lanmadaw Grove. She opened the centre desk drawer to find the key, she felt for it with her slender fingertips. But it was gone.

For the second time that evening the air shifted. Cold gripped her scalp. Thoughts came at her in a thick, fierce rush that forced her down into her chair.

Mrs Goode. Winsome Goode would have the key.

If Winsome Goode was at the house in Lanmadaw Grove she would not be there alone. She would be meeting Dr Grace, as had once been her habit. She was taking her last chance, for she was to leave Rangoon with her fool of a husband in a matter of days.

Killed a white man. The men of the delta had murdered that forestry officer and in response hundreds more had rallied to join them. What if such a blow were to be struck here, in Rangoon, where there were a hundred *thousand* Burmese? Could it be the spark, the explosion that ignited a conflagration? A revolution?

Daw Sein's hands shook. Dr Grace was vain and arrogant. Gauche too. British vanity and arrogance, their sense of entitlement, their *greed* diminished Burma and the Burmese. In his own country he would be nothing. Here he was important.

But could she really bring herself to harm him?

Daw Sein turned her gaze to the man across the room as he gulped his whisky, one hand resting on the hilt of his dah. Not so ordinary after all. Beside him, Aye looked as tender as a boy. She thought back to her sense of famine during those days in Europe and felt a sudden stab of self-loathing. This man eating her rice and drinking her whisky had never known that kind of hunger. His Burma was not some ideal, some calcified dream; it was as real, as sharp as the edge of his dah. She fed him, yes, but it was she who starved.

Daw Sein stood up from behind her desk. She steadied herself. She began to think what might be done.

By the time he reached the city, the sun was already setting and Rangoon's outlandishness, bathed in a violet light, was for once enchanting rather than bizarre. Jonathan admired the smooth flanks of brown bullocks pulling the day's last load, the Christmas villages in the windows of English shops, complete with cotton-wool snow. Along Fraser Street uniformed ranks of police gathered as if for a parade or some Christmas celebration. A Burman watched them from her little stall, brightly coloured with fruit and flowers.

When he came to the Sule Pagoda the golden spires had taken on an amethyst glow. As a child he remembered craning his head to see the top of a church steeple, its height and squareness stirring in him a sense of awe. But here, all that gold leaf had been applied by the hands of the faithful, the impression of those meticulous fingers retained by the soft metal and moulded plaster. The thought of it filled him with tenderness.

The driver turned into Dalhousie Street and as he smelled the river he began to think of Winsome, her newfound self-containment, her mystery; it made him want to prise her open with his fingers to find what had changed; the prospect raised the hairs on his skin. When the tarmac gave out, he let the rickshaw go and walked the rest of the way, as had been his habit.

Lanmadaw Grove was no longer muddy but dry and hard packed underfoot, the stench of decay had gone and the opium fiends were sleeping it off somewhere else. Burmans in cotton jackets and velvet slippers lit their fires, moved up and down the street in the twilight; women with sleepy children on their hips, sombre-faced men, their cheroot smoke forking upwards in sweet-scented arcs, one ragged fellow with a blood-stained cloth wrapped around the sore on his forearm…they all watched him as he passed.

At the house he did not pause even for a moment on the stairs, she had said she would be waiting. He pushed the door; it was open. He stepped inside.

'Jonathan.'

The room was dim, lit only by a blue window. He could not see her, but the air was full of her scent, he felt his pulse quicken, saliva spring to his mouth. He caught a pale flicker of movement as she drew towards him, but she checked herself and did not come immediately to his side as she once had. 'Why are you in the dark?'

She knelt down and struck a match, lighting a kerosene lamp on the floor. It blazed blue-white, sending out its oily scent, before the wick took, and the room was bathed in yellow light. She stood up and looked at him, the lamp spitting and fizzing at her feet. 'I hoped you would come,' and he was struck again by the shift in her.

'Winsome.' He reached out for her with his voice, but still she held herself back.

With slow, deliberate steps, she traced an arc along the floor, her eyes never leaving his face. As she moved, the light caught the curve of her waist bending, unbending beneath the fabric. He took a step towards her, then another and grasped at her, his hand clutching the fabric of her dress, bunching the coarse material. He pulled her close to him and perhaps he was a little rough, a little too hungry. He moved his hands across her lips, over her hair, her breasts, he rubbed his face against her skin, his fingers searching for this new woman, measuring her against the one he had known.

'I knew you would come.' She held her body against him and he grasped her by the shoulders and pressed her into a teak beam. He caught her wrist and held the underside of it against his throat to feel her pulse jumping against his own. He kissed that wrist, then her face, her open mouth, tasted her with his tongue. Her fingers brushed across his groin, along his thigh.

He held her flat against the beam with his chest, kissing her still, gathering up her skirt, her breath was ragged in his ear. He found the waistband of her underpants, ran his fingers through her pubic hair, found her sex, slippery, slid his finger into her, heard her moan then rubbed her creaminess across her mouth and kissed her again, falling into that sweet-salt taste of her, like a spiralling descent to the bottom of a river. He pulled his mouth away, gasped for breath. 'We can start again.'

'Yes.'

Beneath him, the beating in her chest like a thing taking flight. 'We'll begin all over again.'

'Yes.'

He caught her wrist, stupefied by the smoothness of her skin, murmuring in broken words his promise never to leave, always to love her, barely taking in her whispered response, 'Jonathan, don't leave me, never leave me.' He kissed her again, sinking, waters closing over his head, grasping at last the truth, that beside her, Ivy was wan, pale, their love a small thing that would never amount to happiness. Here, with Winsome, he finally knew himself. She gave him courage and he would take her for his true wife, she would be his forever. He would prove himself, he would atone for his mistrust, he would give her a better life and together they would make something fine. He kissed her once more, deeply, and in the murmur of the lamp, the sigh of the thatch they both heard the sweetness that was to come. Months of it, years.

'I knew if I asked you wouldn't refuse me.' 'How could I?' 'So I will stay here, with you...' 'Yes stay...' '...here in Rangoon.'

Now he saw that in every plaster god there was a jewelled heart, in every pile of excrement, flakes of gold, in the suffering of the sick, the silver chime of temple bells. This was Rangoon and it would be his home, for where else had he ever been enfolded, mind, body, heart as he was now enfolded in her?

And there was all that he would do—the work of healing was to worship her and in so doing, honour himself. England was a puny and miserable place, a world with disease eating at its heart. He would not be a man if he did not choose this. Rangoon, Rangoon, the words in a prayer. 'No, don't leave,' he repeated, loving her always, 'never leave me.'

He held her by the shoulders, held her away from him so he could see her face. At their feet the kerosene lamp blazed, sucking the oxygen from the air, the light glazing the walls of the room. Nothing would move him from this. She spoke and he shook his head, still dazed. 'What did you say?'

But at that moment the lamp flickered and she jumped away from him.

'Oh,' her voice still an erotic rasp as she smoothed her dress, touched her hair, her face, hot and guilty. 'Oh.' The door creaking on its hinges. He caught her fingers but she pulled them from his grasp, her attention elsewhere. He turned—and a Burman, a woman, stood in the door, framed by the deep blue evening light. It was the talking woman from the photographic studio.

Daw Sein bobbed her enormous head in greeting, the movement awkward, puppet-like. 'Mrs Goode,' she said. 'Dr Grace.'

He wanted to laugh—he who had just vowed to embrace Rangoon—and now Rangoon had come through the door, inopportune and gawking.

She closed the door behind her with a sly click and stepped a little further into the room, oblivious to the scent of love in the air. 'We met once at my studio, you may remember,' she said, then she gave him another bow, a true Burmese shiko this time, low and so painfully deferential that he knew instantly she was ridiculing him. His face flushed with annoyance.

Now the three of them stood staring at one another, polite, bewildered, as if they were at one of those awful government mixers intended to break down the barriers between races. Waiting for the moment when they could decently part company. He could not understand it—what did she want? He glanced at Winsome, who stood there awkwardly, silent, her dark eyes opaque. Had she been expecting the woman?

Daw Sein bared her teeth in a grin. 'I see, Dr Grace, that you have survived the rains.' Could she really be talking about the weather? 'Cyclones, typhoons, they are common here in Burmah,' she pronounced it with an exhalation of breath at the end, as if that huge head were deflating. 'We are prone to such storms. Not at all like English rains.'

'No, it was not like English rain.' He spoke carefully, suddenly aware how much he had drunk. 'Nothing about Rangoon is the least bit like England.' He supposed it was up to him to tell Daw Sein to go. Politely, but firmly. He looked to Winsome for some sort of clue. Beside him she flickered in the lamplight.

Daw Sein took another step towards him. 'You are right, doctor. Rangoon, Burma, is not England. And yet the English come here. You consider yourselves at home...'

On and on she went, prattling, a parody of conversation—the weather, the English, but nothing making sense, or none that he could hear, her words like a tight band around his head. He couldn't stand to listen any longer.

'Enough. Please, if you have business here with Mrs Goode, then explain what it is. Otherwise you are intruding,' he glanced at Winsome, 'Mrs Goode and I are—'

She smiled coolly. 'Yes, I understand your business with Mrs Goode.'

'Jonathan.' Winsome's voice was stiff and small. 'This is Daw Sein's house. I borrow the key from her.'

Jonathan wiped his hand across his mouth. He could not bring himself to look at Winsome. Never once during the monsoon had he thought to ask how she had arranged things. He had blindly put himself in her hands. So this was Daw Sein's house. How delighted she must be at his faux pas. 'Well, then, I beg your pardon.'

'But you are very welcome here, Dr Grace. In fact, I am *so* very pleased to find you here. I had not dared hope to meet you again.' Daw Sein took a step closer and bowed, she gave him a wolfish grin. 'You asked to know my business here? You are my business, Dr Grace.'

Daw Sein's eyes had an intensity disconcerting in such a pathologically bulbous skull. His own head was throbbing insistently and his dry mouth tasted sour from the whisky. And now there was some vague and ludicrous menace to her words. It made him thirsty. Was there any water to drink here?

'You white men, everything is your business, you wish to know all, as if we Burmese are children who must tell so we may be scolded.' Her voice was rising, becoming shrill. 'But we are not children. We are not satisfied by presents and tall-tales, Father Christmas and goodwill. We see through your lies, lies.'

He stared at her. He still couldn't make out her meaning, not fully; her talk was like those inky headlines in the gutter newspapers. 'Burmah is not your business.'

He would put an end to this. 'I do not care about politics, they do not concern me, I am not a political man. But I cannot tolerate that kind of talk.'

This time Daw Sein's laughter was hollow and bitter. 'You tolerate me. Me, a Burman in Burmah.'

Jonathan was filled with a sober loathing for this woman. He knew that, had he been a different sort of man, a true sahib like the clubmen, then she wouldn't even dare voice these opinions in front of him. She mocked his tolerance, yet took for granted that he would be tolerant. His intentions had been compromised, his goodwill turned into the worst sort of blunder. He wondered if it were some sort of transparent flaw in his character that a certain person saw and exploited, a patent weakness in him.

Beside him Winsome stood silent, absorbing this talk, perhaps believing it. He couldn't tell. In the lamplight, her face was shadowy, her beauty not so very different from strangeness. Was this, his humiliation, what she had in mind when she had spoken to him at the bookshop? Why had she never told him whose house this was?

There was a violent banging at the door and then, with a push, a young man burst through. His hair was slicked back from a handsome face and a red stone sparkled in the ring on his little finger. Over one shoulder hung a Shan bag, which he cradled against his body. A sullen youth got up like some badmash in a tuppenny movie.

Two steps into the room and the boy staggered to a stop. He

stared at Jonathan then looked to Daw Sein as if for some sign.

'Aye Sein, my brother,' Daw Sein said. 'Dr Grace.'

But the boy did not even greet him, instead he spoke to his sister in rapid Burmese. Daw Sein raised a pleased eyebrow. 'Aye Sein has some news. Perhaps it is you, Dr Grace, and your friends who will need my tolerance now.'

Jonathan felt a cold and visceral dread. This woman meant harm. 'Come,' he held out his hand to Winsome, 'come with me now,' as she stood spellbound. He made a move towards the door.

'But doctor,' Daw Sein stepped into his path, blocked his way with her slight body, her expression triumphant, 'you can't leave yet. You have not even heard the news, Dr Grace. Let me inform you. There is an army gathering, one force confirmed at Insein, another seen at Tharrawaddy. And, I assure you, there are others all over the country. British blood has already been spilled. The people are rising and soon they will converge here, in Rangoon. We must be ready for them.' He knew he must be gaping, his face incredulous because she gave a low laugh. 'Have you not seen the people in this street? Have you not heard what they are talking about? Did you not see their dahs?' Her eyes glittered. 'Ahh, but you do not understand. It will be like the riots, except that it will not be Indians but Europeans who are killed.'

He could have sworn that the walls blinked. Her words would have been comical if she were not so clearly deranged. 'I'll take my chances,' he said, and moved towards the door. 'Let me pass.'

Daw Sein took a step back, she planted her puny legs, she gave no ground. 'No. You are a white man with an important job, Dr Grace, and therefore useful. We would like you to stay. We require it.'

And now they came to the point of it. Was it possible that he was not the equal of this delusional husk of a woman? That her will was greater? This was what other men sensed in him, the failure of authority. A man living on his nerves. *In every plaster god, a jewelled heart.*

'Please,' it was Winsome. 'Please, just let him go.'

'Be quiet.' His tone was harsh; but this was her fault.

'He only came out of pity for me.'

Daw Sein did not take her eyes from his. 'Oh, I don't think he came here because he pities you.'

Winsome stepped forward. 'You misjudge him, he is not like other Englishmen. He is a decent man.'

Disgusting to hear her pleading. Still Daw Sein did not look away from Jonathan. 'What are the affairs of Burma to you, Mrs Goode? You do not understand them. I would not expect it of you. Dr Grace says he is not concerned with politics, but he is not blind. He and I, we see a larger picture.' She spoke these words calmly, her eyes trained only on him, intent as a lover. 'Women like you, women like your mother...who go with anyone...well.'

Winsome cut her off. 'But he is not your enemy.'

And now he saw how she diminished him. For in this he was their enemy and they should fear him. Fear, respect—the tolerance, now mocked by Daw Sein, that was a mark of his strength—this was what he had traded for Winsome and now he knew it meant he was left with nothing.

'Please,' she said again, his great love, 'he is only kind, he only wanted to help.'

'Shut up,' he hissed, 'just shut up.'

'Yes, Winsome, please do shut up. You think I don't know what you are?' Little flecks of spittle appeared at the corner of Daw Sein's mouth. 'You sniff after white men even now, you foul the air. So do, please, shut up.' Daw Sein wiped her mouth. 'Sit down now, Dr Grace. Wait.'

Jonathan struggled to keep his voice low, to sound calm. 'I have given you fair warning, now let me pass.' He made a move towards to the door, but she stepped directly into his path again. He tried to push past; again she moved but this time he was prepared to act. He dropped his shoulder, hitting her squarely in the chest and shoved her to the ground. He was at the door in a moment, but Aye Sein was quicker, lunging, his Shan bag smashing to the floor. Something heavy spilled from the bag with a metallic thud. Aye Sein snatched it up, and Jonathan turned his head to see a gun pointing at him.

It was a pistol, an old German Luger. Rusted and clumsy-looking, the muzzle bent and badly repaired. Aye Sein pointed it directly at Jonathan's belly.

Now all he could hear was the hiss of the kerosene lamp. Daw Sein was silent, Winsome seemingly mesmerised by the gleam of the pistol.

He broke the silence. 'Come now,' his voice gentle and without malice. He kept his eyes on Aye Sein, the twisted uncertain face, the shaky hands, and he knew that this was a boy whose talent was in the talking. This boy would be reasonable. He would be logical.

Jonathan licked his lips and took a step towards him. He let his arms dangle. 'Surely we should speak to one another properly before we resort to this?' He watched Aye Sein relax his arm a little. He took another step.

Daw Sein hissed in urgent merciless Burmese and Jonathan felt an unexpected compassion for the boy. What courage it would take to give up the gun; and what courage to hold your purpose, perhaps even to fire. He moved closer, and whispered, soothing, 'We are men, surely we may decide for ourselves?' And with these words, slowly, gently he held out his hand for the pistol, he was already touching the gun's barrel, wrapping his fingers around it as if the pistol were nothing more than a branch of bamboo, as if the bullets might be made of air, as if he were charmed against them, as if nothing this boy could do, nothing anyone could do, would harm him.

'Come now, we'll start again.' Through the weight of the metal, he felt the boy's arm slacken and as the pistol began to drop he marvelled that it was he, Jonathan, who held his nerve, it was he who was the stronger after all.

For a moment, Jonathan and Aye's fingers were interlaced around the gun. Jonathan looked into Aye's face. 'Don't worry,' he wanted to say, 'this feeling of failure will pass,' was in fact opening his mouth to speak when again the room seemed to blink, a little sliver of darkness and then a bright white light that made the walls shimmer.

Aye Sein held his hand up into the air. The ruby still sparkled on his little finger, but there was a meaty space where the rest of his fingers had been, bright blood rushing from the gaps. He gazed at this absence in wonder while from his lips came a thin keening. That was the last thing Jonathan saw clearly before darkness overcame him and he slumped to the floor, his own bright blood pooling around him.

Winsome ran along the tarmacadam, she ran through mown grass, the scent of it rising up to her like water, she jumped over drains and tripped on a kerb, but she did not stop. She heard trams, shouts, Christmas carollers, and the pounding of feet, running like hers. Daw Sein's words had made her fear the blue gleam of metal, but her army had not yet arrived. Besides, it was another fear that kept her going, that and the hammer strike of her heart.

She came from the direction of the river, arriving at the little outbuildings, the bulk of the hospital a shadow behind them. There was a light on. It was in the mortuary and she knew that it would be Desmond alone in the building, his party over, packing up his office.

He was standing over a table, handling some metal implements, sorting the ones he wanted from the ones he would leave. Beside him was a canvas bag, already heavy with his things and all around the room, long shapes beneath grey shrouds. She called to him from the doorway and he gave a startled shout.

'Help me,' she said.

He stared at her; her dress was stained and her face, she knew, would be awful. She moved into the room. 'There's been an accident, Jonathan is hurt. There was a gun. Aye Sein's gun. They say there is an army coming.' He blinked his eyes, not taking it in. 'He is *hurt*. He needs help.'

'Aye Sein,' he turned the name over in his mouth, 'Aye Sein?' Winsome heard again that dreadful keening, Daw Sein's shrill voice raging and grieving over Aye Sein as if he were dead, binding his bloodied fingers, mewing, 'Help him Mrs Goode.' But Winsome was bent over Jonathan. By the time she looked up, Daw Sein had already taken her brother away.

'He was hit here,' she put her hand against her hip. 'We have to find a doctor to go to him.' Blood on the floor, an oily slick of it, she had had to be careful not to slip. Aye Sein's blood, Jonathan's blood, and Jonathan himself, clammy and white.

When he finally woke, mad with pain and incredulity, he cursed her and pleaded with her, 'Don't leave me to die, save me, you must save me.' She had found him water, she had brought the light closer to him, she had fetched the new sheets, tearing them into strips, wet them, cleaned his face, but she had been unable to look at the wound, his clothes were stuck to his skin and each time they tried to pull away his shirt, to open his trousers, the pain had been too much to bear—'Get someone,' he cried, 'get someone else, quickly.'

Now she began to cry, uselessly, and was ashamed of it. Desmond put down the metal clamp. He took the steps between them jerkily, like a sleepwalker, then he pushed her so hard, so cleanly she felt herself lifted from her feet. She slammed against a table, her head snapped sideways against the wooden leg and instruments from a dissection tray clattered around her face. She let the lights dazzle her for a moment, let herself just lie there.

Desmond paced around the room, his fingers tugging along the items of the mortuary, grasping some, caressing others. He picked up a bundle of gauze; put down the metal handle of a saw, gripped a cone of powder. As he went, she realised that he was gathering objects as he gathered his thoughts. He rolled up the tools from a dissection tray. Picked up a bucket. These things he placed beside his canvas bag.

'We will have to take some things from the infirmary.' He looked across at her. 'And you will need to change your clothes.'

He glanced around the room, picked up a small bundle from beneath the body of a boy. 'Here.' He tossed the rolled-up clothes to her.

Her head hurt and her jaw was numb. She struggled to understand him. Had he said *we*?

'You don't mean to go yourself?' But he seemed not to have heard her, only continued around the room, his deft fingers moving quickly, in a blur. She hauled herself to her feet. 'He needs a real doctor, Desmond.' She stumbled over the words, held her hand to her face. 'Help me find a real doctor.'

Desmond picked up a little clamp. 'Even if you were to convince any one of those hospital men to go with you, no matter who, he will want to know how it happened, he will want to know who and when and why. And then he will want a policeman. You have to protect yourself. We have to protect ourselves.'

'Jonathan might die.'

'And what if he doesn't die?' Desmond looked up at her. 'Have you thought of that?'

Jonathan's face in the lamplight, his narrowed eyes, *Save me, you must save me*. She hadn't meant harm, she had meant love, but they had turned out to be the same. All of it—Daw Sein, Aye Sein, the gun, Desmond's angry pain, everything—was her fault.

When Jonathan left her, she had consoled herself with the thought that there was truth only in ruin, that some truths were only possible at the point when someone failed you.

Now she had failed him. She was failing him as she stood here, in this room with Desmond, listening to what he had to say, wasting precious time.

And yet she had come here first.

'You have to protect yourself.'

'I don't care about myself.'

'Very well. *I* have to protect myself. *I* have to protect *us*.' He dumped his own small things from the canvas bag and began to refill it. 'Don't worry. If he wasn't dead when you left him, then he won't be dead now. Death takes time. Besides, this is not the way white men die. Trust me.'

Jonathan was dreaming dry-mouthed of yellow plums. When he felt rather than saw the light in the door, he thought it was the sun through the leaves of a plum tree. Then he heard a woman's voice and a man's heavy tread, he looked up but he could not see properly, everything was blurred; there was sweat or blood in his eyes, or worse. 'Here,' he called to them, 'over here.'

The man raised the lamp and he saw a pale oval that might have been a face. 'I told you once, Dr Grace, that I was the police surgeon's assistant.'

Dear God, she had brought her husband.

He lay in a pool of congealing blood, a small pool, his face pale and his skin clammy. There were streaked tears along his cheeks and mucus smeared below his nose. Seeing him like this, Desmond felt a brief revulsion, as if this were some unnatural violation, some perverse intimacy pushed on him. He turned away from Jonathan and set his bag down. Perhaps he would not be able to touch Jonathan after all, perhaps he would fail and Dr Grace would die, they would be arrested, he would be hanged. Well, then, what were his options?

On the floor Dr Grace writhed, he cursed and moaned, he pleaded. 'Desmond, get a doctor, don't be a fool. I beg you.'

In the face of this, it was crucial to remain calm. To begin with some kind of ordering of things. 'Winsome, move the lamp over here.'

'Winsome,' Dr Grace whispered, 'please don't let him touch me.' Desmond opened his canvas bag and pulled out a cloth. He smoothed it over a clean bit of floor. He unpacked the knives, tweezers, the little metal clamp, the green papers of golden turmeric with its bitter smell. He set these on the cloth and poured clean water from the bucket into a basin. He washed his hands with the soap he had brought. Then he held each of his instruments up to the flame of a candle, and one by one laid them back down. He poured powder from the paper into a basin.

Jonathan turned his head towards him, his eyes narrowed to focus on the shine of steel. 'A knife, you touch me with your knife and you have as good as killed me. You are as good as a murderer.'

'Desmond, he's right, *please*,' Winsome's voice was small.

'Shh,' he said, cutting her off. Already she was beginning to lose her nerve, just when he most needed her. 'You will have to hold onto him.' He took a deep breath, his hands poised above Jonathan's body.

At the touch of his fingers, Jonathan began to shout and Winsome shrank back, she did not hold him as she had been instructed. 'I can go back to the hospital, Desmond, I can try to find someone—I don't care what happens to me.'

'No.'

236

With one hand, he felt along Dr Grace's chest, the ribs were rising and falling quickly, his heart was beating too rapidly and Desmond could smell terror on his rancid breath. 'Dr Grace, you must trust me.' But Dr Grace did not trust him, he lashed out blindly.

'For God's sake, hold him,' Desmond shouted as the doctor screamed and flailed, each violent jerk a new wave of agony, almost certainly tearing his flesh further; but he would not stop.

'Don't, don't,' Winsome cried, 'you're making it worse.'

He tried to hold Jonathan still with his own body, but with a writhing kick Jonathan sent the basin of water, the carefully laid instruments spinning across the floor. Desmond's knife leaped in his hand and cut into his palm. He jumped back, yelping with the pain of it. He knocked over the kerosene lamp. It cracked then fizzed out. The candle guttered out and they were left in near darkness.

Quickly Desmond righted the lamp, choking on the scorching stink of it. He found a cloth and used it to stanch the blood from his hand. Gathered himself. Took a breath; in the dark, his voice was calm. 'Winsome, you'll need to get another lamp, we will need more water too.'

'I'm not leaving Jonathan.' Her voice was clear as his in the night.

'We need to clean his wounds at least.'

'He doesn't trust you.' And she meant, 'I don't trust you,' which infuriated him.

'*He has no choice*,' he shouted, but then controlled his voice again. 'If we wait there is a chance Dr Grace will die. Then we all lose.'

He could hear her thinking it over. 'You won't touch him while I am gone?'

'I won't.'

'You swear it?'

'What can I do in the dark?' He heard her pick up the bucket for water, caught her movements through the gloom, and although Jonathan begged her not to leave him, she was stronger this time.

'Remember what you've promised, Desmond,' she said, her voice resigned. Then she went for the door.

Desmond sat on his haunches and nursed his palm. Dr Grace was silent, but Desmond could feel him watching, could hear his laboured breath. The fool, kicking out like that, the effort of it would have cost him, torn things, made them bleed. From his pocket, Desmond took a box of matches. He fumbled for the candle and lit it, then, in the pale, flickering light, looked about him for the spilled instruments. He found a damp strip of sheet. Kneeling, he held it up to wipe Dr Grace's face.

'You fear me because you've harmed me,' he said. Dr Grace didn't reply. 'Do you know, if we call someone else to come, then we will have to explain how you were injured. That will look bad for Winsome. And, of course, for me.'

'I give you my word I won't say a thing.'

Desmond shook his head sadly. 'You say that now. But what is your word worth, Dr Grace?' He folded the cloth in on itself and turned back to wipe Jonathan's face again. 'Even if you do keep your peace, one day perhaps you will think about these Seins and you will think them not worth your silence after all. Because if you shield Winsome, then they must remain unpunished. Is one woman worth that to you? Either way, you will betray someone or something.' He paused. 'But I can't have Winsome arrested. I was a policeman once.'

He needed to speak plainly, to be very, very clear. 'You are not like other white men, Dr Grace.' He could feel the doctor flinch beside him, even now insulted by his remark and Desmond wanted to laugh but found that he was trembling instead, furious, already

238

grieving for what he was about to lose. He controlled himself. 'If you die, there will be questions, Winsome will not be safe. Nor will I. But if you live, then for all of our lives, we will be reliant upon your word; you will have the upper hand as you have always had. So you see, we are both afraid, we both face a dilemma.'

Desmond could feel the flicker of emotion across Jonathan's face, although he did not say anything. He put the cloth down beside him and, with his fingers, resumed his search of the floor. He found the metal basin, water droplets still clinging to its sides. He found a paper twist of turmeric powder. He touched his knife on the floor near his foot.

'Should I call out one of your colleagues, hang the consequences? That would be the courageous thing to do. Or should I row you out to the centre of Pazundaung Creek and let the current do the rest? Muddy waters, Dr Grace. What would you do in my position?' But still Jonathan didn't speak.

Desmond picked up the cloth and sponged his face once more. 'Men like you should not come to Burma.' He said this as gently as he could, because it was a harsh truth and he did not wish to be merely cruel. 'You are not fit for this life, you should have left it to others who are. Look where we find ourselves.'

He let silence fall between them now. Here was that abyss that had frightened him on the tram; here was that nothing where he might make himself anew—all that he had said was true, yet it got him nowhere. Was it like this for all men? He imagined Dr Grace, open-faced and passionately excited, standing at the rail of a ship somewhere between here and England, a man made daring by the sight of unfamiliar constellations, by the ocean's luminescence, by unheard-of fish and unimagined beasts; all of it would have seemed portentous, all of it would have seemed as if it were just for him. In those circumstances, would he have behaved any differently?

'Desmond,' Jonathan whispered, 'I will do whatever you want me to do.'

'You should go back to England, Dr Grace.'

'I am begging you.'

'Hush.' He smiled and rested his palm lightly against Jonathan's cheek. Then he picked up his knife.

He was properly ready this time and Jonathan was weaker. He used his heavy boxer's body to pin Dr Grace down. He held his knife steady in his strong boxer's hand. Jonathan screamed, he begged, he made rash promises.

'It's all right, Dr Grace,' Desmond soothed, 'it may hurt but it won't be for very long,' and despite the screams, the awful pleading, the flailing limbs beneath him, he began to cut.

When it was over, there was a purple-black mess exposed on Jonathan's skin. Desmond held the candle above it then ran his fingers across this mess, until he could feel a hole just below the ball of Jonathan's right hip. He probed the back of the hip and, in the fleshy part of the buttocks, found another, larger wound. Gently, he parted the edges of skin, searching for the bullet. Once he was done, he folded the shredded ends of twill back over Jonathan's hipbone before turning back to his instruments.

'I've examined your wound and shall I tell you what I have found?' He gave a dry little laugh. 'It was a clean through-and-through shot, I am fairly certain of it. I will wash it out with antiseptic. I am using turmeric, like we used to do up country.' With expert fingers he began to smooth the paste across the wound. 'It would seem, Dr Grace, that you are in luck.'

But beside him Jonathan was not listening. He was weeping.

*

It was the darkest part of the night when they left Jonathan at the hospital. Once the sight of him had been a provocation. Now, as she watched him carried along the hall, Desmond at his side, she recognised this as their final parting. She was at the end of things, she had known it as soon as she'd stepped back into the house at Lanmadaw Grove; when she'd returned Desmond was already cleaning Jonathan's wound, and Jonathan was silent, almost calm, his face turned away from her.

No, she had known it before. The end of things was announced at their beginning. In Daw Sein's black handwriting; in skin the colour of sugar syrup; in the green filigree tracing the printed pages of a book.

She waited for Desmond in the street below. She sat down on the stone. A rat ran past. She heard a distant boom, a low powdery rumble, ending almost as soon as it began—Daw Sein's rebels at the outskirts of the city. But she was no longer afraid. Let them come. She longed to put her head down, to lie flat like any opium dreamer, sleeping where they lay, a wake of ruin behind them.

All about her was the sound of settling, of creeping, of vines snaking through grass, of men shifting in their sleep beneath bushes, the voice of a shrew calling, like a child for its mother; and in it she could hear the cries of a rebel army, the death rattle of patients in hospital beds, the sigh of a nurse fighting sleep, of wives lying awake in the big houses on the ridge, a policeman whistling, the murmur of the driver to his mule as the wheels of the conservancy cart creaked past.

Then once again that thunder, distant and brief, like a change in the deep blue of the night sky. Only the hospital windows glowed grey, only the stars gave light. She was so tired. They might come and wake her, any of them. They would find her here, sleeping. She put her head down against the cold stone.

'Get up, get up.' Someone was shaking her thigh. She would not open her eyes. Let them shake. 'Winsome.' Why would they not let her alone? 'Winsome.' Desmond's voice.

Reluctantly she raised her head. 'It is done,' he whispered. 'He has given his word not to implicate you in any of this, for what that is worth. He says they will probably send him home. For the moment I think we are safe.'

Safe. The words of a dream. She did not deserve it; she had betrayed Jonathan, Desmond. And yet she was safe. It was so easy to do harm and she had never intended it. She had not known herself capable of it. If Jonathan's word kept her safe, then they kept Daw Sein safe too, Daw Sein who mewed with rage and fear as she stanched the blood from Aye Sein's hand, who promised murder.

Winsome raised herself up on one hand but it was no good, her head drooped, her face throbbed. She was so tired. Desmond exhaled, sat down beside her, his body sagging like hers. They were beyond the ordinary recriminations of man and wife now. Jonathan would live, but before them was the darkness of Rangoon. He felt for her hand and she understood that it was not out of love, or duty or even fellow feeling, but simply to hold onto someone in that blackness, to touch something he knew.

She was a liar, she was a cheat, a dissembler, she was ruthless, reckless; but those seemed like the words of a story rather than the truth. Reason was not enough, the body would have its way— and that was the opposite of meaning, the opposite of safety and nothing short of death would stop it. But she did not want to die.

The wisest course of action would have been to take Desmond's hand, to stand when he stood, to turn and walk towards home with him, the two of them like sleepwalkers in the velvet night. From such small decisions, lives were made, and there were worse things than that.

But look now and you will see her stand up from the kerb. Watch her as she turns away from him. She begins to walk. He doesn't follow her.

And where does she go?

She is walking towards the smell of water, following the scent of the river. Rangoon is a city cradled in the arms of rivers.

You may catch sight of her again at the Barr Street Jetty. Before her, moored at the centre of the river, the big boats. The ocean-going passenger ships: Bibby Line, P&O, Van Strenkel. She might stop a sailor with braid on his peaked cap and ask him for work. She might stow herself in the bottom of one of those ships and sail along the Rangoon River until they are clear into the Bay of Bengal, and then out into the world beyond. In the dead boy's clothes she will be just another labourer, just another fantasist trying their luck. Who wouldn't give her a chance? All around her are the bodies of the sleeping men and boys who work the docks, grey bundles like outsized cocoons, flesh and thought beneath the blankets, each one as mysterious as the dawn. She lays her head on the boards of the wharf to wait.

Look up, and you will see that the dome of the Shwe Dagon has just caught the light; it is gleaming cerise just as it did the first time she saw it. Around her the darkness begins to lift, and the air seems to flutter, like a storm of ash. She has never seen anything like it. Have you ever seen that? Have you seen night precipitate into the morning? Have you ever seen how, sometimes, darkness flutters?

ACKNOWLEDGMENTS

Thanks to Mandy Brett, Senior Editor at Text, who applied her pencil with taste and tact. Brian Castro encouraged me to push my writing further, no matter how uncomfortable, and that made all the difference. Jim Aung Thin answered all my questions about Rangoon and Burmese culture and Pam Aung Thin started the whole thing rolling with her childhood stories of Burma. Warren Shnider was a mensch. Margaret McCarthy, Steven Amsterdam and Glenice Whitting gave me great advice. Lauren Melton introduced me to various experts, including Ryan Propst who kindly shared his professional knowledge of gunshot wounds. Melanie Hendrata took my author photographs. Jean Cameron found and sent on a map of 1930s Rangoon.

I spent time researching this book at the British Library and the Wellcome Collection, London; the State Library of Victoria, Melbourne; and the Barr Smith Library, Adelaide. I wrote this book with the financial support of an Australian Postgraduate Award as well as a travel and research grant from the University of Adelaide.

Thanks to the Victorian Premier's Literary Awards. And to the Readings Foundation and the Wheeler Centre, who fund the Unpublished Manuscript Fellowship awarded to *The Monsoon Bride* in an earlier incarnation.

Early versions of two chapters were published in the journals *Strange3* and *antithesis*.

I have taken various liberties with the actualities of 1930s Rangoon. If you look for flowering padauk flowers in late May, you will be disappointed as they generally bloom a little earlier (but it is true that they flower only for a day). Aye Sein and Daw Sein's association of activists is loosely based on actual student groups formed after the Lewis Street Jetty riots. I don't know if anyone connected with the Saya San rebellion ever made it to Rangoon, but it seems pretty likely to me. I have reconfigured some of the titles and ranks within the Indian civil and medical services. Winsome's convent school in Kalaw is also a fiction, but there were schools just like it throughout Burma.